PATRIOT PARTNERS

DEWAYNE RUCKER

authorHOUSE'

AuthorHouse™
1663 Liberty Drive
Bloomington, IN 47403
www.authorhouse.com
Phone: 833-262-8899

Published by AuthorHouse 07/19/2024

ISBN: 979-8-8230-2905-6 (sc)
ISBN: 979-8-8230-2906-3 (e)

Library of Congress Control Number: 2024912558

Print information available on the last page.

CONTENTS

DEDICATION

This story is dedicated to the men and women who served and protected the communities in which they live, and to those who continue to do so. To those who work behind the scenes supporting those who devote their lives to protecting others, thank you for your service.

ACKNOWLEDGEMENT

To the reader, thank you for your interest in this story. If you wore, or currently wear a uniform to serve and protect, this is for you. You have your own stories to tell if you so desire. To my family and friends who continue to support my ventures of creativity, I thank you. A sincere thanks to those who were willing and unselfishly took their time to support my book. Whatever form of editing you participated in, I sincerely appreciate what you have done to bring my story to life. Without the help of Kris, Vicki C., and Ralph R., my dream would not have become reality. A special thanks goes to my wife Maureen. Her encouragement of my journey, and the multiple editing stages she performed cannot be overstated. Most of all, her patience in my creativity is lovingly supported. I appreciate all you have done and continue to do in all aspects of my being.

CHAPTER 1

S moke filled the parking garage of the Missouri State Capitol. The smoke was not the result of fire, but a deliberate scheme. A successful scheme. Firemen scurried from the garage to safety as did visitors, employees, and elected officials. It was a sight never witnessed or exhibited by public safety heroes. Firefighters are seen hurrying to extinguish flames, not run from them. The smoke and presumed flames were not the reason for the mass exodus, although the ear-piercing fire alarm did suggest one to leave the premises. It was the gunfire coming from directions unknown. Gunshots echoed off the concrete pillars of the basement garage. Car alarms were blaring from the noise concussion. People were screaming while attempting to escape. The wounded laying on the concrete floor were victims of hate and evil. A gunman donned in fireman gear was shooting at the state's elected Chief Executive. His security detail surrounded their protectee sacrificing their own safety. It was their job.

Chad Jerguson aimed at the assailant and pulled the trigger on his Glock. He missed. His aim was jarred by someone running scared into him when his gun discharged. Another assailant was identified as smoke filled the death chamber. The other face of evil wasn't dressed as a firefighter. He too fired shots at the security detail protecting Missouri's Governor. Although wounded, he was resilient. The gunning firefighter and his wounded co-assailant left their protected steel and glass car shields to continued their suicidal mayhem. That is where it ended.

Megan Swift was on assignment when terror erupted. She crouched below the smoke that filled the garage. She was deathly close to the lethal threat. She aimed and pulled the trigger on her Glock. With her aim came a different result. She didn't miss. The assault ended nearly as fast as it started, although witnesses would later contest differently.

Chad Jerguson was Megan Swift's handler. Chad and Megan were members of an elite group. This group was not part of any state, city, or county law enforcement, although police presence was more than evident that sultry summer day. Chad and Megan were employed by the federal government. They were there to defend democracy. They were there to prevent terrorism. Terrorism occurred, but the ultimate plot did not. Chad and Megan were members of Missouri's Tactical Analysis Force. MoTAF was federally funded and clandestine.

Thanks to Missouri's security detail, the Chief Executive remained safe. Security protocols to the State House changed after the attack. The probability of another attack caused the focus of securing democracy to be paramount. Memorials were held to honor the heroes and remember lives lost. Half a decade later, nobody talked about it ever occurring. It was finished. Done. It was over.

Memorials planned on the anniversary of the attack ceased to happen. News faded away to current events the viewing audiences craved. It wasn't any surprise, that's the way news cycles worked. Families were compensated for any losses they may have incurred. Finger pointing is part of the process, but who was to blame? The Missouri State Capitol remained the focal point of the most heinous and historical domestic terror event in the state's history. Those who worked inside the granite fortress would not soon forget the horror, although they would try. Sick minds created destruction. Those same sick minds also perished before the sun sat that day. That is what most would believe.

Chad Jerguson remembers the day as if it occurred only a few hours prior. Sleepless nights were less of an issue, but the memory resurfaced more often than he preferred. People go about their everyday business as expected. Chad understood what could go wrong behind the scene of any given day. It wasn't because he was elected by the people to do the work for the people, although he did take an oath. Capitol employees weren't aware of his presence that dreadful day, or that he was there for them, and the visiting public.

Chad was a hero, although nobody would recall his name. He was one of many unsung heroes who stood in the face danger. He didn't wear a uniform.

There was nothing noticeable about his attire, until he pulled the Glock from its holster. Every member of MoTAF participated in their multi-phase aftermath debrief program. It was mandatory. Although other states utilized similar programs, there was no cause in Missouri for a federally funded critical incident debriefing to occur. Then the unimaginable occurred. Debriefing programs proved a beneficial element of ones' emotional and psychological well being following traumatic incidents. Chad worked to conquer his demons of blame. He understood, following several one-on-one sessions, he alone couldn't have prevented the loss of life.

Chad was MoTAF's computer analyst and communicated information regarding intel from other states as well as Washington DC. Chad signed his name with the initials C J on handwritten or electronic communication. He communicated with Washington on a regular basis.

Chad succeeded in challenges he confronted early on in life. Any failures he experienced resulted in victories for his next challenge. A poster success story of the foster care system, he would mentor others as a way of giving back to the program. Young minds soaked up his encouragement. They too flourished in achievements no matter how big or small. He was never far from his roots and helped in any way he could lending a voice for youth. His desire was the solace in friends and associates. Relationships sustained his purpose. Megan Swift was a close friend and that purpose.

Their friendship was bound by MoTAF membership. They faced tyranny together on that memorable day. If not for Megan and Chad, Missouri's notable mark in history would have resulted a different outcome.

Megan's life story was much different than her handler, but she too experienced adversity. Friends gave her purpose as well. Chad was that friend who often connected the dots when she couldn't find the link. Although experiencing different upbringings, Chad and Megan were bound by secrecy. Their bond went beyond friendship. They knew they could count on each other. It proved evident when the possibility of not surviving became probable.

Megan never questioned where she got her attitude, her backbone, or her confidence. Life lessons taught by her parents were never far from the surface. She held her own in any circumstance. Her extended family didn't exist. Shallow facades surfaced when a tragic traffic accident took her parents' lives. There was no family support, only greed and self-righteousness. Aunts and uncles were interested only in potential monetary gain.

She had fallen into a dark hole of self-pity and hadn't found her footing until Chad came into her life. Not only did he throw her a lifeline, he made sure she grabbed hold of it and held on tight. Out of the deep dark hole surfaced a force to be reckoned with. A force she forgot existed. Chad nurtured and pruned that force allowing it to grow like a rose bush full of blossoms as well of thorns.

Both MoTAF confidants extended an arm of hope to a young lost soul on the day democracy was threatened. This young activist found religion that summer afternoon, although faith had nothing to do with it. He sided with the right to save his own life. When smoke filled the halls, as well as the air ducts of the Capitol, Brody Wesson who was captivated by the left, found his voice. Simply put, he got scared. The law enforcement intel world taught Brody the opposite side of left. He not only believed in falsehoods, he became obsessed. It took WITSEC, Witness Protection Services, for him to understand life as he knew it no longer existed. There was no trial because there were no arrests. Those who started the chaos perished. Brody found WITSEC as his safe haven from those promising to continue in the fight. Starting over wasn't easy although there was a playbook established for that very thing. Brody agreed to his new start and became comfortable in his surroundings. The hardest adaptation was his name. Leaving behind Brody took some getting used to.

Sovereign Patriots learned the fate of their comrades while watching news of their foiled attempt to destroy democracy. Social media served its purpose recruiting the wrong side of democracy. The same social media became a viable tool for the investigative arm of law enforcement.

Although the day of remembrances were no longer held, visitors tour the Capitol museum daily. Pictorials, educational displays, political historians, and interactive learning tools of Missouri's history are bountiful. Brochures of the infamous day in history depicted locations of notoriety to be viewed if one cared.

The self-guided tour, by mother and her middle school age daughter, described the story of mayhem from years past. The mother hugged her daughter lovingly as they made their way along the tour. It was a beautiful day for a Capitol tour. Parents accompanied children, out of school for Spring Break. The halls were exuberant with visitors. Monogram plagues told the story of the cornage as the mom wrapped an arm around the shoulder of her child in a protective manner. No danger loomed on this self-guided tour.

"Mom, is this what you were telling me about?" The daughter quizzed her mom about the story she heard for the first time on the short journey to the Capitol.

"Yes. This is the history lesson I told you about. It's the part of history that nobody discusses, but you can read about it here."

The journey through the legislative hallways told the story by the numbering system. This story began in a senator's office, ending in the Statehouse parking garage. A plaque hung at each numbered location explaining how a loved one's life was taken. The Roman numeral five depicted final steps the college intern took from her legislators' office to the garage where she and others attempted to exit the building. Some were successful, some were not.

Missouri's clandestine security force weren't remembered for their heroics when memorials were held. The elite group required anonymity and stayed clear.

It was a Wednesday afternoon and the matinée featured comedy. It was Chad's turn to pick the movie. Rom com was again top of the list. It wasn't a box office hit but it didn't have to be. The movie resembled a Hallmark holiday feature. A motion picture you didn't have to think about the plot, you just smiled and laughed at the humor. It became a ritual filling their weeks if a movie suited them. Matinees became a norm for both Chad and Megan. It wasn't as if they were frugal, finances were of no concern for either of them. Each held lucrative employment after securing notable law degrees. MoTAF made way for early retirement opportunities. They liked lighthearted entertainment and theaters in the area often featured showings of the genre. Following a movie, they often decided to have an early dinner at one of their favorite restaurants.

Chad and Megan sat enjoying their meal. Conversation was light, hearty and with unending humor. Their meal was the finale to a much-anticipated evening. Chad leaned to one side to retrieve his cell from his pocket. The vibration pulse summoned him to look at his text message. He stared at the message, not understanding the meaning or from whom it was sent. The number wasn't listed in his phone address book. He read it twice but couldn't decipher it.

As if on cue, a vibration erupted inside Megans' purse. Both cell phones remained on vibrate from the movie theater. Megan reached for her purse to retrieve hers. She opened the phone screen to read it.

A quizzical glance made its way to Chad across their unfinished meals.

"Weird."

"What's weird?" Chad responded.

"Oh nothing. Just a text that makes no sense." Megan changed her phone setting from vibrate before replacing it in her purse.

"I got a weird text too which wasn't for me. Some poor schmuck is in trouble."

"What do you mean?" she ask.

Chad smiled and handed her his phone, "Read it."

The look on her face was indescribable. Chad didn't expect a response. He wasn't expecting much of anything.

"Oh my gosh!"

Chad looked to the closest dining table from where they sat. He was relieved others hadn't been disturbed by Megan's outburst response to reading his message.

Megan grabbed her purse and retrieved her phone. She stared at the screens and shifted her eyes to Chad. Her eyes moved from the phone screens to Chad without the slightest movement of her head. Chad's smile faded. His now blank expression was that of holding the winning hand of high stakes poker game, only to learn his bluff had failed on a million-dollar payout.

"They're the same! Our messages are the same!" Megan voice elevated to a decibel others could hear. She didn't notice nor did she care.

Chad took both phones from her outreached hands and glanced around the restaurant again with an apologetic look. His eyes shifted from one phone to the other. He repeated the shift as if he couldn't believe what he was reading. He couldn't.

"U will regret what you did. We will hunt u both down."

CHAPTER 2

Megan looked around the restaurant, as did Chad. Nobody looked in their direction. Nothing changed from when they entered. Patrons continue to enjoy each other's company. Nobody looked at them, no one cared about the others business.

"Megan, we've got this. No big deal. Don't worry about it."

The words came from his mouth with the confidence of a four-year-old wearing a batman t-shirt.

"You should tell your face that," she said. "What's this mean, and why should we be regretting anything? Who's hunting us?"

Her voice was unmistakably elevated. This was not her. Normally calm, cool, and collected, she was not herself. The atmosphere from a sunny spring day turned to a tornadic whirlwind.

"Megan, it's going to be OK. We'll think this through." His calming tone wasn't working, and he knew it. They both received identical messages and it was unlikely they were sent to wrong numbers in a group text.

"We've got to get in front of this." Her voice was now at a whisper, as if someone was trying to ease drop.

"Who has both our numbers and how could they? Our numbers are private."

Megan now had both phones in her hands. Chad barely remembered relinquishing his phone back to her. She held up both phones, one in each hand. Shock and despair reigned again in a forced elevated tone. Her face flushed, and her soft green eyes were no longer disarming. It was a look never witnessed from the friend sitting across the table.

Chad again looked around as if someone could overhear her displeasure. It was the all-familiar movie scene when the jaded female rose from a romantic dinner restaurant setting. She shouts for all to hear that it was over, right before the cloth napkin is slammed on her plate, and the glass of ice water splashed in the face of an unsuspecting fiancée.

Chad knew when not to speak. He had never been married, but witnessed many relationships crash and burn for the lack of communication. No explanations to irrational conclusions. Danger found them both.

Their waiter approached but his gate slowed as his gaze met Megans. He took the unspoken answer to the unspoken question. The stare on Megan's face spoke loud and clear as he approached their table. The fierce glance screamed "not yet!"

The waiter, well versed in the unspoken language, looked at Megan and said, "I'll return in a little while."

Chad wanted to smile but now wasn't the time. The waiter got "the look." The all too often glance one receives from another when the obvious need not be spoken. The silence between them was deafening.

"Chad, we need to find this guy. Where do we start?"

It wasn't like they had been at this juncture before because they hadn't. He wasn't sure what steps to take. As her handler, he needed to show calm, resolve, and take charge. He retained tenure within MoTAF. There had never been a breach and he was confident his Washington counterparts would be all over it. As the thought entered his mind, he wasn't as sure. He began troubleshooting the possibilities. The breach should have been alerted throughout MoTAF's network. There were no notifications of any sort. No false alerts were ever tested. Notifications were routinely forwarded and advising systems were in fact tested and functioning as expected.

"I'll send out emails. It'll be from a secure account and sent to secure accounts. They'll know it's not from my cell when they respond."

"But what if they have been compromised as well? Whoever's taunting will know who else to threaten."

"You're right, but emails are a start."

Chads eyes averted from hers as the words came out of his mouth. Breached security was something MoTAF hadn't experienced. Megan looked at him as if deciding where to insert the butter knife. Her eyes were on fire, and she was certain he could hear her displeasure without uttering a single syllable. This was not the quiet before a storm. They were thrust directly into a torrential rain and the horrendous winds encircled their tranquil surroundings.

"Chad you're a computer analyst, how could something like this even happen?"

Chad took a deep breath and exaggerated his exhale. His body language offered a surrender. Her eyes diverted down to her lap, and she eased the grip on her phone. Her shoulders slumped forward, and she too took in a similar breath. The tightness in her chess waned and she put both elbows on the crisp tablecloth. The much-anticipated desert was out of the question.

"I'm sorry. No pressure," she lied.

"No need to be sorry, I'm at a loss with this too," he continued. "There are techs who know what to do. They'll handle it."

"But what should we do in the meantime."

"Once I notify them, we'll be assigned new phones."

"What about our phone numbers, wont they have to change?"

"Yes, but we can use our personal ones until we get new ones."

"Problem solved?" A rhetorical question accompanied by her deadpan stare.

"I didn't say that. I'm just not sure how long it will take to learn exactly where the breach originated."

Chad stared into the eye of the storm. He understood the severity of the circumstance they found themselves in. He would not make light of it and wouldn't try.

"I've got an idea who I can call about our messages. I'll use my unlisted landline from my place."

"Let me know what they say."

"Megan, I'm in this with you. MoTAF will keep us both in the loop on how this happened."

Megan remained diligent regarding safety. It is one of many things ingrained by her parents. She couldn't recall an incident where it didn't work to her advantage. Her self-imposed shield kept her safe. She took in a deep breath to calm the misgivings. Her eyes softened, tenseness in her shoulders eased. His sky-blue pupils would soften an angry baby or even a knife wielding assailant. That was her reasoning at the moment. Megan bowed her head and exhaled, as if apologizing for not giving him a chance to understand the circumstance they were both thrust into.

A changed person now sat across from Chad. She didn't know it, but she was his confidant. Their simple lunches, movies, and workouts were both their small circle of existence. An existence they both enjoyed, and he vowed not to complicate things. He knew his boundaries. Every gentleman did. Chad stated what should have been readily apparent.

"Let me know when it's OK to smile again." Chad looked at her with one raised eyebrow.

In his mind, and only his mind, he wanted to laugh and laugh loud. It wasn't a laughing matter. He was looking forward to the evening, but it quickly turned into a dumpster fire. Chad dipped his pointing finger into his glass of water, then flirtatiously flipped his finger in her direction. He wasn't sure the intent hit its mark. She looked at him, expressionless. He waited. Eternity passed. Megan picked up her half glass of water and looked deep into his eyes, raising both her eyebrows.

"I got your message, do you get mine?" She ask.

They both realized the complexity of their phones being compromised. Finding out the who and why would be daunting. Humor would not change the realization of it all.

"Of course, and I deciphered it as well. I'll let you know when I find something out."

CHAPTER 3

Brody Wesson, a few years shy of his thirtieth birthday, planned his life different than what he was now experiencing. A forced withdrawal from, not one but two colleges was the beginning. He didn't envision WITSEC being any part of his future. Lessons learned, is how he described his plight. Repeated missteps and misguided teachings pulled at every turn. Those lessons were self-taught. He gravitated to misplaced schools of thought.

A believer of Sovereign Patriot rhetoric, Brody was rescued from the bowels of hatred. He witnessed violence in its extreme form during the attack at Missouri's State House. The product of those decisions, poor chosen paths, and the proverbial forks in the road almost ended his life. He made more wrong turns than he cared to admit.

A self-proclaimed loner, his belief system was deeply rooted. When the opportunity presented itself, Brody shared his concerns knowing full well those opinions differed from others. He didn't care. He was a quick study but a slow learner. The choices he made were not paths he should have taken.

In a small town, with a name resembling a foreign country, Brody started his new life as a different person. With a population around 15,000, the small community of Lebanon was thriving. He found the community, divided by Interstate 44, as good a place as any to call home. Starting over seemed to be the answer. It wasn't like there was a choice. WITSEC was home for Brody Wesson. The willful participation of the unthinkable was his choice. Chad and Megan helped manufacture this juncture in what he was now experiencing.

He assimilated well into the small south-central town. His safe haven became his life. The construction trade sustained his livelihood. At least that was the ruse if ever pressed by inquiring minds about his finances. What he didn't know he learned. The median age was 40 plus years for the construction trade. He felt out of place, and he was. Although he wanted to be removed from the slow and mundane, he was decades from thinking of any comfortable career for retirement. Construction was not for the faint and not his favorite pastime. Computers were his passion. His nightlife was nonexistent for a young man his age.

Brody lived a double life. Years ago, he celebrated birthdays. Now he couldn't name any close acquaintances to celebrate any milestones. Holidays were no different. In the beginning, he cursed the two people who saved his life and rationalized them being responsible for ruining it. Retribution on his terms would be his sweet revenge.

Self-reflection brought on maturity. It was nearly a month of Sundays in the protection program before he was permitted to use electronics. A fate worse than death for a hacker. This revelation assisted in his maturity. The smart phone he used belonged to the government and the laptop came months after. Each device came with restrictions. Every keystroke was monitored by Big Brother.

Brody opened the lid of his lunch cooler and grabbed a chilled Mountain Dew. It was break time at work. He was young, strong, and healthy but liked his caffeine. He would joke to coworkers about them being off their old man meds and they would return the banter. What he had been through he called his multi-step program, and food for the soul. With what he witnessed, he was thankful for being alive. Brody had his so-called friends to be forever grateful. He still had his faults, but maturity kept him honest. It was simplistic, it was who he was. Retribution had different meanings for different people. Brody didn't have any misgivings or problems with his moral compass. As complicated as it was, he was comfortable with it.

"Hey! Seven Up! Come to life! We got the weekend ahead of us and I for one ain't hanging around any longer than I have to."

Brody turned to his cohorts with a smirk on his face and bantered back.

"Give it a break clowns. Got ya covered, I'm all but done."

He hadn't been called Brody for a very long time. He wasn't even sure he would react to being called his birth name if someone looked him in the eye while calling him out. Brody changed, not just inward but on the outside as well. Along with everything else, the facial hair went well with the 20-pound weight gain to his 5'9" stance. It wasn't by accident and was welcomed. An exercise plan at any gym would do it, but hanging drywall prevented money being wasted on gym membership.

He was forced to change his life to save his life. It's not like family would come calling to check up on him. He had no family and no friends worthy of the term. There wasn't a handful of people who thought of his existence, and he was ok with that as well. Acquaintances perhaps, but better odds would be waged on the lottery than him being recognized as Brody Wesson. Those who once knew his name, had long forgotten who that guy was. He unwillingly understood change was needed.

The most welcomed change was his art. It started small and broaden to tell a story. His story. Everyone has a story, however, not everyone will have their story painted on canvas. Whether huge like a Rembrandt or subtle like a freckle between two fingers, body art would be the connection in his two-sided world. What he hadn't yet decided, would the story be sad and resemble a faded polaroid, or a priceless memoir.

WITSEC have secured the identities of individuals since the early 1970's. Brody Wesson found himself part of a program he wanted nothing to do with. He was convinced by his arch nemeses, the benefits outweighed his objections. He never thought he would acquire that much money and lodging without holding down a job. Being a freeloader wasn't what he was about. He despised those who sponged off the government and yet he found himself thankful to those who helped him get his life back.

Brody Wesson's appearance changed as did his identity. It didn't take much to create a person who pretty much maintained a nonexistent life history. Thanks to WITSEC, Brody Wesson became Tenor Upshaw.

He became accustomed to the name, however, he found it difficult writing it or introducing himself as his new identity. It took practice. Tenor was a unique name to have since he couldn't sing a note to save his life. The indoctrination into the program was invaluable and obtaining employment was a true test. Practice makes perfect, and he finally assimilated himself into the workforce. The caveat was to avoid anything even closely related to computer technology.

Tenor was strongly encouraged to enroll into an apprentice trade school. It wasn't like he had a choice. He found construction to be somewhat interesting. It fit his already stale and boring life. It filled his time as a loner, but he soon realized he had purpose. He looked forward to a job earning his keep. He wasn't sure about the union labor, but he didn't concern himself with politics.

Tenor liked his new name. The lines easily blurred from a Brody to a Tenor. However, Tenor Upshaw acquired a nickname. Ten became short for his first name Tenor. Up became short for his last name Upshaw. To make it fun, the number ten became seven because of his consumption of caffeine. The nickname 'Seven Up' was born from Tenor Upshaw by his workmates.

He enjoyed his drywall coworkers. They needed his help and didn't want to chase the new guy away which occurred often in construction. Contractors frowned on multiple requests of apprentices out of training. The heavy work wasn't all that demanding, and he didn't shy from manual labor.

Tenor could do no wrong if jobs were completed on time. The company appreciated good help. He didn't need the income but enjoyed earning a salary. WITSEC provided a stipend he was more than comfortable with. He was told when he signed on, the freebies wouldn't last long, but a deadline wasn't forthcoming as he was let on to be. The boring life he led, cost the government very little. Sitting in his one-bedroom apartment and doing nothing began to bothered him. The trade school was perfect, but he soon tired of learning something he had little desire to stay with long term. His skillset was way beyond the trade he was taught. He didn't mind the work and the strenuous tasks was of no concern. He enjoyed the camaraderie but wanted more, much more. The new life, as he called it, was a work in progress. His peer group did not bother with the world around them, only the present tense was of any importance.

Seven Up became accustomed to living his double life. He not only became accustomed, but he became an asset. A valued asset. After what seemed like forever, his was able to purchase a toy with his own money. Not everything belonged to Uncle Sam, and he was granted some freedom.

There would be no reason to believe every keystroke of his new computer would be monitored. He was a realist, and that thought quickly vacated. He understood his previous life warranted a watchful eye.

People change and he had proven, thus far, he can be trusted. His technological asset became his drug. That drug became his enemy. Escaping the enemy was the lifeline he needed. He was going to enjoy his new computer even if big brother lurked at every download or search inquiry. He knew there were lines he couldn't cross. He was fortunate to be in a position where he was given latitude. Time would soon tell. Tenor was anxious to spread his wings. Getting wings clipped by Uncle Sam would require relocation. Another life interruption wasn't something he wanted to pursue.

CHAPTER 4

Sovereign Patriots became a household name in years past. A name that became synonymous with hate. The Sovereign Patriots did not dissolve. Law enforcement intel determined, a name change kept discontent on the forefront. Evil resembled a double headed snake. Cut one head off, one remains. Cut the remaining head off only to learn the mating process had already occurred.

That two-headed slithering monster had struck leaving poisonous venom. Trojan safeguards were in place and activated. Alarms were set and bells rang unbeknownst to the watchful eye of law enforcement. It was an antiquated term, but sleeper cells were easily awakened.

"How can we be certain they got their message or that it was even delivered." Alia was not shy especially when talking to her brother.

"The main question you should be asking yourself is why even doubt they didn't get it. They got their message," Alec replied.

Alia Noble was pointed as an icepick. Her bluntness came down with the force it took to chip away any opposition. It was who she was. She never, under any circumstance, apologized for being herself.

Her brother, Alec, maintained a peaceful and tranquil persona, most of the time. Alia was the older of the two, a whopping 5 minutes older. It was not that Alia wasn't a nice person, because she was. Her heart was solid gold. However, if crossed, it was like being seared by molten lava. It didn't just burn, it would scald a life scar deep in one's soul, not soon forgotten. She was protective of her baby brother. They were close as fraternal twins in a Yin Yang way. Like many siblings, they didn't always agree with each other. If one knew the others viewpoint was misguided or different, diplomacy was required to sort out the differences.

They understood each other. Their minds communicated like osmosis. They joked many times about the unspoken thoughts of the other. The unspoken word would soon be confirmed by actions or deed.

One of the most memorable circumstances happened while seated at an outside diner eating oven hearth pizza. The evening was quiet except for the crowded traffic on East Battlefield in Springfield, Missouri. The normal sights and sounds of the night blended with all other ambient sounds. The comfortable breeze under the umbrella table was an evening like any other. An ambulance, with activated red lights and siren, streamed through yielding traffic like the turning of a Rubik's cube. Alia and Alec would recall the memorable episode often but with a smile and grin. People will watch YouTube videos of a train wreck as it unfolds. The difference to the commotion, the normal person would not laugh at those killed or injured. That is what set Alia and Alec apart.

On that same evening, both ate their huge single slices, at ED's Pizzeria. Alec's choice was without fail, pepperoni and mushroom. Alia would not differ from her usual Canadian bacon with an extra layer of yellow peppers. No green, only yellow. The diner made that mistake once, and only once. The order included green peppers on her deep pan slice. Alia had made certain the manager understood the cook would not return to work the next day after succumbing to an unfortunate accident if green peppers found their way in her order again. Who threatens an employee and gets away with it? The employees at ED's would always identify Alia when she dined there.

Alia found her niche working for mental health professionals. She worked her way from ground floor clerical to administrative assistant. She would tire of the monotony, start a job search for vacancies in another healthcare facility, and do it all over again.

Alec wasn't all that different. He too worked from the ground up but wasn't at all authoritarian and shied away from any leadership responsibility. He was a follower. Opinionated like his sister but didn't have the drive or desire to take control. He observed all too often how the chosen few would sell their souls to lead.

Alec found his adrenalin rush in his work. He flourished when observing a task progress to the desired result. Alec would say he was self-taught. He acquired his tech knowledge off the teachings of others. He resembled a two-year-old soaking up knowledge like a sponge. He would take it all in until there was nothing left to siphon.

He needed assurance and affirmation that his talents were appreciated. At work it was expected and appreciated. Living with his sister, he didn't want or expect his talents to be rewarded. As roommates, they got along well. They understood each other like any young adult sibling. Any outside recognition of any of their joint computer tech ventures could mean incarceration. He wanted to observe from a distance like he was accustomed. This time was risky. He had to know for himself and not take his sister's word for it. He trusted his sister with every breath of life. He needed something more in this circumstance and it was vitally important for the plan to work. He knew it and Alia had led him to believe it. All things had their purpose, and this was no different.

A few simple keystrokes and he would have his answer. Programming was Alec's foreign language and he spoke it fluently. He worked for Com Tech, an up and coming, flourishing computer tech company. He and a close friend at work created tech language only they understood. Complicated to a novice graduate from a large, accredited computer engineering university, simple addition and subtraction mathematics to Alec and his close coworker.

The alphanumeric sequence forwarded through his message delivered its response. A time code was attached causing the delayed response he was expecting, although the wait was unbearable. The suspected targets got their message. The time stamp gave delivery and the receipt of the message. The trained eye would know how to decipher the encrypted language. Alec was the trained eye, and the message was the digital footprint he attached to the text message he sent. It was no different than with current smart phones. In this case, the sender wanted a response, but the receiver wasn't aware one was being returned. To those who didn't understand, it was as if being blind and told there was nothing to look at. You would have knowledge to the contrary. It didn't mean anything to the untrained eye. If you weren't schooled in that language, you couldn't read or speak it. It meant something, you just didn't understand what.

Alec was smart and calculated with his multi-tech attributes. Hacking was his skillset. Numbers, symbols, and letters told a story or requested one be told. The language was foreign to anyone not knowing what was beyond each key stroke formula. The visualization came from knowing what to look for and understanding what was in the coded language. It was his addictive high. He sat in silence and basked in simplicity. The thrill was an amphetamine rush.

It was his drug, their drug, and he was on a high. He knew the chase was on. They were the hunters.

Thirty minutes later, and as expected, there it was. The confirmation of his handy work told him what he already knew. His facial up-tick was the only jubilation he exerted. To him, it was like a nightclub party. The DJ was spinning tunes to make him breakout in a happy dance, if only in his mind.

Like clockwork, or a timer that was set to go off on her bedside table, Alia stepped to her brothers room. She knocked lightly as she always did without entering. She never entered without invitation. It was her request of him. The request was misunderstood once and was never repeated.

"Did you get confirmation our friends got your message?" She ask.

"It was our message, not mine. And yes, they got their message."

"Good. We're going to send another one before long. You've got to make sure they know you mean business."

"Alia, you're doing it again."

"Doing what?

"We send them messages. Not me."

"Whatever," Alia retorted. "You hit the send key. You and you alone send the messages."

CHAPTER 5

Two weeks passed. No other messages were received by MoTAF members. Some even suggested it could have been a prank instead of believing encrypted private cell phones could be compromised. Chad and Megan knew no pranksters existed. The intel world had been quiet way too long for something as simple as a prank to even develop. Nothing alarming occurred and no serious threat developed for Missouri's clandestine security force.

MoTAF had its underground as well. A lot of intellectuals make up the tech world. They know the language, spoke it professionally amongst themselves and anyone vetted to inquire of their expertise. They were clandestine as well, although sanctioned by big brother. DC analysts could not only blend in but needed to be invisible. They operated, funded, and were sanctioned under the Department of Homeland Security.

Chad's request for red flag clarification sounded the alarm and the response was instantaneous. No red tape or roadblocks to overcome. A red flag clarification was pretty much unheard of until things got dire. It was the DC analysts who corresponded to tactical forces across the U.S. warning of potential threats to the country. Threats were vetted by analysts then sent to task force members to neutralize or eliminate any threat encountered or suspected. These cautionary notifications never became commonplace. Even though the country was polarized now more than ever before, falsehoods never surfaced. Particularly, no high clearance federal employee, played games with security of the country.

Chad and Megan, the only members who received the unwarranted message, remained concerned. Alarming as it first seemed, their mindset did change over time. The threat was believed random and isolated. It was easier to forget about it, although any threat remained in the back of their minds. The powers to be would not take any chances. That was what they were led to believe until learning different. The search of any breach continued and was soon determined nothing brought to the level of concern near or abroad. Their new phones were encrypted as the previous phones. Creating cell numbers that don't exist to the outside world is not as complicated as one would think. Any red tape or any political maze to weave through was one in the same. The purse strings were controlled by the same unknowns that created the complicated maze.

Whatever MoTAF needed, they received. Wants and needs are two separate monsters. Not one person ever requested tech toys, even if a new item of potential use was on the market. That mindset was child's play. MoTAF did not play games. The thought quickly faded for Chad and Megan of there being a jokester amongst them. Their heads became swivels.

Chad and Megan's concern never brought them to the level of fearing for their safety. The smartest minds in the tech world were on their side. It was explained encrypted software had not been thwarted on either of their phones. Chad and Megan wanted to move on. There were concerns about the phones, but they were not able to brush off thoughts about receiving any more unsolicited messages. Their personal safety, as with other task force members was always priority. No shortcuts were ever taken with training or keeping abreast of trending threats across the country and even around the world. They had entered uncharted waters.

Nothing traced to any viruses, hacks or any other backdoor disturbances linking any groups or persons disrupting communications. In other words, it was as if nothing happened. The person or persons linking the text messages sent to Chad and Megan's cell phones would perhaps forever be a mystery. What was undeniable, the person or persons who sent the message were as clever as the analysts trying to find out who it was. No familiar tech signatures surfaced. Nothing of this nature had ever occurred before. Every avenue of inquiry turned out to be a dead end. They were good, perhaps too good. They would make the mistake that would unmask their deeds.

Games or no games, techies like challenges and didn't like being outdone. The war between cyber pros was on. The only assurances were that neither knew their adversary. The only question was if a war even existed, and if so, who was the perceived nemesis?

Seven Up gave a quizzical glance at his cell. The uncertain glance was because the sound coming from his phone wasn't expected. It wasn't that he hadn't heard it before. The notification on his phone was the alert confirming the underground network securing his admittance into WITSEC was alive and well. He didn't have to wonder, but the audible was reassurance, if he needed any help, all he had to do was ask for it. The cell sounded again. This brought Seven Up to his feet because he knew what was coming. It would be a call from an unknown number, from an unknown person, for an unknown reason. He was informed about a call prefaced by the all-familiar alert in a sequence meant something was afoul. It could have meant he crossed a security protocol. A breach in protocol was a flagrant violation of his contract. The same contract he unwillingly agreed to but was more than willing to accept due to the options placed before him.

He knew he had to answer it. His number was an unlisted government number. There was no chance of a nuisance call with the promise of a week-long Caribbean cruise. Not that they didn't exist because they did. There wasn't a snowball of a chance a call of that nature would be on his phone.

"Hello, who is this?" he said.

"My name is irrelevant. It's why I'm calling that's important."

The soft young female voice was puzzling to listen to. She was command bearing, but in a polite way. She was good at what she did, the only question to be answered was, what was her job and what was it she did?

"I haven't done anything wrong. Why are you calling me?"

The soft-spoken voice of obedience didn't waver. There was no reason to question what may be asked of him. There was an undeniable truth anything could be asked of him while he was in the program. Tenor called WITSEC 'The Program.'

"We are going to need your continued assistance." The calming woman continued her lecture.

"You've been stellar in providing the continuance in security of our nation. Your continued participation is that of more of a hands-on approach."

Tenor wanted to laugh but he needed to understand exactly what she was trying to tell him. He had to play their game and not ruffle feathers. He summoned his professional tone to ask what he needed to know.

"I'm grateful of the courtesy you've extended on my behalf thus far. How can I be of service?"

"The exact extent of service hasn't been approved as of date. What I can assure you, your talents will be utilized, and you will be handsomely rewarded."

"I've got to know more about what you're asking of me. What exactly do you mean by saying I will have a hands-on approach and what kind of talents are you talking about?"

"I'm sorry, I'm not at liberty to discuss the specifics at this time. I will be in touch."

"Hold on a minute, hello. Hello, are you there?"

The line went dead. No name, no answers to his question. Nothing. Tenor wanted to open his second-floor apartment bedroom widow and throw the phone into the busy street. Screaming was the only rational thing he could think of to do, but it was also childish. An unprofessional call from the government. That was exactly what he should have expected.

Megan and Chad saved his life. He understood it was up to him to repay his debt even though it hadn't previously been asked of him. It was the government. His part was different than other program participants. He'd been given a pass because someone stood up for him. The voice on the phone wasn't familiar. Soft spoken but commanded obedience in a feminine way. The caller made a request for Tenor to remain available. The request was in and of itself offensive. He was always available. His life was controlled by others, and he knew it. It wasn't like he was being told when to get up or when to go to bed. He was free, sort of. He could make meals for himself or could freely dine anywhere he chose. He could turn out the lights or turn them on when he wanted. His sleeping quarters could be altered anytime he desired. He wasn't incarcerated.

The puppet strings always pulled at him, but they weren't what defined him. He could only take care of things he could control. All other things would work themselves out. He convinced himself of that years ago and that mindset served him well.

He was intrigued by the call but didn't appreciate the abrupt conclusion. It wasn't clear what roadmap he was being given or where that road led. He may be told he was sitting in the driver's seat with both hands on the wheel, but there was no denying who was in control.

CHAPTER 6

Alia entered her apartment with a scowl across her brow. Her day was long. Alec heard a deep exhale as she slung her leather-bound satchel strap over the back of a kitchen chair. It missed its mark with a thud on the floor. Alec knew not to ask what her issue was. He'd been through this scenario many times prior. She would open the cupboard, grab two mint tea bags, and pour water into the coffee pot. The routine was mundane. Alec could almost count down to the second when she would sit at the table with her tea rubbing both temples. Her migraine would diminish but his nightmare would begin. Alia began her rant about her boss's concern with appearances. The good of those who worked for him or the mission they were trying to accomplish played second fiddle.

Alec could write the script because he heard it - often. Those in power making decisions without remorse, adversely affecting those they propose to advocate for. Alec remained silent until the script concluded. Without warning an occasional rebuke of power broke the silence in the room. Alec knew when the headache diminished. She would refresh her cup of tea and he would embraced the calm. Computer programming was not her forte although her grasp of programming was impressive. Her patience wouldn't allow the nuances. If an electronic device would power on, there would be no need to understand why.

Alia finally spoke calmly. "Enough time has passed. We're moving on to the next phase."

It was time for sensical discussion. He knew full well she would require his expertise.

Alec braced himself and responded. "I'm clueless to your next phase."

"I'm kinda winging it." she said.

"Seriously Alia, work with me. You've got to have a plan and how we're going to execute it."

Alia refused to allow her migraine to return. Sipping her tea, she looked at her brother atop the oversized mug while savoring the aroma. She'd seen his displeasure before and didn't care for it. She could smolder whatever backbone he could muster. This time she didn't have the desire to engage.

"I'm not saying I haven't thought about our next move, I just haven't decided which move to make."

Alec wanted to debate the issue, but the aggravation would be futile. Not knowing when his talents would be needed for any of her plans was painful in and of itself. He was smart enough to know which buttons to push and the sequence in which to push them. The game of taunting would be entertaining for anyone watching, but not for him. For him it was painful.

"Alia, I know we need to keep the fire burning and can't let them rest on their laurels."

"Exactly. We're going to play this one right. They'll have no idea who we are and most of all, where we are coming from."

"Let me know what you want me to do. It could be tricky to pull off."

"It's always tricky with you," Alia mumbled. "We're gonna send them another message. This time it will be specific."

Scenarios flowed through his mind like melting snow careening down a mountain side. He seldom questioned her decision making, at least not out loud. Why would she revisit sending another message so soon? It wasn't wise. Being aggressive with Alia was like searching for landmines with a hammer in knee high grass.

Creative programming and cryptic Java language was complicated regardless of how skilled he was. She didn't concern herself with complicated technicalities. He fought that battle all too often. She didn't like it when he made her less capable than himself. The fact was, she was intelligent, but in a different way. She researched every angle for state resources for well-deserved clients. With modesty, she would proclaim it was part of her job when commended for going the extra mile. They both maintained IQ's upward of 160. There was never a need to compete with the other's intellect. Competitiveness, however, was a suitable synonym when it came to being involved in something they both believed in.

"You're correct in your assumption. It's time to send another message and today is the day."

"What? I didn't say I should send another text."

He knew what he said as the words came out of his mouth. They functioned as one, not as two. The landslide could not be stopped once it started. He fell for it, like many times prior. She would engage and taunt his being unsuspecting and naive. He never saw it coming. It frustrated him and she reveled in his short sightedness.

"Alia, it's too soon. I can't send another message."

"It's not too soon and we can send one anytime we think it's appropriate."

Alia was as calm as a gentle breeze in the late spring morning. She humored at his quick rebuke. No need to write down the phases for memory recall. She knew what was next even when she kept her brother in the dark. Some things are better left unsaid.

It took a while for her to come up with the exact wording. Alec was in his room finding comfort. It was she who pushed that infamous button. The mute button during tense moments became the only one he preferred when it came to his sister. The thought brought a smile to his face. It faded to a frown when he heard the hinges of his door and her soft knuckle taps. It drowned out all his tranquil thoughts. There was no need to turn around.

She stepped halfway around the door looking toward his desk where he always sat. She cleared her throat as if she were an executive administrative assistant interrupting a board meeting.

"Alec, I know what I want it to say, and I want you to send it now."

"I'm assuming I don't have a say in it, so let's have it."

The displeasure tone wasn't received well, but she knew he was right. He didn't have a say and it didn't bother her knowing it. His brashness only resonated when she let it and now wasn't one of those times.

"You have no integrity. Get your affairs in order."

As the words came out of her mouth, his eyebrows flinched upwards. She waited for him to say something. His pause was long and unintended.

"Nicely worded," he said. "They'll know we mean business."

CHAPTER 7

Sovereign Patriots. Who are they? Nothing could be found giving any worthwhile understanding of the name. Except perhaps Wikipedia. But even the word patriot gave pause to any name it was attached requiring a deeper query. Sovereign Patriots were a force to be taken seriously. The watchful eye of big brother continues to scour different allegiances attempting to thwart democracy. There are those defending the will of the people as well. A strong democracy is the defense to polarizing forces. History proved the lines can be blurred.

Tenor took pride in doing something productive and positive. He liked small gestures, nods, and thanks for a job well done. He recognized his debt and was paying it forward. He didn't recognize the poison he previously ingested until the sickness was malignant. He didn't even notice the warning signs. Radicalization seldom has a proven course of treatment. Tenor missed the curve signs, directional arrows, and all warning prompts designed for vulnerable and unexpecting souls. Like an undercurrent, he was drawn into the deep end.

Social media was a powerful force. Purposely and by chance, people are connected. The same can be said for news media outlets. Sovereign Patriots formed an allegiance that could not be shaken. At least not until the tightly woven web of hate withered under the weight of decency.

Tenor Upshaw learned the hard way. It all began when classmates became friends. Friends became vulnerable to similar mindsets. Those mindsets lined with others, then more mirrored the same. Young minds with the need to assimilate are drawn together for a cause not yet understood. When in doubt, it was too late for one to think for themselves.

Law enforcement professionals are just that, professionals. They are good at what they do and are comfortable with the reward of knowing they accomplished missions of protecting others without fanfare. None is ever needed for those wanting to do what they took an oath to uphold. Serve and protect those who look to them for their wellbeing was a calling.

Tenor tried not to dwell on the past. Incapable of separating his past from the present, the future didn't hold a lot of promise either. At least not until now. He would go about his mundane until he would be informed what he would be doing for The Program. He was certain he would be politely ask and he could graciously decline. After all, it was Uncle Sam who was kind enough to eliminate the draft and only ask for volunteers. Marketing could learn a thing are two from them. There is likely a study somewhere, how the government learned tricks of the trade from the tobacco companies. You can't argue with success.

There would be nothing subtle about requesting his assistance. Tenor thought of being aligned with other tech professionals. There wasn't a second thought on the subject. There was no chance he would be allowed anywhere near a room full of government keyboards and software. He did push aside thoughts of sitting in an uncomfortable chair and in front of a directional floodlight.

They could dangle the carrot all they wanted. The entree was prepared. The concern, of course, what was on the menu? His patriot friends were inactivated, that he was assured of when The Program changed his name. He had no desire to partake what they previously served. He preferred a straight and narrow diet moving forward.

The twins were susceptible to social media like anyone with large friend circles. The definition of friendship became narrowly defined, like a friendship with a next-door neighbor. Or a friendship sustained through an employment coworker. Justification to his or her way of thinking could easily be theorized by the many likes or heartface emojis. When a wave of social media gained momentum, the tide could drown all sensible thought processes, reason, and morality. Influencers were of all sects. All one had to do was a simple search and align themselves quite easily for the good, or evil.

Alia was a melody of mystery and intrigue. Alec was not like his sister when it came to patience. He did not throw caution to the wind. He tolerated her lack of decision making because there wasn't any other choice.

Without warning Alia started a rant. An unsolicited berate of what was wrong with the world. That was her M.O. She was curt with him, more so than normal. This time it was personal. She raised her voice in a vial tone with relinquishing disdain for his not being supportive. Alec surmised her migraine returned. She accused him of betrayal and at the least, being on the wrong side of democracy.

"Enough is enough. I've had it!" Alec shouted and kicked a chair before walking to the door.

He paused momentarily, glancing back as the chair tumbled to the floor. He was able to hide his surprise. It was the first time the chair didn't slide across the tile. It couldn't have been planned any better. His point was made as the apartment door thundered shut behind him. The door was the explanation point and climatic effect after the chair. To further make his point, he turned off his cell. She wasn't talking him down, not this time. He needed to clear his head. This time her apology would be authentic and sincere.

Alia composed herself and walked from Alec's room to pick up the chair. She could have said what she did with more of a diplomatic approach, but she didn't. That wasn't her style. Standing in his room and questioning his loyalty wasn't the smartest play in her bag of tricks. It was time to give him space. She would call him after he'd cooled down. She would have him drive by one of their favorite eateries, her treat of course, as a peace offering. After all, it was nearing the supper hour. She was certain her neighbors could hear her rant as well as her brothers. If heirlooms remained on nearby shelving, the concussion from Alec slamming their door would have sent them crashing to the floor. There were advantages to bottom floor apartments.

Alec drove in a fury and cursed like a sailor. He abhorred not being part of the equation. He made all things plausible by persuading reason to the chaos. When she was willing, she learned calmness. She would show promise with understanding his tech world. She was gracious every time he showed her how to perform complicated tech nuances. How dare she challenge his loyalty.

He slammed his palm on the center of the steering column, not once but three times. Alec glanced in his rear-view. No car behind him, none in front. It was the steady red light that caused the noise of someone's car horn.

The sound of screeching tires. A loud noise, and glass shattered all over him as his driver door collapsed inward. He knew what was happening but had no control over his car spinning from his lane and off the pavement. The spinning went on for what must have been minutes, although only a few seconds passed. He closed his eyes and gripped tightly to the steering wheel. The spinning stopped. He understood he was upside down. The seatbelt did its job. The ringing in his ears became louder. He hurt all over. His head hurt the most. He wanted to open his eyes but couldn't. The pain was intense. Trying to decipher what hurt most was futile. He finally opened his eyes but could not focus. Everything was all a blur. The blur faded to darkness.

CHAPTER 8

Alia paced the polished comfortable surroundings she called home. She became accustomed to how secure it made her. She pressed the end key on her cell for the third time. It was unlike Alec not to pick up, especially after multiple calls. Her calls were unlike previous ones. One ring and it went to voicemail. She knew not to leave a message. It didn't go well for her the last time. It wasn't like him turning off his cell, which is what she surmised. She was sure of it. Alec left a couple hours prior. She would forego the thought of take out. He wasn't going to pick up anything for supper. That ship already sailed.

Alia enjoyed meaningful conversations with her brother. She got him to understand why she worked so hard for those who couldn't find their voice. The mothers who would do anything for their kids only to observe the bureaucratic system throw them away. She was now frustrated with herself. Where was her empathy? She knew not to push his buttons but found it entertaining. Him not answering his phone was finding its mark. She was sure he was now intentionally pushing hers.

"No pizza tonight," Alia proclaimed out loud to near silent surroundings.

Her musical genre filled the air with what normally would be conversation with her brother at this hour. He made his point and it landed with an exclamation point. She wasn't one to apologize, however this time, she knew a sincere explanation was warranted and she would deliver. The corners of her mouth turn upward. She held the smirk on her face. The knock on the door was a test and she wasn't falling for it. He had done it to her before. It wasn't going to work this time. It wasn't like he went out grocery shopping. That was the surprise she got from him about a year ago. He proved to her he could grocery shop without her help. The problem was when he got to the apartment door, he knocked by kicking the door with his foot. With his hands full of groceries, he had no choice but to have Alia open the door for him.

She waited for the kick on the door like before. It didn't happen. The smirk on her face turned to a full smile as she recalled opening the door and her brother grimacing from the weight of the groceries. Once inside, one of the plastic bags failed and groceries careened all over the floor. They both laughed until their sides hurt from the lack of oxygen.

Alec didn't leave the apartment to prove anything. Well, perhaps he did, but it wasn't to grocery shop. He wasn't angry, he was livid. She hoped he would calm down and they could talk it out. She waited a little longer and it came - another knock.

"Nice try, Alec. Get your own door."

She called out from her reclined and favorite seat of the couch. Another knock and then came a voice she didn't recognize.

"Hello, Mrs. Noble."

Her smile faded. Alia rose from the couch and hastily made her way to the door. Who was it and why did they think she was married? Cautiously she leaned to the peephole and nearly gasp out loud as she backed from the door. She hadn't expected the police. They can't know. Nothing had been put into motion, not yet anyway. It wasn't really a threat. An anonymous warning is not a threat. How could they have known where they lived? She wasn't going to open the door, she decided she couldn't. They hadn't planned for this.

"Mrs. Noble, it's the police. We need to talk to you about your husband."

Alia never experienced fear. She's been mad at her boss, but she knew how controlling and manipulative he was. The pounding in her chest was at uncomfortable proportions. Incarceration is not something she planned. She was not going down without an understanding and sympathetic audience. She had demands but was not prepared to put anything into motion. Not yet, not this way. She could hardly breathe. Alia never experienced asthma symptoms, but she was gasping for air. She felt faint. The pounding heartbeat in her temples became unbearable. The rise and fall of her chest to every breath was deep, but not fully exhaled. The hyperventilating persisted. She steadied and willed herself not to faint.

In a whisper, leaning on her door with her t-shirt balled up in fists to her chest, she responded to the knocking.

"Who is it?"

The words came out softly, knowing full well the people on the other side couldn't hear them. She slowly looked again through the door eye hole seeing the uniform officers waiting patiently. She gained all the composure she could muster and ask again what she already knew. This time it was in a tone not of the faint, but of command and nearing that of anger.

"Who is it?"

The door pounding stopped but was interrupted by a deep authoritarian tone.

"Mrs. Noble, it's the police. We need to speak with you."

The knocks and the booming voice was followed by uncomfortable silence. Stepping back into the safety of her surroundings, she attempted to calm herself. Alia responded loudly as if she could only be heard through the peephole.

"You have my name right, but I'm not married. You must have the wrong address."

She tried to take another deep breath, and another. She closed her eyes momentarily, before tiptoeing again to the door still gasping for a deep lung exhale. Looking through the peep hole at two uniformed officers, she steadied her breathing. They were still standing, waiting for her to respond.

"Ma'am, we need to speak to you. Please open the door."

"Show me your ID." Both officers held their identification separately to the door eye piece to be viewed. Remaining defiant, she again refused their request.

"They're hard to see, slide them under the door."

She heard one of the officers say something she couldn't clearly hear. She looked again through the security eye piece. They were not going to hand over their identification. She unlocked the dead bolt but left the chain link connected to the door frame.

"Your ID please. Show me your IDs."

Alia opened the door to the length of the chain. In her mind, the metal link connected her between safety and danger. That link now resembled a log chain preventing unwelcome intrusion.

"Ma'am, we would like to talk to you about your husband.

"I'm sorry, you have my name correct, but I'm not married. I'm rather busy, so you must excuse me."

"Ma'am, your husband's name isn't Alex?"

"I told you I'm not married. My brother lives here, and his name is Alec. It could be him you're wanting to see. I'll tell him to call your department when he returns."

"Mam, we are sorry for the confusion. It must be your brother we're talking about. He's been in an accident and was taken to Methodist University Hospital."

Alia unclasped the door with frantic expectation. She stepped back to allow the officers entry, still grasping the cloth of her t-shirt in fists.

The onset of faint persisted. She leaned back against the closed door as the officers continued to look at her after they entered. They would make sure she would be fine after their visit. They've experienced notifications previously in their line of work. They weren't going to let her do a header on the floor. The paperwork would be an aggravation they preferred to avoid.

While keeping a watchful eye, they apologized again for the mix up and politely gave enough personal space so not to be abrasive with their presence. The officers gave Alia all the information they had at their disposal including the hospital contact information. Alia declined to seat herself at their suggestion. She assured them she would be fine even though she wasn't as sure as she lead them to believe. She ask all the questions she could think to ask. They answered the best they could with the information provided to them. The officers made a sympathetic and graceful exit. Alia wanted her privacy to return to the moment before the intrusion. That would have to wait. She needed to get to the hospital.

CHAPTER 9

Seven Up perused his electronic devices. The invigorating empowerment of freedom was addictive. He was free to look at anything online he wanted, within reason of course. His new freedom did come with restrictions. While living a double life of hidden identity, he accepted every keystroke was viewed by the all-mighty Big Brother. It took a while, but this juncture in life was patriotic. He would be doing good for others. Whatever they were going to ask, he was sure it would be for the positive.

While reading nonsensical news sites, he received an alert on his cell. Startling as it was, he pondered whether to answer his phone with a snide sarcastic greeting. Proving he could be a trusted professional, he calmly answered his cell.

"This is Tenor."

"Hello Tenor, it's me."

Tenor could not resist the temptation. He was to get as much enjoyment from the anonymous caller as he could. He was the present day 007.

"And who might you be? We haven't established that yet, have we?"

"Don't be coy. Something has altered a change in current affairs. An alert in national security may cause our level of urgency to be altered."

"Yeah, whatever. I've proven my sincerity so quit jerking me around."

The unknown calm voice responded. She continued as if she did not hear what he said.

"Go to the Methodist University Hospital. Say you're a friend of Alec Noble. Find out what you can and report back to us."

"Are you serious? Who is Adam Nobody and why am I pretending to be his friend? I know that hospital. It's in Memphis."

"His name is Alec Noble. Write it down, Tenor. It was the closest hospital to the traffic accident he was involved in."

Tenor got a lot of information about a guy he was ask to meet. It was unfortunate he was in a car wreck but maybe they could be good friends. Anyone who was a computer tech junkie like himself, couldn't be all bad.

Tenor was near mid-sentence when the line went dead. He was about to ask about mileage reimbursement for his drive to Memphis. It would have been a joke, but he liked the sound of her voice and preferred to keep her on the phone a little longer. He was on his own and charting new waters. The wind was in his sail. He acquired tenacity from his time in WITSEC. He would prove to his anonymous friend he was up to the task. It was a challenge he looked forward to.

Work conflict surprisingly didn't happen. A late morning trip proved to be a positive proposition. The drive to Memphis was not only tolerable, it was informative. Finding an interesting podcast about social justice made the trip bearable. Hearing a different viewpoint spurred thoughts he hadn't pondered. He was looking forward to his return trip. He wanted to engage the topic with someone, although he wasn't so sure bringing up the topic to coworkers would be so inviting. He was very much aware other viewpoints weren't as cultured as his own. He was his own worst critic and believed he could empathize with other viewpoints.

He never in his wildest imagination believed his life would have turned into an educational research project. But there he was, continuing to give back to a community he was now calling home. He was being ask to do something he wouldn't have thought possible. Be a spy. How difficult could it be? Find the guy, talk to him, learn about his craft, and tell an unknown person over the phone what he learned. No problem.

Hospital parking was terrible. In the middle of the day, and middle of the week, there's so many people with a multitude of health issues. What could be the similarities of so many to require him to park in the farthest forty-acres of a parking lot? As he gave up looking for the nearest vacant spot, he noticed several reserved handicap parking. He thought it briefly, his moral compass would not allow him to park there. Not anymore.

He slowed to a stop in front of the large UPS panel truck taking up not one but two handicap parking locations. He rolled down his passenger window taking a quick photo with the thought of confronting the driver or at least the company. Not long ago he would have dared to be confronted for the same infraction.

The futile search for a close parking spot ended as did the thought of confronting the UPS driver. He would park and prepare for the longest, unintentional walk he had ever taken. If it would have been a scheduled doctor appointment, or perhaps an employment interview, he would have plenty of time to change his mind and cancel the appointment.

The lobby was larger than he expected. Tenor prepared himself for the audition of his life. He rehearsed his performance during his drive. His confidence sored. *Adapt And Improvise* was the name of the movie he was auditioning for. With composer, he walked to the information desk. The young lady looked him in the eye and ask the question before he could speak.

"What is the name of the patient?"

Tenor was taken back by the receptionist's question. He must have looked like a tourist on a sidewalk approaching a historic landmark. Note to self. Never, ever, be transparent. Keep them guessing or at least show how unpredictable you can be.

"Alec Noble, he was brought in earlier today. Can you tell me what room he's in?"

"We have nobody admitted by that name. Is it N O B L E.?" She spelled the last name like he was in second grade.

"Yes, that's correct."

"Sorry sir, we have no Alex Noble admitted or recently discharged in our records."

"No, it's Alec Noble. A L E C."

Tenor spelled the name with the most annoying patronizing tone he could muster.

She, without a doubt, took offense to his rude reply.

"Second floor. He hasn't been assigned a private room yet. The elevators are just beyond the gift shop."

Her pointing in the direction of the gift shop, without looking, telegraphed that one side of her body was robotic. He would kindly thank her, but she continued looking down at her cell phone without eye contact. She subconsciously waived him on so she could continue reading her social media. Tenor walked toward the elevators, vowing vindication when he would undoubtedly see her again. He loathed rudeness. Mainly because he was that same, uninterested smug self in a previous life.

The rehearsal was back on track. His earnest face of concern was easily practiced in the reflective elevator door. It was a good thing he was the only person in the oversized compartment. He practiced the sloping of his shoulders and serious concern look as he leaned into his reflection. He imagined a crowded cart with others as they avoided looking into other faces in hopes they wouldn't looked at yours in such close quarters.

The elevator gave an audible tone to announce the anticipated floor Miss Personality informed him about. It was a quiet slow ride up one floor. The hospital layout was odd. He stepped off the elevator and noticed the sign to the receptionist straight ahead. No turning, no long hallways, no need to ask further directions.

"Good afternoon sir, how can I help you?"

She was at least 30 years older than Miss Personality and wore no ring on her left hand or indentation of there ever being one. There were none on her right hand, leading to the assumption rings and dangling necklaces were prohibited. She had a smile of warmth that would melt any glacier. So much for the earnest, down looking sorrow facade he had been rehearsing. Before he could respond to Ms. Cordial, duty called. Her desk phone rang and another employee in scrubs called her by her birth name. She ignored the phone call and drew her attention to her coworker. Tenor was occupied with the calmness displayed by Ms. Cordial. This was not her first day on the job.

Tenor looked at the surroundings. Computer terminals on rollable carts. Partially opened doors leading inside patient rooms. Patient charts resting in holding trays attached to each door appearing to be occupied. The odor of disinfectant permeated throughout. An inessential smirk appeared on his face when he noticed the strategically placed security cameras facing the reception desk. His face returned to normalcy when he heard the arrival tone of the elevator. The same tone announcing the arrival after he pushed the number to the floor. An excited man in his late twenties walked briskly to Ms. Cordial.

"Ma'am, I need to find my fiancé. Tell me what room Alec Noble's in."

"Sir, please calm down. Let me help this gentleman and I'll be right with you."

Ignoring the annoying ringing phone, Ms. Cordial turned to Tenor. "I'm sorry sir, how can I help you?"

Tenor wanted to apologize for the incredible busy moment she was having. Multitasking was not new to her. He couldn't wait to see this play out. Tenor stepped aside and let Mr. Anxiety shuffle the deck and play his hand.

"That's fine ma'am, I can wait," Tenor moved only slightly to the side and let Mr. Anxiety get the answers he so desperately needed.

The man had already invaded that uncomfortable personal breathing space to ask his one question. The curtesy of a normal human being would have noticed the awkwardness. Entitlement took on a whole new meaning. Tenor became an enemy of his previous life. How quickly things changed. He liked his new self.

Tenor overheard the conversation between Ms. Cordial and Mr. Anxiety. EMS earlier explained to attending nurses and the on-call physician the seriousness of injuries to Alec Noble. The on-duty nurses and doctors understood the potential onslaught of visitors. Notifications of the accident were ongoing.

Tenor knew he needed to find out all he could before the potential onslaught of arriving family members. Ms. Cordial and Mr. Anxiety were going to be an invaluable resource.

CHAPTER 10

Applying make-up and changing clothes was out of the question. She needed to hurry. Alia found herself running a race in quicksand. She was moving as fast as she could, making little progress and soon overcome with anxiety. The calming effect was knowing she didn't have to get gas in her car. She closed her eyes and took a much-needed slow deep breath. The dizziness she experienced earlier no longer held her captive. She was able to take deep breaths, fully exhale and repeat. She was fine but she was in haste to find out about her brother.

The hastened trip to see Alec was not without concern of traffic violations. Sadly, she couldn't remember much about how she got there, only that she arrived safely. Miss Personality was on her perch but didn't see Alia enter the hospital. Alia navigated through the lobby to the elevators. Remembering what the officers told her, she pressed the number 2 and was pleased to be the lone passenger going up.

She composed herself as best she could and willed herself to be calm for Alec. She was angry with herself for playing her stupid game. She always had fun pulling his strings and making him laugh or making him angry. What made this different from all the others wasn't clear. She couldn't wait to apologize. Hopefully, he would forgive her. They only had each other. There was nobody else. She looked at her mirrored door reflection. She would not cry in front of him.

Tenor patiently sat in the not so comfortable waiting room. He was making notations in his phone for easy recall. The request was to forward a narrative to his unknown mentors. It wasn't much of a request although the congenial unknown caller made it appear so.

Ms. Cordial was her same professional, passionate self when the elevator alerted to another arriving passenger. Tenor got the answer to his awaiting question. Her name was Alia Noble. She was the sister of the man he was there to meet. Tenor heard the lady tell Ms. Cordial the story of the police coming to her apartment. Tenor tried not to show any reaction to the information. Ms. Cordial told the new arrival, her brother's fiancé was with her brother in recovery.

Ms. Cordial was calm. "Ma'am, he said he was your brothers' fiancé. I couldn't refuse anyone who stated they were close to the family."

"There's a guy in with my brother who said he's my brother's fiancé?"

Tenor wasn't going to allow anything from accomplishing why he was there. The sister's arrival gave his assignment intrigue. Staring down at his cell, the sister paid little attention, if any, to his presence. Ms. Cordial's pleasant persona melted his heart. Not so much for the patients sister.

"I'll go talk to him and make sure he is who he says he is. I'll get my supervisor and be right back."

Tenor dropped the magazine he was holding. He wasn't in a library, but the commotion caused both ladies to turn in his direction. Opportunity presented itself. It was time to put into action what he rehearsed. He had to sell it.

"Hello, I'm Tenor. I know your brother and I heard about him being involved in an accident. Is there anything I can do for you?"

"Thank you. I'm Alia, you've probably heard I'm his sister. The lady is going to get her supervisor and find out why some guy is in my brother's room."

Tenor improvised. He would have to think fast to find out all he could and not draw suspicion himself.

"I'm sure she'll be able to help you. She seems really nice. Can I get you anything, a bottle of water?"

He was asked the same thing when he was greeted by Ms. Cordial. He refused but was told where vending machines and a stocked beverage refrigerator was located. Boredom could be soothed by beverage. The room served as a kitchenette and was filled with snacks, coffee, iced tea, hot water dispenser with an assortment of flavored tea, and as many flavored creamers. He didn't plan to be there long enough to use the microwave for the popcorn.

The look on Alia's face was of shock and dismay. She stared at the back of the computer monitor as if reading a message specifically for visitors. There was nothing to read on the rear of the computer monitor. She was in another world.

Tenor's rehearsals required fine tuning. Getting what he needed was more of a problem than anticipated.

"Ma'am, are you ok? Can I get you something to drink? Water or a soda?"

Alia reacted like she had seen a two-headed cyclops monster. She looked at him with no expression. Her blank stare was as if she was on medication which required one not drive, operate machinery, or even stand upright.

"No thank you. I just can't wrap my head around what's happening."

"I know what you mean. It's surreal," Tenor said.

Tenor couldn't reveal much about himself or how he supposedly knew her brother. If a true coworker would come to the hospital while he was there, his facade would be up.

"So how do you know my brother?"

And there it was. The question he was expecting. The one he had rehearsed. The one answer he had to sell like his life depended on it.

"I was recently hired at Com Tech. I haven't been there but a couple weeks, but I remember Alec's welcome was genuine."

"That's so nice of you to say. I'm surprised anyone would have heard anything. It just happened."

It was time to deflect. She bought it, but her fishing expedition needed to end and end quickly. If she asked much about him being a new hire, she may easily learn that was not the case. She could know her brother's coworkers by name and have met several of them.

"I was wondering if I could do something for you. I thought perhaps I could help in some way."

"OK, you win. I'll take that bottle of water if the offer still stands."

"Of course. Right this way." Tenor silently thought to himself, scene 1, act 2.

CHAPTER 11

I t was late April, and a Wednesday morning. Chad and Megan went on their weekly morning run, weather permitting. They discussed current challenging work issues, without compromising any client confidentiality. Invigorating conversation included notable city, state, or national headlines. Never confrontational, only educational. Challenging to the mind, good for the soul, addicting as a new weight loss pill approved by the FDA.

Megan's junior year at the University of Missouri, Columbia, was the most memorable. Tragedy made it that way. She propelled through the storm finishing her law degree. Never in her wildest dreams would she have thought both her mom and dad would not see her accomplishments. Life took a different turn at the fork in the road of her planned future.

What she didn't know at the time, her financial future was secure. As their only child, her parents made it a priority. She hadn't seen coming the part of something much bigger than herself. MoTAF was home for her. Her true friend, Chad, was protective as any brother would be. She became part of a legacy her parents paved the road for.

Megan was not one to shy away from competition. She held her own and accepted any challenge. An early morning summer jog wasn't exactly a challenge. She accepted the exercise especially when Chad was along to break up any monotony. It was their normal Wednesday morning routine when Chad got the call. Megan could have received the call as well. Chad was not expecting any call particularly during a run. Neither received any calls during their aerobic routine. The pace resembled that of an elder man recovering from cardiac bypass. Slow but steady. It was how they were able to converse without having to take a breath between sentences.

Chad slowed their jog to a brisk walk. He answered his phone in a jovial way knowing full well who was on the other end. It was a short conversation with minimal response from Chad. Unexpected and out of character, the call ended with a quizzical glance to his now walking companion.

There wasn't anything on the horizon which would cause any intel to warrant an alert from MoTAF. The call Chad received was to the contrary. Chad raised his cell to Megan, with a tilt of his head and questionable brow.

"That was Ted. I've got to make sure the conference room is meeting worthy. I'll have guest coming late this afternoon."

"Do they think you have frat alumni parties during the week?"

Megan had been to Chad's home several times. Each time his place was immaculate. No overflow of trash cans, dirty kitchen counter tops, or wadded t-shirts thrown on chairs or over the back of a couch.

"Cute. I'm no party planner and this ain't no party," Chad responded. "We're being alerted. Something's up."

Chad could match her humor. Siblings they were not, but it was as if they could sense each other's thoughts. There were things about each other that hadn't been broached. It wasn't important to deep dive into the other's life history. He knew of Megan's loss. It was a tragedy not needing to be brought up in any conversation for any reason. Megan understood a glimpse of Chad's history as well. He didn't freely explain his childhood, she didn't ask. Bringing up his past seemed to open her wounds and they both avoided family history.

There was plenty of time to complete the morning exercise. There wasn't much preparation needed. Meetings seldom occurred and when they did, he was already aware of the meeting agenda. He was given the agenda and prepared all necessary documentation MoTAF members needed. They would discuss whatever current event causing taskforce activation. Activation generally meant something of notoriety had already taken place and reactionary measures were needed to prevent further harm to any Missouri interests. Those interests could include any public or private commercial, governmental, financial, or industrial relationship, or even personal injury. Domestic terrorism had no boundaries.

On the wall of the conference room in Chad's basement were various pictures. A couple of notable monuments in DC, and of notable historians. One item hanging on his wall was the creed every MoTAF member were familiar with. The elegant, framed motto read the sworn creed of MoTAF members.

The oath wasn't required to be memorized, just understood. It read in part:

*"The men and women of **MoTAF** are dedicated to preserve freedom and democracy*

within the boundaries of the United States. This mission will not be taken lightly by those who have sworn to uphold it. Those who propose to alter the will of the people will be dealt with extreme prejudice......"

A lot of forethought was put into the creation of the membership creed. Every member in each of the 50 states knew the importance of a functioning democracy. Although MoTAF had formulated after the events of 9/11, the purpose of their foundation had not changed.

MoTAF members sat swiveling in their high back leather chairs as they visited. There weren't any seat assignments however, they all gravitated to a chair they previously sat in. Jovial conversations filled the room. Without cue, the conversations came to an obvious pause. All eyes turned to the chair.

"Good afternoon everyone, it's good to be with friends again."

Dr. Theodore "Ted" Morris was upbeat and set the tone for their gathering. He didn't act or carry himself as a boss, a leader, or mentor but that is exactly how others perceived him. He was the epitome of professionalism, compassion and frankness all rolled up in one. Many leaders demanded respect. Those type of leaders taught those who worked for them a valuable lesson - how not to treat others.

Close friends and associates called him Ted. That's what he preferred and how he introduce himself. No introduction was ever needed when MoTAF members met. Any first-time introduction would address him as Dr. Morris. He would, without missing a step, correct his address as Ted and would prefer that over any other. Pure humbleness. He taught political history and several law courses at Missouri's flag staff university. Megan and Chad were required to complete several of his courses in completion of their law degrees. Dr. Morris had several acronyms and abbreviated letters after his name.

He opened a binder and began addressing the members. It was as if the CEO of a Fortune 500 company was addressing his managers about their progress at a quarterly meeting. The seriousness was not lost. Any remaining murmur of voices ceased as he stood to begin the meeting. Ted's opening was sharp.

"I will fill you all in on what I know. Anything other than what I'm presenting will be nothing more than speculation. There are a multitude of unknowns, but we have been put on alert."

He looked into each of their eyes to reassure them of the importance of what was about to convey. Some in the room were prior students of his. He would tell his students about the aspects of law. It was he who would tell others how he learned from his students.

"I was contacted directly by DC and there have been apparent chatter regarding a faction of Patriots we have previously encountered."

Dr. Morris related the intel gathered by their DC, MoTAF analyst counterparts. A sector of so-called patriots were becoming boisterous. The word patriot had taken on new meaning over the last several years. It was referenced several times through his presentation.

Each member was captivated by the storyline. Interface software and the application of a trojan to leftwing extremist communications caused the alert. These interface communications resembled law enforcement officers chatting online with pedophiles who assumed they were talking to underage girls or boys. Unbeknownst to the so-called patriots, the applied software could be used as a backdoor locator. If suspicious or boisterous communications were exchanged, the analyst would have to be enticed to engage in felonious activity. The trained analyst engaging in the activity would flag the IP address so other analysts could engage and the sting could be successfully completed.

Ted looked directly at Chad and across the conference room table where Megan was seated.

"Guys, this is where it gets a little dicey. These guys are not novice techies. Their tech advances have become quite sophisticated."

Megan ask, "Does this have anything to do with my phone and Chad's being compromised?"

"That's what is expected. However, nothing can be verified, and speculation can lead to unwanted consequences."

"In other words, we still don't know who hacked our phones." Chad offered his comment, not in the form of a question.

"I know it's frustrating. It could have happened to any of us. I'm confident they will get to the bottom of it." Ted was reassuring.

"I for one recommend we all get new phones. Whomever it was could just be toying with us, waiting to hack a different phone and send another message." Brian was a silent member of MoTAF. Seldom did he speak during any of their meetings. This time however, heads were nodding to his comment. Nobody wanted to be the next recipient.

"I understand everyone's concern," Ted continued. "I've already petitioned that solution without any success."

Even though each member was aware of Chad and Megan's cell phones being compromised, Ted left no stone unturned regarding what steps being taken to locate the perpetrator or perpetrators.

The perpetrators had also placed an alert on a trojan to alert them of unwarranted breaches. It was like a virus detection put on a trojan virus itself. DC analysts used the same techniques as well, however, the bad guys developed software to again detect what is supposed to not be detected. It was not only the chatter within activists, but it was also the fact it was encrypted.

Chatter with an IP address had become increasingly active. A specific communicator had expressed the time had finally arrived to raise the flag. The chatter went back and forth for weeks and immediately following was a discussion about something taking place. The raising of the flag was common language for followers and members to be placed into action. Soon thereafter, all communications from one specific alarmist ceased.

MoTAF members were engaged. These revelations charted new waters. The game was always dangerous, but the table had turned. It was personal. What magnified the unknown was not the why, but when. It was more than palpable that something was imminent. What could be done to prevent it was the bigger question. Waiting for something to happen was like being a passenger on a runaway train. Everyone assumed a collision was imminent, they just didn't know when. The rails could be switched for safe passage if someone could figure out how.

Members were informed of an acquaintance placed into service. Dr. Morris reminded everyone how Megan recommended the young man, known for his hacking ability, to assist MoTAF. Chad overwhelmingly agreed with Megan's recommendation. Although they couldn't connect the dots of how their long-time friend could help, they all were intrigued by the possibility, although with skepticism and caution.

Ted was meticulous with his timeline of events as they knew them. A multitude of information resulted in an analytical solution to a problem. Smart minds were the link to solving what seemed like the impossible.

Department of Homeland Security, DHS, and defense contractors responsible for defending our country's interests needed all the assistance they could get to accomplish their mission. Technology was the exciting piece to what was yet to be realized. Not to be overstated, software was being used to obtain information most people didn't think was possible. In fact, it wasn't just possible, it was necessary, although most ACLU litigants would argue case by case otherwise. Rightfully so, the sharing of information had to be carefully funneled to the agencies who needed it the most. Privacy concerns always came first. MoTAF would be the stealth force offering up the tools needed to remain unknown.

Dr. Morris continued to explain why they were meeting.

"The catalyst causing the alert was a traffic accident by a member of a previous Sovereign Patriot group. Police officers alerted to a business card in the driver's billfold and glove box of the wrecked car."

Megan politely interrupted, "The Sovereign Patriots are active again?"

"It's believed they were never inactive," Ted continued.

"The card, which was located right behind his driver's license, listed an extreme right-wing group. In the glove box were several hundred cards like the one in his billfold. The detectives did an intel online search which alerted MoTAF's database."

Megan couldn't hold back her enthusiasm. It was as if she was ready to suit up for a playoff game and she was a starting forward playing in front of scouts for the WBA.

"I'm assuming we are back in the game," Megan stated.

"No reason to assume, it's game on," Dr Morris said.

As if lecturing his students in one of his advanced pre-law classes, he used a dry erase board to explain the break they got. He wrote a series of numbers and letters on the board. When turned upside down the number seven equated to the letter L. The number three equated to the letter E. Dr. Morris explained the card meaning and how it was deciphered.

"This business card had a sequence of letters and numbers on the reverse side. The sequence of letters and numbers were upside down. When read backwards, it was ultimately the password to log into the Patriot website."

Chad couldn't help but chime in. "DC analysts deserve a Christmas bonus. How does our friend from the past figure into our mission?"

"Thanks for asking, Chad. We all know Tenor has been successful acclimating himself into society. Ever since the Marshal Service gave him his name change, he's been a willing participant of anything relating to helping MoTAF succeed in our endeavors.

Dr. Morris understood all in the room agreed with a certain WITSEC acquaintance joining forces. However, it remained a delicate subject.

"He's been given liberties which have not been violated. Thus far, Tenor is a success story. He is thankful for the safe haven we have provided. DC has ask him to obtain some personal intel on the Patriot extremist who once infiltrated right here in our backyard. It's believed they've resurfaced under a similar name. Tenor is engaging in person rather than electronically."

CHAPTER 12

Ms. Cordial returned from conversing with her supervisor. Due to the seriousness of the injuries, the on-duty charge nurse cleared visitation for family or serious relationships. Tenor did not fit into that category and didn't want to be included. Any other visitors could be granted visitation upon family members' request.

Ms. Cordial approached Alia and Tenor in the waiting room.

"Sorry for you having to wait. I spoke with my supervisor. Only one visitor is allowed at this time. I can escort you to the room now. The current visitor says he's ready to leave to allow others to see your brother."

Alia's eyes remained bloodshot from the time local law enforcement arrived at her door. The angst on her face would scare any hardened criminal. Ms. Cordial again apologized for the wait after looking at the distraught Alia.

"He is heavily medicated and may not stay awake during your visit. Follow me please."

Alia said, "I want to meet the guy who's with my brother before he leaves. But first I want to apologize for my impatience. I do appreciate you helping me Beverly."

Alia glanced at the name tag of the receptionist and extend her thanks in a more personal heartfelt manner.

"You're very welcome, Alia. The gentleman brought a laptop with him. Your brother needed assistance with the hospital Wi-Fi or a secure hotspot."

"Again, thank you. Your job is difficult, I appreciate what you do."

They turned the corner at the end of the long hallway. Alia didn't realize another pod of rooms and a nurses' station were down an adjacent hall. She was lost. Assistance would be needed to lead her from the hospital room to the elevator that brought her to the floor.

Alia lowered her guard to the guy in the visitors' waiting room. He was genuinely concerned and lowering her guard was a result of her rattled nerves. Alia was always guarded. She was uncharacteristically talkative to a total stranger. He introduced himself, but she couldn't recall his name. Alia did remember he was easy on the eyes. She needed to express gratitude for him coming to visit her brother. They conversed for a long while but couldn't remember everything they talked about. He seemed nice enough but asked a lot of questions. He mentioned how patriotic he became after meeting Alec and appreciated what he was doing at work. She was taken back by what he said and why he suggested she was as patriotic as her brother. It wasn't the time to ask.

Beverly stopped abruptly. "This is his room. The guest must have left. The stairs are faster than the slow boat ride most people take."

Tenor sat down after watching Ms. Cordial and his new acquaintance walk down the hall. He opened the notepad app in his phone and started entering information into the Cloud. The changes forced upon him gave him something more powerful to ponder. Maybe he was a patriot after all.

Alia unlocked the door to her guarded soul with vulnerability front and center. Tenor stepped on the porch, read the welcome mat, and walked right in. He took the positive approach to her shocking revelation, and it paid off. She agreed with Tenor. She loved her brother no matter what his sexual orientation. Alia described her job, and he complimented her on how much compassion she had for the disadvantaged.

Tenor logged all he could remember into his phone which was pretty much everything. He wanted to witness the tongue lashing she was going to give her brother for not telling her he was gay and for nearly killing himself.

Tenor feverously recalled more and entered the information into his cell phone document. He was glad she let her guard down if ever a shield was up. Two siblings, probably in their late 20's, would likely have a significant other whom they would be building their lives around.

He put himself into the false story line. Painfully aware of no social life whatsoever, Tenor did relate to the friend he had not yet met or learned much about. Alia's life centered around her work and her brother. She was fascinated by how computer savvy her brother had become and was grateful for what she was learning from him. Bragging on his personal accomplishments enlightened Tenor into his own life history. She too had become a tech novice and was considering changing careers because of it. Her openness with Alec took away the anxiety and reason they both were in a hospital waiting room. If only he could believe her story as he related his falsehoods to her.

The word patriot was a catalyst in the conversation Tenor had with his new acquaintance. He was enjoying his assignment. The two of them possessed similar mindsets for causes he was familiar with. Antigovernment theorists have not changed over the years. Now, however, they are brazened. The in-your-face nonapologetic tone is taking a strong hold across America. In his humble opinion, the moral majority was becoming less of a majority.

Alia was distraught about her brother's health and especially regarding the friend she was about to meet. It struck a chord with her about shared patriotism. Tenor meticulously led her down the path of deception while taking her mind off her brother.

Tenor continued to summarize their conversation. Understanding what was said and piecing it all together would be the job of someone else who was aware of more than he was privy to. The trick to any puzzle, of course, is finding all the pieces to bring the picture into focus. His ability to assume the position ask of him was shocking. So many people were unsuspecting of who he was. It was who he was and more important, he was comfortable with the persona.

Alia stood at the hospital room door. Ms. Cordial instructed Alia to fill out the family visitor's information form attached to the clipboard inside the room. The last visitor failed to return it to the reception desk. Alia noticed the turned-up brow of the receptionist and the defined wrinkled facial lines of disappointment. The information was used for contact information for patients in critical condition. Alia was more than disappointed. She wanted the friend's name and number as well.

As if tiptoeing to avoid waking her brother, Alia cautiously walked through the room threshold while taking in her brothers' appearance. His left arm was taped securing the IV drip. Two fluid bags hung from the irrigation tower. Bandages wrapped his head and covered his left eye. His right eye was closed. She stared at the rise and fall of the white blanket covering him, relieved to see movement. There was bruising already showing around his unbandaged eye. Under the blanket, his left leg was elevated, the raised foot was wrapped in a boot stirrup preventing movement. A mist of moisture formed in both her eyes as she stood next to his bedside. She pulled a tissue from the box sitting on the food tray dabbing the corners of her eyes. Pulling a chair to his bed the coasters made the familiar fingernails on a chalkboard sound. Alec stirred as Alia took the seat grimacing at the noise.

With a tone just above a whisper she said, "Hey baby brother, you scared me."

His visible eye was open slightly. Alec turned his head to the right, looked at his sister while trying to focus. He blinked several times and with his bass voice, deep in his diaphragm, he bellowed out his all-familiar greeting.

"Hey big sis, what's up?"

She didn't grab another tissue. Alia let the tears flow down both cheeks. She smiled at the unrecognizable person who sounded like her brother. He was the only family member she cared anything about.

"You're pretty banged up. How do you feel?"

"I feel like I've been in a bad car wreck," he lifted his right hand and grasped hers. "Sorry for you having to come to see me."

"No problem. What else do you think I would have done?"

Even with his head bandaged, she could see the bewilderment on his broken face. To minimize the awkwardness, she told him where he was and how she found out about his accident.

"Wow, I had no idea how you found out and I didn't even know where I ended up."

Alia, still bewildered about her brother's fiancé, took that moment to sneak the question she desperately needed answered.

"Your friend didn't tell you what hospital you were at? You're at Methodist University, you failed to tell me about this special friend of yours. Who is he?"

Alec appeared to drift off, then abruptly opened his right eye responding to her question. "Special friend? What do you mean, what did he say to you?"

Alia stumbled for a good answer. The pause resembled an opera singer running out of breath after extending the last note to a song.

"Your friend told the doctors and the nurses he was your fiancé."

"Well, of course he did. That's funny."

He released his sisters hand and grabbed his side, holding it tight as he coughed. He started coughing uncontrollably. Alia stood from her seat while watching his painful cough. She gasped out loud and grabbed the nurses station call button when she noticed droplets of blood from his closed eye lid and from his right ear.

Tenor edited his notes and added his own commentary to the insightful visit he had with Alia. He truthfully believed they could be friends under normal circumstances. Audible tones began making a musical performance at the nurses' station. Tenor leaned toward the reception counter in hopes to hear some of the commotion. The nurses' attention were glued to a monitor screen. Ms. Cordial spun in her seat, leaned toward a microphone on her desk. While looking at her monitor, she responded to a voice requesting room nurse.

"Can I help you?"

A loud booming voice came through the speaker. "I need some help! My brother needs help!"

Nurses moved from their huddled conversation at the reception counter and looked at Ms. Cordial's computer screen. Ms. Cordial confirmed the call for a nurse. Two nurses looking over her shoulder quickly walked down the hall. The receptionist stood from her comfortable seat, moved from the nurses station, and sauntered toward Tenor.

"Sir, I'm sorry to inform you, your visit will be delayed. You'll have to return at another suitable visiting time."

CHAPTER 13

Taking the stairway from the hospital room was brilliant. Drake had no interest in nonsensical conversation with somebody he didn't know. The gig was up when a nurse came to the room asking for identification. It was a good thing Alec was awake at that moment. He was in and out of consciousness ever since Drake walked into the room. Alec immediately inquired why he had to produce identification. He didn't have any problem showing his ID but had to decide which fictitious one to produce.

The receptionist announced the sister was waiting to see her brother. That was his cue. He wasn't prepared to meet the sister, the twin sister. Drake assured him he understood what he was to do. He pressed Alec to rest and get well. Alec's fail-safe plan was being tested. The apartment key he gave him would have to be returned after he made a copy.

During the visit, the brother and sister relationship was better explained. Perhaps a little controlling, but Alec was proud of his sister. Alia was one not to cross, but gentle as a butterfly landing on a fully blossomed flower petal.

Drake decided to take the stairs. If he were asked how close he was to her brother, his lie would not have ended well. The drive back was in haste. This was his best opportunity to enter Alec's apartment. She would be miles away at the hospital when he returned. Any other scenario placed her in the same town and the chance of her looking at a stranger when she walked through her own door.

Alia and Alec paid a price for the ground floor and surface patio. That made the visit a little more pleasant knowing if he heard a visitor, he could leave out the back door. The apartment was easily located but an uneasiness came over him. He listened intently, making sure he heard nobody inside. He pulled the key from his pocket and pushed it into the lock. He heard a noise and wasn't sure if it came from Alec's apartment or another one. Pure paranoia. If he knocked and somebody answered, the mystery would be solved. He would make a name of who he was looking for and apologize for the disturbance.

He heard footsteps. Not from inside the apartment, but on the steps above him which lead to other apartments in the building. The steps sounded rough, as if stumbling down several stairs. Someone was descending the stairs in a hurry. They would likely exchange a neighborly greeting. He needed to avoid any greeting at all costs.

He turned the key, nothing. It wouldn't turn. The steps were closer, and the key wasn't working. It was similar but the wrong one. He fumbled nervously then inserted the correct key. He opened the door as footsteps bound onto the landing to the main hallway. He escaped a near catastrophe.

He exhaled, not realizing he was holding his breath. Nothing was what he envisioned but why would it? He had no idea what was beyond the closed door. He didn't break into the apartment, he was holding the key. He made sure he would leave nothing behind. He walked to Alex and Alia's bedroom doors as if he owned the apartment. With that thought he placed the apartment key in his pants pocket. This wasn't a crime, but it was like his first act as a criminal. He left his billfold, watch, comb, and baseball cap in his car. What a travesty it would be if he unknowingly left behind fictitious identification.

He looked around admiring his surroundings. It was a well-kept apartment. There was no reason to be uncomfortable in the surroundings he found himself in. He was alone and he was invited to be there. He was rethinking his hasty hospital room departure. The mysterious apartment gave way to his wishing he would have met Alec's sister. The wall pictorials were welcoming. No photos of friends and family, although not absent perhaps for those who lived there. Everything was in their proper place as if guests were soon to arrive. Angst crept back into the present tense of his reality. A request from a friend was dependent on him. A short hallway led to several doors. He assumed the closed doors was to a linen or utility closet. The first room on his left was Alec's room. He stood in the entrance for only a moment. It was apparent Alec, and his sister were loners. One question from a visitor about his computer setup would undoubtedly create all kinds of interest.

Back to reality, time to get to work. The faraday cage around the computer was what drew him in like a magnet. In the corner of the room was a stencil picture of an eagle in flight. The majestic fowl was lifelike in the 3D framed pictorial. He didn't know how much he liked eagles but by the look of the apartment, he marveled at their beauty like many others. His sister must be a fan as well. Several colorful pictures hung of eagles in flight or perched high on treetops in her room and around the apartment.

There would be no mistake logging into Alecs' system. Alec explained after three password attempts, a reboot would be required. He had to finish his task before the sister returned. A hurried exit through the rear patio door would result in a high-profile manhunt.

Drake snickered at the word eagle as he looked at the letters written on the piece of paper – his cheat sheet. The pronunciation of the word was the same. The letters on the page were oddly different. EGOL, in capital letters, was on the paper Alec gave him. He turned the page upside down reading the numbers the capital letters displayed; 7093. Not exactly, but close enough. He touched the space bar and the cursor blinked waiting for the password. He typed carefully and both thirty-two-inch screens came to life.

Different pictures on each monitor depicted up close majestic views of Bald Eagles. He quickly found the settings icon on the left monitor and disabled the lock screen and sleep mode settings. Alec had shortcuts to these settings but finding them would be asking someone to walk blind through a mine field. The settings prevented shutdown of the computer until he could get what he needed downloaded. Reaching into his cargo pants, he pulled out two USB flash drives. He brought two, not knowing exactly how much info needed to be loaded or how long it would take.

A door slammed in the hallway causing him to spin on the swivel high-back computer chair. He had to leave the place without disturbing anything. He nearly ran out of the bedroom toward the back door. He needed a plan in case things went south. The possibility of needing a plan became plausible as he watched the slow transfer of files being copied to the flash drive. Six minutes remaining was eternity. The promise to Alec was not without risk. He breached into the danger zone as soon as he turned the apartment door key.

Drake and Alec were close, but this was different. Alec talked about his distrust of supervisors and corporate icons a long time ago. He would always follow his stories up with circumstances and reasons for his optimistic beginnings. He would mention how he drank the Kool-Aid for many years until he learned of the ingredients. He would hope for change, only to witness an unfortunate reoccurring story. Drake knew he would not let Alec down and he could be trusted.

Alec would say, "Change is good until you would see the knife in someone's back."

The sound of a doorbell startled him. There was no doorbell to the apartment. The Windows 11 alert on one of the monitors announced download complete. It obviously didn't take six minutes. Mission accomplished. He needed to call Alec as he promised. They had already discussed the what, the who, and the why, as if the why was even part of the equation.

Preppers. They joked about it several times. They were being prepared. Solidifying this one step was a sure way of completing the ultimate task. It was hard for him to believe he was part of the plan. They talked of the plan, believed in the plan, but to be a part of something bigger than himself was surreal. He picked up his cell to make the call. He was prepared to whisper so no neighbors could hear what he was saying.

The download was completed, and he could help with whatever Alec needed for him to do. Since he was incapacitated for who knows how long, he was more than willing to do what was expected. He wanted to do exactly what they had talked about during their lunch meetings. It was even patriotic, which was the only way it could be explained.

Alec told him he may have someone in the room with him when he called. He was not to be surprised if Alec sounded like he was uninterested in a telemarketer calling him. He was going to turn the table on Alec though. He was going to tell Alec the wedding venue was available, and they could get married as soon as they picked out matching wedding bands.

He laughed at the thought of getting married, especially to Alec. There was no way he was going to introduce himself to his sister as Alec's fiancé. It was funny and they both laughed until the pain meds failed. They agreed how uncontrollably angry she would be when she found the joke was on her. He never met Alec's sister, but he knew her inner soul. He heard so much about her, he sometimes questioned if he weren't her sibling as well. The controlling dark side was hard to envision.

He dialed Alec's cell number. He hoped Alec was awake and not heavily sedated to carry on a conversation. He considered disguising his voice but decided against it. On his person was a key to a strange apartment while standing in a strange bedroom. There was no reason to add another rendition of strange to the equation.

He put his cell on speaker and listened to it ring. It rang several times. There was no doubt the call was going to voicemail. Until it didn't. Then the call was answered.

"Hello." A weak timid female voice came through the speaker. "Hello," the voice repeated.

He hadn't planned for this. He wasn't ready. He looked at his phone to make sure he dialed the correct number. There was no mistake, it was Alec's number, but who was the woman that answered his phone.

With caution he responded, "Hi, I'm trying to reach Alec. Can you please hand him the phone?"

The women on the phone ask the question he immediately knew he couldn't answer.

"Who is this? I'm Alec's sister. I'm answering his phone, and the name listed under this number says - sister. Who is this?"

The faint voice became clearer. The game was no longer a game. He didn't smile when the female voice said she was his sister. Alec had not prepared to talk to his sister. He and Alec talked so much about his twin sister, he couldn't believe he was now talking to her. She might as well be standing right next to him.

"I'm sorry, I'll call him back or you can just tell him I did what he asked me to do."

There was a long pause. The same pause a comedian would endure to a joke nobody understood. Drake wanted to disconnect the call but was afraid to.

Alia said, "You can't call him back, and I can't tell him what you want me to." Her voice trickled down to a whisper. It was the same whisper as she answered the call when her brother's phone rang. "My brother. You can't call him back, and I can't deliver your message. My brother he ... he... My brother, he died."

CHAPTER 14

C had sat in his study reviewing his notes from the MoTAF meeting. He couldn't remember being called to a meeting where he didn't prepare the itinerary. He had no idea what the meeting was about to formulate one. Everyone had the same question at its conclusion: what was next? It was the way things worked in DC. It was only when red tape needed circumventing that miracles happened.

The vibration from his cell and the simultaneous ring was a much-needed break. Reviewing documents sent to him from analysts across the country had quickly become an overwhelming and daunting task.

He glanced at his phone before answering. Weeks prior, he received an unknown text at the same time Megan got one. That created a reaction of new circumstances. He was acute to the term of one keeping their head on a swivel. It became more meaningful when the realization of one's personal safety looked you square in the face. He smiled and answered the call.

"Hey Meg."

Meg responded without saying hello. "It's my pick, please tell me you remembered."

He remembered but wanted to make a play for one of his quirky comments. He couldn't come up with anything fast enough, leaving more than enough awkwardness to the silence.

"Seriously, you forgot. I can't believe you forgot."

"Meg, of course I didn't forget. I Googled the restaurant to make reservations."

"You're stupid, but you know that already. Taco Bell doesn't take reservations."

And there it was. Her contagious laugh warms any troubled soul. He looked forward to their weekly sit downs. The choice wasn't Taco Bell and they both knew it. The back-and-forth bantering resembled a brother and sister relationship. This was no sibling relationship although it would appear so to an outsider. The working friendship was indescribable. Oddly enough, neither one of them were able to describe it. It was obvious to them. As the friendship grew it became special.

Chad knew he would not ruin a friendship by attempting to chisel at the invisible wall. Megan didn't cross the line either. She too placed a barrier between them. There was no forcing anything that was not there. Nor would she show how vulnerable she was.

"OK, same time, 6:30?" She said.

"Yes and let's not do the one on Campbell today. Let's try Panera on Sunshine."

"Wow, all the way across town."

"Do you hear that?" Chad smirked as if she could see his face.

"Hear what?"

"That sound. Do ya hear it?"

"What are you talking about, I don't hear anything."

"You don't hear that?" he chuckled, "it's the sound of you not talking."

"I'm hanging up now," Megan uttered, "you're getting weird as if that's any surprise."

"OK. See ya there."

It happened again. This time a little stronger than the previous. Not that it was an everyday occurrence. But it happen every once in a while. She couldn't remember when it happened, but there it was. That flutter, which could only be described as butterflies. Then the tightness in her stomach that had nothing to do with appetite. She was ready to eat, but she wasn't famished. She pushed back the feeling and went to look for something to wear. She wasn't hungry but she wasn't fooling herself either.

No crowd, no waiting in line and nearly the pick of the place for seating. Chad waited in his car for Megan to show before going inside. He would suggest eating outside since it was a gorgeous evening. He instinctively knew an umbrella table would be her choice. He watched as she pulled into the parking lot. He watched everyone who pulled into the lot. It wasn't as if he was paranoid, he liked watching people. It had served him well and it made him comfortable for a multitude of reasons. Chad recalled the not so long-ago Panera Bread incident. It was still fresh in his mind, as well as for Megan.

Megan noticed Chad right away. He almost reached her car before she was able to park and get out. She met him with a bright smile, and he extended his right fist, and she reciprocated. It was a trademark between them. Oddly enough it started with Megan. She played competitive sports throughout high school and into college. Extending high fives were the trademark of her softball and basketball careers. It wasn't until she met Chad at a gym where they both exercised became fist bumping buds. He soon became her unofficial fitness trainer and encouragement coach. She would extend a fist and he would graciously complete the ensemble.

The baked bread, the fresh baked cookies, the prepared meal orders permeated from the kitchen. Outside seating was without question Megan's choice. They sat thoroughly enjoying each other's company. The laughter between them caused other patrons to turn in their direction with smiles as if they were part of the same joke.

Time would pass like all meals did between them. The conversation topics circled the world twice and began on a third. Although they both attended the University of Missouri in Columbia, their graduate years briefly overlapped. They knew the same professors and took similar courses. Law school was their love, and both had promising careers with prestigious firms. Chad focused on family law specializing foster care unions. Meg was drawn to legal defense.

Law school was a challenging curriculum but rewarding. Chad mentioned an ethics course he took during his senior year. Megan didn't recall the class but thought it would have been interesting. He explained the course curriculum and that debates were all part of the class discussion.

"There were some interesting debates. Some uncomfortable and controversial," Chad continued to explain.

"One discussion was about an attorney bringing a frivolous case to court. Classroom debate got very interesting. A law firm client was fired after complaining about her supervisor's advances, so she sued."

"My classes had similar topics," Megan responded. "I don't understand why the lady got fired, sounds like her attorney had a good case unless her attorney flunked pre-law 101."

"She didn't follow protocol, Meg. The company had regulations and she didn't follow them when she made her complaint."

"You're saying she should have put up with the unwelcome advances," Megan tried not to reveal the vial boiling in the pit her stomach.

Chad continued to explain, "All I'm saying is the lady didn't follow regulations."

Megan replied sarcastically. "Let me guess, she went to her boss. That boss went to his boss to make a complaint against him. That boss tells the other boss not to worry about it. Yeah, I get it."

Politely excusing herself, Megan left to use the restroom. She returned moments later although time had reverted to slow motion. If Chad hadn't a bird's eye view of her car, he would have bet a million bucks she had left the restaurant. She continued to sip her sweet tea without eye contact. The outside temperature had taken a quick dive from a record high to an unseasonable chill in the air.

He wasn't a genius, and rocket science was not in question. He recognized his mistake but for the life of him, couldn't figure out how to alter the slow-motion scene playing out. A change in the topic was needed.

"I want to ask you a question and I want an honest answer," Megan said.

If he answered wrong, he would risk Megan pulling a sharp object from her purse and forcibly inserting it into his carotid. She leaned forward and looked directly into his eyes. She uttered what she had rehearsed since returning from the bathroom.

Megan said, "Picture a foster care child being interviewed by a child psychiatrists. The child is sitting in a defensible fetal position on a chair in a room she's never been in before. The guardians are obviously present. This child is describing unimaginable abuse. Would you as a children's judge advocate, after listening to all of it, tell the child to return and play nice?"

The slow-motion effect returned at the most impeccable timing. Chad paused to gather his thoughts. Megan's eyes were locked in on his. Chad's cell phone vibrated breaking the silence. Her cell phone vibrated as well. As if an atom bomb exploded from under their table, neither wanted to say the obvious.

Chad looked at his phone, Megan did not. She continued staring at Chad until he looked up from his phone. Him being occupied by his phone didn't go unnoticed.

CHAPTER 15

Tenor reviewed his notes. With all he was able to acquire, questions remained unanswered. Bluntly stated in his brief, there may be more questions than answers. He wasn't even sure what he had achieved with his endeavor, but it was exciting. He wondered what espionage would be like. If you were a spy, and given an assignment, would it be as exhilarating, or would it become mundane?

He finished his draft. He was given a task, and it was complete. It was to his satisfaction and that is what mattered. With what he was given there wasn't any more he could add. He sat in the car with the front windows rolled down. It was warm, but the breeze was nice as it circulated through his car. The drop in temperature was apparent. He hadn't moved from the so-called south forty area of the parking lot. It would be prudent to take the shuttle than hike to the hospital entrance. He was young and it wouldn't be a big deal until you found yourself walking it. He watched another poor soul making the same stroll. It was comforting to know he wasn't alone in that endeavor.

Tenor wondered why she hadn't waited for the shuttle that was continuously making circles through parking lanes. She exited the hospital door and just started walking. He diverted his attention back to his tablet where he transferred the notes he documented in his cell.

The lady navigating through vehicles walked close to where he parked. They could have taken the route together and found out about each other's family tree. He laughed as she retrieved keys from her purse and pushed the alarm button on the key fob. She spun around like numbers on a roulette tabletop while looking for her car. She turned toward the repetitive car horn, finally locating it. To his surprise, the lost car was one row up from where he parked. He immediately recognized her.

He put his phone down on top of his tablet, got out of his car and started his approach with a huge smile on his face knowing she too would be surprised. He almost arrived at the flashing parking lamp noise maker before she did. She finally unlocked her car with the fob before his migraine ensued.

"Hello there," Tenor smiled with his greeting.

His smile quickly turned to a blank stare. From a distance, he couldn't see her blood shot eyes. As they stood face to face, she looked as if she had an appointment for allergies and it was a colossal failure.

"It's me Tenor."

That's all he could come up with in a feeble attempt to calm her nervous and tense retreat.

"I'm sorry, I didn't mean to startle you. Are you alright? Is there something I can do for you?"

Alia turned away to hide her watery eyes. He wasn't sure what he could do but was glad to help. They had just met, and she was obviously distraught over something. Time to be a gentleman.

"Oh, hi. I didn't see you. I'm okay."

She was not doing well. She fumbled with her purse replacing the key fob. She found a wadded tissue and daintily dobbed the corner of her eyes and wiped her nose. She attempted a smile which didn't resonate through tear smeared makeup.

"I can tell something is wrong. Allow me to buy you a coffee or an early dinner."

Immediately after the words came out of his mouth and with the look she gave, his mistake was front and center. The ripple effect resulted in a tsunami.

"Seriously, coffee?" The look on her face told more than a little problem. Tenor accepted the stare as it was meant. It was time for him to listen from this point forward, wait for an opening and choose his words carefully.

"Why would I accept you buying me coffee, let alone dinner? I can't even think about eating right now."

Tenor didn't move, he couldn't. He lowered his head to telegraph his soon to be delivered apology. He took off his sunglasses to make sure she could see the honesty in his eyes.

"I'm so sorry, I didn't mean we should go out to eat.. I'll let you go."

"No, I'm sorry, I don't mean to be rude. I've been handed something I can't wrap my head around."

Tenor stepped to her car door, opened it, allowing her to sit. She didn't take the gesture. She took a deep breath, looked at him and in almost a whisper, she spoke.

"There is something you can do for me. Please tell Alec's friends at work that he died from his injuries. I'm sorry you didn't get to see him."

Tenor's reaction was not an act. He was speechless. He didn't have to say a word. She could tell he was shocked by what she told him.

Tenor was glad his thoughts couldn't be read. He shouted aloud in his head Whiskey Tango Foxtrot, but not the cliche. It was so loud in his head he wasn't so sure she didn't hear it.

"I'm so sorry," he responded. "Yes, of course, I'll call people for you at work."

It was at that moment he hoped she didn't ask for numbers she would assume he had readily available to give her. Tenor didn't want a coffee or to eat and regretted he made the offer.

Alia placed her purse on the driver's seat and closed the door without sitting. Leaning back onto her car, she took another breath, and with poise, she started talking.

"He laughed about his friend I demanded to know about. I can't believe he'd keep anything from me."

Tenor let her talk and talk she did. She exemplified the early stages of shock and grief. However, these stages took on a whole new meaning. Her anger was something Tenor hadn't witnessed in any person. Sure, he had seen people upset, but this woman had reached a whole new level of animosity. He was seriously wondering if he should be concerned about his safety. There was more to her story. If a weapon were in her purse, he could at least prevent her from getting it.

"There is so much I need to do," she continued. "We planned to do things together, but now I'll have to do it by myself."

Tenor was at a loss but knew not to interrupt. She rambled on and her sentences were not logical. She was upset about her loss but more upset at her brother for leaving her. He would have to do some research on the different levels of despair. He wasn't sure what he witnessed was called grief. It was more self-indulgence. She mentioned reaching out to his friends and moving up some timeline. Her anger returned with a vengeance explaining how her brother's anger got the best of him. At that point she paused and wiped tears from both cheeks.

"It's all my fault. If I hadn't made him mad," her voice trailed once again to a whisper.

He wanted to record the conversation but hadn't thought of it in time and his phone was in his car. She would not have noticed if a stand-alone microphone were inches from her face. Tenor was positive he would have to append his document before sending it.

It would be hard making sense of it all, but she liked to talk. Although he was a stranger, their short visit allowed her to project otherwise. He capitalized on her shortcoming.

Tenor masterfully backdoored the conversation. It was like a trojan horse of make-believe storyline. He was sorry for her being so gullible - almost. Business was business. It wasn't his concern that she was open to his goodwill. Besides, it wasn't exploitation. He held back his thoughts at that moment. He didn't enjoy exploiting her emotions and particularly her loss. He would consider ill thoughts about it later, but now he was doing what was asked of him and he was not going to fail his assignment. Not a chance.

Her anger became displaced. Her grief engulfed multiple layers of emotions in a matter of seconds. Tenor would have to theorize how her brother's boss, her boss and government officials fit into any equation of their moral compass. He wasn't sure how patriotism underscored what she was telling him. Tenor was at a loss for what she was saying. She recounted her statement about her brother being a patriot and moving up a timetable in his honor. Without a doubt, he was at a loss to what he was hearing.

CHAPTER 16

Drake couldn't believe his ears. Alia was clearly devastated and understandably so. To make it worse, he was in disbelief as well. He and Alec were joking around. Although he was in pain, fading in and out of a deep sleep, he would be fine. At least that is what he told him, and Alec of course agreed. He knew he couldn't find out what exactly happened, and it didn't matter. His visit was a facade, at least the ruse to get in the hospital room in the first place. It was Alec who had sent him a text asking him to come. It was his sister relaying the disturbing news with his phone - her brother's phone. Alec's phone.

The sister now had his phone number. There wasn't a chance she would understand why some guy would be labeled as her in Alec's phone address book. He immediately considered blocking Alec's number but would have to wait in case there were any contacts, including his sister's, that he needed to be weary of. He was not looking forward to hearing from her again.

Being in Alec's apartment now was without question uncomfortable. He tried to push it aside but couldn't. There he stood in his friend's apartment having done what he was asked to do. The big question remained. Now what? They talked about his unfortunate stay in the hospital. Their talks were in generalities. They often considered themselves as preppers. However, they both theorized scenarios of what if this, and what if that. Their bond of friendship was indeed unique. A wave of sadness engulfed him. He looked at the simplistic confines of where he stood. He knew why he was there, but he couldn't get over the circumstance he found himself in. He couldn't let Alec down, but he didn't know what exactly he was to do. Nor did he know how to do it.

The anxiety wasn't going away. He needed to get out of the place before Alia returned. But first, he needed to make sure there wasn't anything he needed to do while there. There wasn't a chance he would return. He had to get it all done. He returned to Alec's room and pulled open a desk drawer. He took out a notepad flipping through pages looking for something, anything that he could use later. Math equations crossed out, scribblings not making any sense, and mostly blank pages. Right before he put the pad back into the drawer, he retrieved an envelope with the capital letters EGOL on the outside. Inside the unsealed envelope was a page with what looked like passwords numbered one through four. Feeling guilty, he folded the business size envelope and placed it in his pants pocket.

Things were getting complicated. It began with entry to an apartment he had never been in before, with a key from someone who no longer existed. Removing an item from a private location in an apartment for his own personal use is the essence of burglary. There's nothing good about the uneasiness. He remained focused and looked around Alec's room. He wasn't changing his mind, he was not going into the sister's room.

Three loud poundings on the apartment door sent a chill up his back. He quickly left the room, light on his feet, heading to the patio exit. He had to get out of there and quick. He almost fell from the floor rug sliding under his feet. Someone yelled from the other side of the door.

"Alec, wake up dude! You can't sleep your day away. Do something worthwhile for a change."

The voice faded away midsentence down the same hallway he had taken. The dimly lit hallway could have been a scene in a horror movie. An echoing barrel laugh that sounded like Santa Clause on Christmas morning vibrated the hallway. The loud bass voice would be an annoyance to anyone working a night shift and trying to sleep in. Drake pulled the sliding glass door to the patio closed with a sigh of relief. He imagined a concerned citizen calling the police after being seen hurdling fences to his burglary. He was done and it was now time for his not so graceful exit. There would be no explaining his whereabouts and what he had been doing to any concerned police officers. No handcuffs and free ride to a place with gated windows.

Only moments later and back at his place he began the download. At first, he believed the virus scans would interfere with each other as if they were in a never-ending conflict. A battle where neither side wins. It was not the case. Not only did they sync with each other, they were in harmonious rhythm. The systems Alec installed married up to his. The integrity of his system was not compromised, it was stronger. Their stuff was cool, and they knew it.

Alec taught Drake what he hadn't picked up on his own. He didn't expect any issue particularly because it was Alec who wanted him to be his back up, his second sister, his twin brother. It was also Alec who enhanced the firewall system for their computers with the additional back door safeguards. The systems married up perfectly. The just-in-case scenario Alec had envisioned was now in effect.

It was at this moment he started reminiscing about their friendship. A wave of emotions engulfed him as the tears flowed. His chest rose and fell in short breaths as he tried gasping for air between exhales. He only knew Alec a short while and would miss him. Their friendship was at a point where 'what if's' were discussed in nearly every tech discussion. Their world was intertwined with how they would deal with different make-believes.

Some of those discussions encompassed oppositions to work assignment and hierarchies in the workforce. Those chats evolved to empowerment for each other. They would feed off each other on how things would be if they were in charge. They even discussed being promoted to authority and how they would pull the others up the corporate ladder to accomplish greatness. Although they were in separate divisions, they looked forward to their lunches. Conversations ranged from them being President and Vice President to espionage. Their most meaningful exchanges were about how to set things right again. To bring the country back to where the founding fathers meant it to be. It was what true patriots lived for.

He was brought out of his trip down memory lane by the familiar tone sounding on his computer monitor. The security scans were complete. He wiped both eyes with his forearm and took a deep breath. He waited until the completion of a successful download so as not to potentially corrupt his opening any of the files. His computer set up mirrored Alec's. It was as if he was sitting right next to him.

Opening the first file took him by surprise. He had no idea he would be reading his name. A word document opened without his keying the icon. A five second countdown by bold numbers preceded the document opening on its own. He couldn't proceed without reading the required Microsoft Word paragraph. It was like reading an introduction to a movie explaining if it were present day or a flashback. He was the main character. The only character.

Their breaks and lunches weren't only for meals. The plots and scenes of true-life scenarios were developed. Although they were tech world preppers, they embraced the title. There were times when they both laughed so hard, Alec would witness carbonated Pepsi spew out Drake's nose. At the same time, Alec would try not choke on his food while watching his friend embarrass himself.

Alec told him, before handing over his apartment key, he wanted him to follow the instructions the best he could. He was to call him if there were any problems but explained it would make more sense once he returned the key. Alec explained he needed to read what was in the first file he was asked to download. What he wasn't told, none of the files could be accessed until the word document was read.

As he read the first sentence, it all became clearer. He was being asked to insert a period at the end of each sentence. This would confirm to Alec that each sentence had been read. After finishing reading the word document the remaining files could be opened. Whomever read the document would admit how ingenious he was in safeguarding privacy. The last sentence instructed the reader to enter the correct spelling of Alec's favorite bird of prey in all caps. The hint to the password was the previous password turned upside down - the four-digit numerical number allowing him to access his computer. Drake opened the envelope he removed from the appartement containing passwords. Seeing Alec's writing caused his already red eyes to flood again. He copied the email address in his cell's address book under Alec's number. It included Alec's sister's email address. He would not delete it. His phone synced with his computer and Alia's information was added as well.

He typed in the word EAGLE. Another word document appeared. This document was surreal. It got his attention right away and kept him reading the short few paragraphs. It was what Alec was trying to convey to whomever was reading his words. It couldn't be as dire as the current situation had presented itself. How could anyone predict what has already occurred with any accuracy?

It was a glimpse of the future. What he was reading couldn't have been anticipated, but it was. Unbeknownst to Alec, he envisioned a time when he would need help finishing what he and his sister had started. They couldn't all be true masterminds of good over evil. They would need help. The paragraph was disturbing because he was reading about himself. The first sentence of the document, which was now in front of him, gave him pause. It was surreal. It was shocking. So much so, he had to read the first sentence more than once.

"Drake. Thank you for doing what I asked. Your friendship means a lot to me, and I genuinely appreciate everything."

Drake's mind drifted again to the times of extended lunches. A lot of what they talked about was now starting to make sense. Many things were discussed since he began working with Alec. Much of their banter was fun and about how they were going to solve all the world's problems. The more serious conversations were now in the front of him. He dabbed at a tear forming again. Reading his name was something he never envisioned, but there it was. The words unfolding from the screen were a request to do something he would forever remember.

Alec mentioned he had no choice but to undergo a surgery that, if successful, would save his life. He was afraid of what lay ahead. Although they both talked about the positive of what was to be, both could see the concern on the other's face. Alec explained he had met with his surgeon who had given him grim news of his injuries. He was telling his friends and any close relatives about the seriousness of his injuries. He was given the option to tell others who visited him the severity of the situation. Drake was glad he was the selected friend who he entrusted to read what was in front of him. Alec being able to sync any document from his cell from any location to his computer was ingenious.

They had joked on the phone about how to make sure he was able to come to his hospital room. He was to tell anyone who asked he was Alec's fiancé. Under those circumstances they couldn't refuse his visit and who would debate the validity of their relationship. There wasn't a chance of that happening, not in today's climate of litigation. More of the puzzle was now laid in front of him. It was his responsibility to find all the pieces and complete the puzzle. It was his job to finish what Alec started. Upon closing the document, another file opened.

Although he was alone in comfortable surroundings, Drake was compelled to turn around to make sure no one else was reading what he was. This was serious, this could be criminal. This is what they joked and talked about.

CHAPTER 17

Megan glared at Chad. An extended pause lingered between them.

"Well, I'm waiting," Megan uttered with disgust.

He stepped in the proverbial cow dung, and the stench would ruin a memorable lunch.

"Mine was an update on the Cards game," Chad replied. "The Cardinal closer through a fast ball to end the game with the go ahead run on second."

His response was the unintrusive ripple in the pond, the onset of a destructive tsunami.

"What are you talking about?" The frustration flooded her patience.

"I get Major League baseball alerts on my phone, and I follow the Cardinals," he replied.

"I'm not asking you about baseball," Megan's voice was rigid. There was no escaping the sharp glare. A glare so sharp, it could slice through the outer layer of a Nasa space shuttle.

"I'm sorry. I assumed you were talking about our phone messages."

"Well, that's obvious," rolling her eyes in disappointment.

It happened again. The silence. The thunderous, indescribable, and unmistakable moment when nothing needed to be explained. It had to be witnessed.

"I'm asking what you would say to the child? You heard a child pour out its heart and soul to you."

Chad understood the question and the symbolism was on point. Gathering his thoughts were making things worse. Silence was not golden.

"Megan," saying her name was calming. His valiant attempt to convey sincerity. "I'm trying to say I do understand -"

"No Chad. You're not understanding," Megan interrupted and leaned forward to solidify her point.

He didn't know how to turn the tide without making matters worse. Chad had no choice but to calm the sea.

Looking directly into her eyes, with all the earnestness he could muster. "Megan, I'm sorry."

She looked up from the churning of her lettuce salad. Her appetite would not return but she was good with it. Her hunger was satisfied by her good friend understanding the seriousness of discriminatory insensitivity. It didn't matter the gender of the perpetrator. It was not only the intent, but it was the impact of inaction. Enablers sanctioned willing participants. She would let him grovel in his explanation.

"There's no excuse for the actions or any sensible reasoning behind why people would exploit wrongful deeds," Chad said in earnest.

Surprised at his response, she almost regretted the seriousness of the topic. She was passionate about squashing belittling attitudes and did not tolerate anything of that nature.

"Thank you for saying that. I really appreciate it." He was wounded by her assault, but he would survive.

Megan continued, "I have one question and again, I want an honest answer."

She leaned forward again from her lounging posture and looked him directly in his eyes. She didn't want to stand down now. She had him right where she wanted. Vulnerable.

"I know what came across on your phone. When my phone vibrated, why didn't you ask me what text I received?"

Chad answered, "I shouldn't have looked at my phone, period. It could have waited. Megan I'm sorry."

"Thank you for the apology. I truly appreciate it. Now let's talk about something else before you wear my salad that I'm no longer eating."

Megan glanced up at stratocumulus clouds. She followed NOAA weather broadcast and hated interruptions from unsuspecting morning or afternoon frog choking monsoons.

"Somebody's going to get wet in a little while."

Chad followed her gaze upward, "you're right, and it might be us."

"Not a chance. This girl's always prepared."

To prove her point, she pulled out her never used travel poncho from her purse and waved it at him.

He wasn't sure if she was pulling at her poncho or her Glock. Tension still loomed. A downpour was imminent. He was now at a crossroads regarding what to do next. Should he mend the fence or rebuild the collapsed bridge? It was up to him to repair the damage he caused.

Her mission was accomplished. She plotted the course through uncharted waters. The sail was set, and they both headed unknowingly into the storm. They both took on more water than their vessel could hold, but they survived. She gave him a lifeline and he feverishly bailed them out of the sinking craft. No life preservers were needed. Their friendship would be stronger. She was sure of it.

The breeze picked up to cause a slight tussle to the patio umbrellas. She winked and smiled at him. Her look was all that was needed to repair his fractured ego and she knew it. He was for sure a Clark Kent replica. Tall, lean, and good looking. An overly cute sheepish grin was formed by his chiseled cheek bone. She laid in front of him kryptonite and he withered as suspected. His vulnerability was front and center. Megan would not soon forget the unassuming trait.

"We better go before everyone finds out my trusted Revlon spray proves my curls are not natural."

She reached across the table and placed her hand on his. Even though Chad was securely holding his iced tea, he could almost see the ice melt through the to-go plastic lid. A distinct contrast from the chilled conversation. She released her touch, smiled, and stood from her seat signaling Chad to do the same.

"My text was an alert from the weather app. Rain is imminent. And by the way, I'm glad the Cards won."

They walked briskly to their cars before any sprinkles were felt. Megan pulled from her parking spot, waved with fingers individually flickering her signature goodbye accompanied with her smile.

"Forgive, but never, ever forget," she whispered to herself. "Thanks Dad."

CHAPTER 18

Tenor edited his document. It was odd not knowing the name of the recipient or why he was requested to send it. After experiencing the day events, he could surmise with certainty several things. He did know his so-called friend was associated with the witness protection arm of the federal government, the infamous U.S. Department of Justice. Tenor didn't have the patience nor desire to delve into finding out who was pulling his strings. He was aware any attempt would be futile only to be thrust back into how he got into his predicament in the first place.

There was no need for him to move from his south forty parking spot. He now found it a personal solitude to finish what he started. Enough parking locations were now open and readily available to hospital visitors without having to look as he did when he arrived. Although there were several cars parked where he was, he assumed they were twelve-hour shift employees. Why else would anyone intentionally park that distance?

He was near done editing and perused through what he was to send. He hoped somebody could make sense of what he had learned. His document was logical and succinct to avoid a ton of questions. That was his hope. After going over it multiple times, he could easily understand the governments interest.

He noted the time when he arrived at the hospital and time of arrival in the intensive care unit. There was no reason to include the receptionist names in his document of events. Although it wasn't up to him to decide what was or wasn't important, he omitted the names of the receptionist. He made his executive decision and stuck to it.

Beverly's name was not important to the mission. He was glad he made note of her name tag although he preferred Ms. Cordial. She was patient and mature. He was certain she could lecture a historical perspective of her life story. Tenor surmised she, at one time, lived in the bowels of a southern state. There was a slight telling sign to her accent. She either witnessed or read next day news stories of church burnings occurring all too often in her younger years. She colored her hair, but hints of gray highlighted her thinning natural brown curls. This women could have been his mom. This women should have been his mom.

Kindness goes a long way. His patience paid off when he learned of the seriousness of his pretend friend. He hoped the game he was playing would pay off. He was feeling less than human under the circumstances. It would have been unfortunate to have learned from all of the worried visitors how well they knew Alec. The gravity of making others think they were linked by friendship was not setting well. He thought more and more of Alec and if he was aware of how dire his injuries were. Tenor would have felt better having the chance to meet him for the first and last time himself.

The sister wasn't a happy camper, especially about the unknown engagement. It was more of a shock than a disappointment. The chance of a meaningful relationship soured her opinion of her brother. What a roller coaster of emotions.

Tenor was shocked. The guy he was there to see, the guy he had never met or spoke to had died. Furthering his stealth visit was pointless.

He finished the editing and pressed send. Now all he had to do was wait for his next assignment. Thinking back on his performance, an Emmy was in order. There was a downside to it all and it couldn't have been avoided. There were some questions he knew should be asked, but he was quite sure and painfully aware things were outlandishly above his pay grade.

It occurred to him to suggest he be utilized for other well-meaning assignments. The financial incentives would be worth it. The truth to the matter, he was asked to do something, and he agreed. Not exactly a willing participant, but he came through for whomever was asking. He admitted to himself, there was no risk in helping. The mixed bag of emotions was creeping back into perspective. He was gloating knowing full well there was devastation, pain, and suffering. He was on their side and was helping them accomplish something obviously important to them. The masterful plan was coming together, or it crashed then burn at the very end.

There it was again. The annoying tone coming from his phone. What he sent wasn't an overly long document, but whoever was reading it, must have taken a speed-reading course. They needed answers to the questions he couldn't provide.

"Hello."

"Tenor. It's me. I need clarification. I need for you to confirm what you sent."

"I need confirmation as well. To whom am I speaking?"

Tenor was expecting dead air from the connection being intentionally lost. The silence was golden but only to him. He was smiling and certain there was vulgarity on the other end. He just couldn't hear it.

"Is it true. Is what you sent correct, did he die?"

"Yes, why would I joke about somebody dying?"

"Tenor, remain available. I'll be getting back with you shortly."

He couldn't believe what he heard. Remain available was like asking someone tied to a chair while being water boarded, to hold on for a minute or maybe two.

She once again ended the call without the customary, so long, farewell, goodbye. Although trivial, rudeness annoyed him to no end. He was not the same person he was in past years. Conscience and morality was now part of his vocabulary.

Pulling away from his favorite parking spot, he hoped he would never have to make the trip again. Perplexed as he was, he was anxiously looking forward to getting his questions answered. The game, if it were to be called one, had taken a turn. The road was no longer one-way. There were four lanes divided in both directions and it was up to him to make sure there were no roadblocks.

"No time for my acceptance speech," Tenor said out loud. "The ovation will have to wait. There is only one American Medal of Patriotism award and I humbly accept."

CHAPTER 19

Drake wrestled with his emotions while reading the downloaded document he obtained from Alec's apartment. The surreal story line and reliving nonchalant conversations with his friend, caused tears to run down both cheeks. He took a deep breath. Normally, he channeled any misfortune into a positive experience. Until now.

He needed to grieve but was aware he must do what was asked of him. At that moment he affirmed his decision. Without any hesitancy whatsoever, he was going to do what needed to be done. Loyalty to a friend favored any misgivings to the contrary.

Drake understood the plot - he helped design it. Talking and joking about a plan was different than implementing one. He hadn't the foggiest idea of it coming to fruition. The script was ever changing which made for memorable scenarios. There is no longer a duo with Alec. He was on his own. At times, the scenarios included the twin, Alec's sister. The question remained of what was to come of the suspected trio. Alia was part of the pact. Now however, it was troubling talking to her about her brother. Even worse, how could he come up with a pretense to join her with pulling off any ideas he and Alec had privately discussed. She had no clue Alec betrayed her trust. He would have to invent a reason for her to patronize the idea of him assisting in what once was their ploy. He had her contact information. He would soon get the courage needed to finish what Alec envisioned.

Alec would mock the injustice of his sister declaring herself a patriot. Although in the present day, Drake was questioning the meaning of a true loyalist. He now wrestled with the idea Alia was not just a willing participant but a well thought out strategy with Alec. He was unknowingly brought into the fold, and perhaps a well-orchestrated plan.

As he continued reading the first document, he was drawn into the plan. It softened the loss of his friend. The plan was a short story but with an alarming climax. With good reason, he was no longer sure of himself. When he conversed with Alec he was in control. He would not call it fear, just uncertainty. He would question, as Alec did, if they were bold enough to do what was being considered. As he recalled the exhilarating moments of their planning, it included understanding the price of reality. It was that idealistic curtain call they both were unsure about. Could they get others to join, would others understand their own plight?

Drake summoned his resolve. This undertaking wasn't thought through. It was all speculation and perhaps even testosterone chest pounding. What he read was not. The painting of this picture came into focus, but it was still a work in progress. Not a Rembrandt by any means, but the idealistic composition carefully constructed onto a canvass was one in the same. As he read about what they had discussed, it became painfully and brutally absolute. This was real.

Intriguing and intellectually brilliant how Alec and his sister were orchestrating their plan. It wasn't all that surprising knowing full well how smart his friend was. He was part of that plan although he was unaware of Alia in the background. That was why he got along so well with Alec. The maze of ideas between them were unsurpassed. They boldly joked about how Albert Einstein was either a descendent or they were his protégé in a Back To The Future scheme of planetary survival.

Alia would have Alec forward a timely message to said X and Y. The program confirmed the message receipt right on schedule. Drake was rarely surprised as scene after scene unfolded. It wasn't brainstorming. He followed the script Alec, as well as Alia, had drafted. In this setting however, Drake was not watching a movie, it was act one, scene one. He could almost follow the script as if knowing the outcome. Something was off in the script, and he couldn't read fast enough to find the part. His part. The one where he and Alec talked and joked about how it would all go down. The screen play wasn't following their storyline.

This wasn't the reminiscing during breaktime and lunches with Alec. He was a willing participant in something he was unaware had been under careful planning with a twin. As he read on, it was clear he not only was part of the storyline, but he also helped draft the playwright.

Something was still missing. Drake was at odds but even so, he was captivated and intrigued. From the onset he was all in. He wasn't aware the finale had already been written. What hadn't been planned was the trio becoming a duo. A trio without the main character. What a mastermind. A mastermind of deceit and frustration or was it anger? How could Alec be so deceptive in their planning? Why hadn't Drake been told about his sister's role? The disappointment described in the loss of a close friend was becoming evident. Alec left him with a mess.

Stay focused. Drake literally shook his head as if to shake off cobwebs. He needed to gain control of his thoughts. They were all over the place and his mind was like his arms flailing to escape the webs which encircled him.

Drake drafted an email to Alia. She needed to be contacted if things went wrong during the plan execution. His reaching out to the sister was the requesting for help. The idea to contact her at a time like this was unreasonable. Alec, although brilliant, wasn't staying in his lane.

CHAPTER 20

Conversation with Megan, following a memorable dinner was normally lighthearted and even informative. They could take either side, prosecution, or the defense. It reminded Megan of debating with her parents who were both attorneys. As a family they would watch the evening news. If a crime incident were reported, they would debate between themselves as if they were in court. If a suspect were at large, or arrested, they would discuss scenarios which led to fun family nights at the Swift residence.

The dinner with Megan fell short, although memorable on multiple fronts. The topic of discussion left a bad taste on both their pallets. He couldn't recall the exact ripple that triggered the tsunami because there were more than one. No matter her acceptance to his apology, he was sure further offerings of peace were warranted. It would require forethought.

Chad prided himself in his culinary skills. Preparing a meal for two was high on his list for a peace offering. He bragged to those who were bold enough to take the bait. Truth be told, which was seldom, he would confess to Googling a recipe, utilize Pinterest or watch Rachel Ray reruns. He disliked additional spices or anything with a hint of jalapeno powder or sauce. He'd frown at network chefs adding their pinch of anything that would result in a flavor stronger than mild. No five alarm cuisines for him.

Most of Chad's meals were spontaneous. A random thought would come to mind of what sounded good. There were times he would plan something that would take time and even required a marinade. Those menus generally started soon after lunch. If there were anything to marinade or sauté, he wanted plenty of time. That's how he rolled. A simple salad or even cereal was often his go to dinner choice. Simplicity was something he preferred. Even with simplicity, he avoided the sugar and was cognizant of anything he put into his body. However, he did like his desserts. Everything in moderation was the familiar motto. Any leftovers were adequate for his next meal.

He pondered with the freezer door open. Chad was often undecided on specialty meats for dinner. This meal of choice was between his personally seasoned ground beef, or the Price Cutter smoked pork chop. Being on a first name basis with a few grocery butchers worked well for him. The refrigerator was lowering the house temperature. Seasoned ground beef it was to be. The ground beef would thaw at refrigerator temperature to fix for his lunch or next evening meal. He learned the multiple kinds of cuts of meat and what to look for. He took time to purchase from behind the counter and often requested a particular cut of meat instead of prepackaged.

His thoughts turned briefly to his dinner with Megan. He would avoid a repeat experience at all costs. Although his apology was accepted, a meal for two at CJ's was in order.

He recalled the gentle touch Megan gave him before they left. Mixed signals indeed. She was not pleased with his explanation and attempt at defusing her displeasure. Her accepting his apology was a good thing, although he didn't expect anything different coming from her.

The three-quarter inch cut would be perfect for a dinner of two. He would offer this to his best friend at a time of her choosing. A truce dinner, that's what he would call it. A truce of dinner, wine, and dessert. He would talk to her to make it happen. It would be perfect. He would make it perfect.

Megan wished she had asked for a to go bowl for the remaining portion of her salad. She knew why she hadn't thought of a to-go container. Chad had never shown that side of insensitivity before. He was attractive in his caring and protective persona. Nothing fake about him but today he was hurtful.

They were friends, best friends. The thought of ruining the relationship was out of the question. Any thought of enhancing what was between them released a flurry of emotions. It wasn't as if she was afraid of a relationship. None of them in her past were lasting or meaningful. It was those relationships which nearly caused her to change her degree and extend her collegiate years of academia. Social work is demanding and rewarding. So was dentistry if you don't mind inflicting pain to get the desired result. Total awkwardness was the only label that fit. Megan was torn with emotions. Navigating a maze where she couldn't find the path leading to clarity. She glared at her reflection in the hallway mirror. The mirror had been placed there many years before. It was surrounded by photos of her mom, dad, and her. She stood in her reflection while her eyes grew misty.

Although it was years prior, the memories were as if they were the day before yesterday. She and her mom arranged the photos laughing and sharing hugs of years past. Megan vividly recalled the moment while wiping away tears. Returning to trips down memory lane, were mom and daughter moments conversing over tea, coffee, hot chocolate, or their favorite wine.

She recalled how they both laughed about silly things. Iced coffee was one of them. Neither could understand the point. She walked from the wall pictorial to the kitchen lightly touching her favorite framed picture with her fingertips. The same picture hung on her dorm room wall and her apartment. It was the facial photo of her mom. It didn't matter where she stood in any room, the eyes of her mother were looking at her. The soft curls partially covering one side of the face accented the slight upturn of the lips. That was her all-time familiar smile. Megan considered it more of a sly mischievous inner thought her mom would often have. During serious reflection between them, her mom would say to her "Girl you got this" or her favorite, "Peace be still."

Megan opened the frig, reached to the back, and grabbed a twist off bottle of wine. Another memory moment. Megan and her mom took several road trips to St. James after confirming a reservation for tours and wine tasting. It was at the St. James Winery they found their favorite. They enjoyed a dessert wine for any mother-daughter occasion.

While sitting in the family library, glancing up through the skylight, Megan leaned back in the recliner. Tipping her second glass of wine, she slid in place a hand knitted doily across the polished oak to protect the delicate tabletop. The doily was one of many of her mother's trademarks. The antique table was a gift to her mom from her dad.

Her eyes watered seeing the engraved wooden plaque on the library wall. The quote, "Peace be still" brought calm to the storms she faced without her mother by her side. She knew why the storms came. Although time had passed, missing her parents, especially her mom, brought on the turbulence.

The home library was where she found calm. It brought her back to the times her mom would say those same words to her. A chilled glass of wine often made those moments special.

Megan would often drive to Nathanael Green Park, which was a short drive from home and an easy commute for her mom's lunch hour at the law firm where she worked. The scenic waterways made the visit all the more special while they sat eating their lunch. During those private talks she would hear soothing words of encouragement. The conversations didn't require a topic.

The trips to the park and outings to the St. James Winery have ceased. Road trips to the quaint small town 15 minutes east of Rolla on interstate 44 for wine tasting were the best. It was their mom and daughter's day adventure. The annual trip brought wisdom only a mother to daughter could convey. It became another anniversary date of jaunts down memory lane becoming immersed with sleepless nights. Thoughts of happier moments while in the library kept the demons at bay.

There were items throughout the house she savored. Memories of the family of years past remained scattered throughout. Crumbs remained on the saucer and the smoked cheddar cheese no longer accompanied the last tastes of her wine. She closed her eyes to further drift off to sleep when the familiar tone accompanied the vibration from her cell on the coffee table. She needn't look at the caller ID, she knew it was Chad. She also knew he couldn't interrupt the moment she had with her mom. He could wait.

Chad pressed end so as not to leave a voicemail. Dinner wasn't that long ago. He hadn't formed any specific thoughts to why he was calling only to mention how he enjoyed their meal. But did he, or more importantly, had she? It was different this time. Like strangers greeting each other in a department store. One stranger offer a simple observation. That simple observation yielding a reply from the other stranger. The only response suitable reply would be friendly unless the recipient held on to a deeper unrelated meaning to the innocent observation.

Chad understood the ship needed to be up righted. He was alone on the proverbial sinking ship.

CHAPTER 21

Drake went to work like any other day. Coworkers greeted him with condolences, and some offered counseling referrals if he was so inclined. It became nauseous before the noon hour. Everyone at Com Tech expressed condolences, and well wishes. Some let Drake know they were willing to listen if he needed somebody to talk to. In the days, months and years prior to his friend's passing, those same people could have cared less who either one of them were. He seriously considered submitting a one-hour resignation notice before cleaning out his desk. He hadn't formulated a no employment plan, so quitting was not practical.

Ingenious. That was how Drake described Alec's forethought to their plan. It was insightful to have safeguards in place in case an unsavory foe attempted to thwart the plan - their plan. He had no clue Alec devised a plan to ensure things would be carried through. How could he have known one of them would not be there to see it to fruition?

He accrued enough sick days and vacation days any employee with any amount of tenure would envy. Neither he nor Alec took time off from work. As loners, they didn't see the point. There was no family they wanted to spend any time with. Alec would joke about taking some time off to get away from his sister but even that didn't seem like a good use of hard-earned leave. Work wasn't strenuous to warrant the need to escape that routine. Drake now understood what vacation really meant to those who looked forward to theirs. He was nearing his ultimate boiling point. One more "how are you doing" would send him over the proverbial cliff.

His employee computer alert was activated at his terminal. Drake, along with every other employee, witnessed alerts during in-service training periods. Currently, training was done through an online portal. Employees would complete the online training and recertification. It was repeated with minimal updates by IT every year for in-service. It became a time management issue. Scheduling employees to attend eight-hour training sessions became unmanageable. It was a private joke throughout the workforce what an innovative concept it was to learn from employees how to improve productivity.

Drake stared with a puzzling squint as he leaned to his computer screen. It was only his computer terminal receiving the alert. On his screen a flashing box required employee password sign-in to proceed. He had signed on to his computer when he arrived at his desk that morning. He entered the information. He looked over his shoulder in case anyone were close to view his screen. The screen prompt requested the eagle code.

Drake entered the corresponding numeric number to code EGOL.

He reached for his glass of water to moisten the sudden dry mouth. Looking up at his screen, the images were out of focus. He cleared his throat. He took another drink and rubbed both eyes before tears would reach each cheek.

There was no doubt where the employee alert came from. The interesting part of it was, he couldn't explain it. There were only two people who understood the password and code. Maybe three, if Alia was part of the equation. One of them was now dead. It was no secret that any personal documents created or viewed on employee-owned electronic systems were no longer private documents of the user. One click of the mouse, and he opened himself to disciplinary actions, or at the least, the powers to be could have access to whatever he viewed. As soon as the thought entered his mind, his grin formed. He's done it again, and from the grave. Absolutely genius. But how could he pull something like this off without anyone being aware?

Drake entered 7093 into the required field. A word document appeared. Surreal. An unintended hunt for the final piece to the puzzle. As he sat taking deep breaths and gathering his thoughts, he was successful in lowering his blood pressure. There was never the need for medication to help maintain healthy blood pressure levels. This morning had him utilizing proven breathing techniques. The document was another safeguard Alec created for them. Drake began to understand how serious his friend was about their effort to secure democracy. It was their desire to ensure those who proclaim to be for the people understood it was in fact the people who made it possible for all to prosper. Not the elitist.

"This backdoor document assures all Patriots win against tyranny," Drake's eyes averted to his left and right making sure he hadn't been approached without his knowing it. He could hear his pulse throbbing at his temples.

"Once you press continue, what you're reading will no longer be recoverable through any means."

Drake knew very well what it meant, and he quickly took a photo. He duplicated it and saved it to his phone SD card. He would retrieve it later to save and duplicate away from prying eyes. He continued to read knowing full well he could finish reading it anytime he wanted while away from work. The alert was sent from Alec's terminal. Alec had programmed it to be delivered after a specified number of hours of no sign-in from his terminal. One could only surmise how it wasn't detected by company antivirus software.

He continued reading with bated anticipation. Words from the grave caused a level of anxiety he'd never experienced. Alec was a jokester and his voice boomed loud in Drake's head. The pounding in his temples was manageable. Webster's third, fourth, or fifth edition, didn't have a word fitting what he was experiencing.

"Olive Branch. What the...."

Conversations with himself were commonplace after Alec's passing. Therapy was something he was seriously considering.

The document was not a short story. "Go to Olive Branch and retrieve the fruit of the tree."

Drake read what could be viewed as a scavenger hunt. A hunt he wasn't inclined to participate in. Could there be participants he hadn't met to help solve the puzzle? He always wanted to be on a team in an Escape Room with an extravagant payout amount for the winners.

The pounding remained as did the forming of a headache. He had to finish reading before leaving. The backdoor program earmarked for both his and Alec's terminals would self-expunge once the document would close, or the screen turned black. Drake and Alec both had their terminals time-out at two minutes if no activity existed during that time frame. The reading of the document was short but straight forward.

"Every Patriot understands our founding father's steadfast commitment to our constitution. We will not fail."

Drake sat up in his computer chair. Shoulders back, feet flat on the floor, chest out. Looking peripheral for any chance of someone walking by, he recalled earlier conversations with Alec. Everything became clear. Very clear. He grabbed a post-it and pen. He added together the numbers one, seven, seven, six in his head and wrote down the summation on the pad. He ripped off the post-it and placed it in his billfold. He opened google maps on his phone. He looked at the words on the document again.

"The Declaration of Independence of 1776 was written from the blood of patriots. Give me Liberty or give me...." The sentence was incomplete or was it.

Drake exhaled unaware his chest was full as well as his emotions. He was reading the document in the voice of his best friend. Chills were visible on both arms. He pressed the left button on his wireless mouse while the curser blinked over the word "exit." He tried to open the document, find the field to enter his password and the required code. It didn't exist. It was like he was in a time warp and when he clicked exit, it brought him back to the present. Ingenious.

Drake opened the Waze mapping app on his cell. He entered Olive Branch, Illinois and looked at the time and distance. He drafted his email and pressed send.

"I'm leaving for the day. I'll be back to work tomorrow. Maybe."

CHAPTER 22

The next morning Chad woke to an unfamiliar chime. It wasn't his alarm, although it was early enough one would assume the setting would be to alert one being late for work. Nine AM. His cell was designed to reflect only a maximum of 5 ring tones. Spam calls never made it through the MoTAF analog system. The government didn't allow the same technology to be afforded to federal employees' business cellular numbers. Cellular lobbyist dollar purse strings prevented such intrusion to big business and of course government clandestine organizations.

Another text from an unknown intruder was the only answer that came to mind. It rang again. It wasn't a text. His cell was ringing an unfamiliar tone. He sat up as if it was the hallway smoke alarm sounding. Rolling onto his right side, he grabbed his cell only to drop it to the floor. He cursed under his breath, fumbling for his phone, in time to hear the last ring before going to voicemail. He slung his upper body back onto the bed forcing his head to assess the comfort of his pillow. He let out a deep breath of disappointment and pressed his right thumb to his action key on his phone.

Holding his thumb steady, he read the words on the screen; "Improper Finger." He placed his forefinger to the action key. "Last Attempt" boldly displayed on the screen. The left thumb was again placed on the action key unlocking his phone.

MoTAF had the same protocols set on each member's cellular phones. Each member used their own sequence of fingers to unlock their phone. Safeguards also included the phones to reformat after several wrong sequence of finger placements on the action key. Facial recognition could also be utilized. All data and information would be deleted and unretrievable from the device but not removed from the clandestine cloud storage.

Chad retrieved the last number calling his phone. It only took a microsecond to recognize it. He intentionally didn't have the number programmed in his address book. He didn't need to recall the number to ever speed dial it. Why would the foster care system call him? Customarily on the first of each month, he would call the Senior Director of Administration for the foster care system. She knew his number when he called, and that number was approved for her to dial at any time. She didn't understand why it was private, only to never reveal that number to anyone or to have anyone call that number on her behalf. Due to privacy issues within the foster care system, she knew not to inquire his reasons for the privacy.

Chad needed coffee. The mojo was not yet percolating. He only set the timer for an early morning rise if he was on an assignment. The coffee would undoubtedly be needed to help him mindfully maneuver through whatever conversation he was about to engage in. He listened to his message. There were two. Both rings were only seconds apart, but each had a message.

"Chad, it's me, Dr. Florra. When you get this, please…."

The voice in the message ended abruptly. Background noise of a knock on a door, and a phone ringing. Chad understood Dr. Florra was in her office. It was the number she gave him. She offered on several occasions her cell number, but he declined. He listened to the last message.

"Chad, it's me, Dr. Florra. Could you please call me? It's about Liam."

Chad, now awake, as if a bucket of ice water landed on his head. The kind an unsuspecting coach of a football team would receive after they won a championship game. He dialed her number, and it went to voicemail.

"Dr. Florra it's me, Chad. I got your message. What's up with Liam? Call me back."

Chad's mind started its overload. Understanding what he couldn't fathom created pain at his temples. Ibuprofen was his dutiful option. It would be futile to try and guess why Dr. Florra contacted him.

Chad met Liam soon after his placement in a foster home. It was a match in heaven. At least that is what the director had told him. Could the match in heaven turn out to have been an unimaginable, unfortunate tragedy? Liam reminded him of himself at the same juncture in adolescence. Perhaps he got an award for his football heroics. The kid was talented in several areas. His abstract art was amazing.

Chad tried to stop the guessing game but couldn't. The foster care program was who he was. The formidable years of his life was attributed to those who saw promise in his abilities to rise up from adversities. Chad enjoyed volunteering with the program. Giving back was one of the many things that brought him purpose.

When he first met Liam, there wasn't anyone to encourage or push him to reach his potential. He didn't have anyone to tell him he was unique, that he had promise, or to believe in himself. His future looked bright especially under the circumstances that brought him to Dr. Florra.

Chad, now awake and his coffee now ready to be consumed, poured several cups in his travel mug. He grabbed his phone to redial and flinched as it wrang in his hand. It was Dr. Florra.

"Hello."

"Chad, hello. It's me, Dr. Florra. Sorry to bother you, but I thought you would want to know about Liam."

Following the call, Chad reclined back in his favorite chair. Holding his Yeti mug, he sipped slowly on his sweet caramel mocha coffee. The creamer made it sweet, the tablespoon of chocolate protein powder made it overly sweet. The throbbing in his head and his brief talk with Dr. Florra prevented him from having much of an appetite. He calmed himself and let the throbbing subside in hopes of avoiding a headache and the ibuprofen.

He opened the address book on his personal cell and dialed Liam. He answered on the first ring. "Hey C. J. how are you?"

Liam sounded exhilarated as he spoke. It had been a while since Chad heard himself called by his initials. It had been too long. He hadn't reached out to Liam mainly because it was his understanding from the director, things were going well. Dr. Florra introduced Chad to Liam and the young bright mind quickly asked him if he could call him by his initials.

"Hey Liam, I'm fine. I'm a little worried about you though. How are you?"

There was an extended pause. Chad listened with his phone on speaker. He turned up the volume and leaned forward.

"Liam, are you there?"

"Yeah, I'm here. I'm good."

Chad could hear the reservation in his voice. Things weren't good. It was time for delicate reflection and not be presumptive to any of his responses. Dr. Florra was correct, he must gingerly navigate through any conversation with Liam.

"Liam, it's me. I can sense something is bothering you. Where are you, let's talk."

"I'm at the 35-yard line. Where else would I be."

"Stay there, I'm on my way."

Chad knew exactly where he was. They sat on the bleachers of the high school football stadium on multiple occasions. Liam had Chad take him there on a foster care mentor meet and greet. Chad was a success story from the same program. It was at the same facility Liam was a graduate from. He was placed in a loving, nurturing home and Chad kept up with Liam's progress and met with the foster family as well. During one of his meet and greet sessions, Liam had Chad take him to a place of reflection. It was the happiest and worst memorable moment in Liam's young life.

It was the night of his sophomore school year. He was second string defense and hadn't seen any action other than on the practice field. On a Friday night, the rival team was leading by a field goal. The home team was moving down the field for a score and possible win. It was in front of the hometown fans, and they were literally inches away from a winning touchdown when their star player fumbled the football and was injured. The opposing team recovered the fumble and needed one first down to run out the clock to win the game.

The coach put Liam in as a linebacker to gain some real game playing time. The opposing team quarterback threw a pass and Liam intercepted. He ran it back for a touchdown and became the hero of the game. Liam was awarded the game ball in the locker room.

His dad never missed a game and promised to see the second half. He worked an extended shift to get some overtime pay. Times were hard after Liam lost his mother to cancer the summer before school resumed that year. Liam told his dad to work the shift and catch the last of the game. An industrial accident occurred, and his dad was killed. Liam was told what happened after the locker room celebration. Liam intercepted the ball on the 35-yard line, the same area his dad would sit to watch the games. For the longest time, Liam blamed himself for his dad working extra hours. It was where Chad could find him.

CHAPTER 23

Megan picked up her cell and dialed Chad's number. What was it he wanted to say when he called the evening prior? More precisely, there were things he needed to say. The out of ordinary happened. Her call went to voicemail. It was like placing a hand on a hot electric stove burner forgetting it was recently turned off. He always answered his phone when she called. There were multiple times she was with him, and he excused himself to take a call. She never knew who or what his call was about. It wasn't any of her business, and she never asked, but it was generally about a client. He would always explain who it was from without her inquiring.

This was a first and she didn't care for the anguish. She listened to his upbeat deep, business professional tone. She hadn't called his personal phone since forever and a day. The voicemail was a new phenomenon. She would not leave a message. However, the message was easy to listen to. It wasn't the message itself, it was how he sounded. The exchange of numbers was platonic when their acquaintance began. It hadn't changed but listening to his voice message was different. She wouldn't mind calling again if he were unavailable.

She hung the phone up before the prompt to leave a message. She gave it some thought and after a few moments, dialed his number again.

His message was worth dialing to hear. It could be viewed several ways, and she accepted every one of them. It was as if listening to a soothing voice on a self-healing, positive uplifting podcast.

"Chad, it's me. Sorry I missed your call. Call me when you get this."

It was at that moment she realized she always answered when he called and not let it go to voicemail. She couldn't even remember what her voicemail message said. She would give him a few minutes and call back. She smiled to herself at the thought.

A flurry of emotions continued from the evening prior. The personal time she took in the family library reminiscing thoughts of her mom was long overdue. It had been years but seemed like only days of receiving the dreadful news about both her parents. The wounds had healed but the scars will remain forever. She wished she had taken the advice to talk to someone with an understanding ear. She opened her eyes and gently smeared a tear with the back of her hand. The tissue was within reach, but she didn't bother. It found its way down her cheek. Still holding her phone, she pressed the speed dial.

"Chad, It's me – again," there was a distinct pause emphasizing it wasn't the first time she had left a message. "These are new phones we have. I got your message, I know you're getting mine. Call me, ok?"

The sharpness in her tone wasn't purposely extended. Megan closed her eyes, breathed in, and exhaled willing herself not to wake. There was a calmness that briefly came over her. The answers came quickly as if her mother was in the room with her. She knew she would get the answers. She always did. She could hear her mom's disappointed tone bringing things into perspective.

"Peace be still, my dearest," the words spoken by her mother caused her to pause and look at her conflict from a different perspective. Things were going to run their course.

Chad sat as comfortable as one could on stadium seating. Liam was all ears. Chad told him stories he had never heard before. It made him gain more respect for his friend. Liam experienced similar circumstances as Chad when he was about the same age. The pain of the loss of Liam's parents resurfaced during school sponsored parent recognition days. Schools throughout the district would have students invite their parents to specific classes for programs the students had been working on. Music, drama, dance, and literary performances were showcased and open to all district families. Multiple suggestions were either overlooked or discounted regarding the printed announcements sent home to students. Not every child were raised by biological parents. There were students from a multitude of unfortunate circumstances. Some were adopted, some were raised by grandparents, some were raised by older siblings, some by single parents, some by similar gender parents. The list goes on.

Liam couldn't have been placed in a better home environment than the one he was currently experiencing, but he missed his biological parents. It was every year during designated parental events where he had difficulty. He needed to talk to someone who understood. His foster parents were in fact a suitable placement for Liam. They understood the emotions Liam went through during school parents day. Although all guardians were welcomed by the school, Liam preferred not to attend. His artistic abilities were displayed in his art class, but he wouldn't attend. It was agreed by his foster parents for Liam not to attend. Chad was his sounding board because he had walked in his shoes. He allowed his vulnerability to show when around Liam. It was one of the many things Liam appreciated in their friendship. No holes barred, frank discussions, judgement prohibited.

Liam agreed to text his foster parents with the expected assurance he was fine and not to worry about him. He was with his trusted friend and would return to his scheduled class after the last school parent program. Liam wasn't the first student with extraordinary circumstances. The school district was a model for other districts around the state that collaborated with community services providing secure safeguards for students. Dr. Florra, with the help of the foster parents and the liaison mentor system, established protocols the student would activate, or the foster parents would initiate when potential issues arose. The reduction of at-risk adolescents and continual home placements were a testament to the program's success. There were many successes, but the program wasn't perfect by any means. Improvement was often hard to sell when those who controlled purse strings remained involved. Chad never envied Dr. Florra's unwavering commitment to the program and how beneficial she was for the students.

Chad promised Liam he would stay with him until the school programs were concluded. They remained in the bleachers through the scheduled time. Chad walked with Liam to the school counselor's office. They both had the understanding their conversation had to change gears once inside.

After a jovial visit with Liam and the school counselor, the librarian entered the office. Chad returned to his car and noticed how the previous rain and pollen changed its overall appearance. A detour to utilize his unlimited In and Out car wash club membership was in order.

Once seated he retrieved both his cell phones from the armrest console. He noticed he had missed calls on his personal cell. He also had two voicemail messages, undoubtedly from law office clients who awaited his return call. They could wait when his concerned thoughts about Liam diminished. The blinking blue light on his phone was an annoyance. He lifted the armrest dropped the phone inside and closed the lid.

Chad customarily turned his ringer phone off when talking to Liam or made sure he left them in his car. It would be a dagger through the heart for a young person requiring your undivided attention only to notice multiple glances at a phone.

Pulling from the parking lot onto the busy street, he was startled by a loud horn. He saw the car coming but didn't think it was that close. He waved in his rearview as if to apologize. Shaking his head to his mistake, he brought his thoughts back on his driving.

The wait line was short as he pulled up to the car wash attendant. He aligned his wheels onto the wash track, put his car in neutral as the sign instructed. Two young faces, one boy one girl, pointed at the signs requesting, car in neutral, hands-off steering wheel, windows closed. Both kids reminded him of Liam, young and the world in the palm of their hands. Or so they thought. At least these kids had jobs and weren't sitting on the hoods of other friends' cars, skipping school, or having dropped out of school altogether. The kids likely excelled in their academics or at least had resources to sponsor teenage employment opportunities.

The movement of his car being pulled by the auto wash allowed him to lean back on his head rest, close his eyes if only for a few short minutes. Even with the noise of the water pounding his car, he could hear and feel the vibration from his armrest. Another job client emergency. Being allowed to work remotely had its advantages.

Chad grabbed his MoTAF cell, opened the address book and called Megan. It went to voicemail. Out of the ordinary, but not unexpected either. It rang once and he surmised she had it turned off. The phone tag game would now begin. He took one long deep breath, and another. He closed his eyes and ended the call without leaving a message.

"Perfect," he said aloud in a disappointed tone. "Just perfect."

He pressed redial and decided to leave a message. He wanted to talk, to get with her and let a close friend listen to what he experienced. Megan wasn't familiar with Liam. It was time she learned another side of him. An important side.

"Hey Megan, it's me. Give me a call when you get this."

His phone was in his hand when it vibrated. He looked at the screen displaying "Meg" as the caller. The roar of forced soapy water slammed simultaneously against his windshield and both driver and passenger side windows. The car jolted forward on the tracks as the soft scrub brushes started turning at the center of his front bumper, license plate and grill. The large wide brush slowly lowered onto his hood moving toward the windshield.

"Hello" he paused, not hearing any reply to his answering. He raised his voice below the shouting decibel.

"Hello. Megan! I'm at the car wash. Megan!"

The line went silent, and the phone screen went to the home screen on the dropped call. He looked at the lost connection, slammed the back of his head to the head rest closing his eyes once again.

It was a perfect day to complete the hand drying of his car after getting it washed, as well as a good vacuuming. A quick detail would take his mind off of things and give him a needed reprieve.

Megan quickly lowered the phone from her ear and slammed it onto her right thigh. Not returning any of her calls is one thing but hanging up once he heard her voice brought things to a whole new level. She wasn't ready or willing to confront him about it, especially today. She didn't have the desire to pamper his ego any more than he needed. She too could play his game.

Chad stepped up on the curve where he parked his prize ride next to the courtesy vacuum hose. The monthly amount deducted from his bank account was well worth it. He could wash his car as many times as he wanted, come rain or shine. He didn't like waiting as long as he did to wash it. He could afford any set of wheels he sat his eyes on. It wasn't the cost of the carriage, it was the style, quality, and options each one afforded him.

He pulled the vacuum hose from its cradle, and the suction commenced. After vacuuming, he repositioned the hose to listen to his clients messages in case he needed to call before detailing his car. At least he could get an idea what his afternoon would look like. He sat down in the driver's seat and opened his phone and retrieved his first message on speaker.

He looked at his phone when he heard Megans voice. He didn't recognize the number and he hadn't listed her personal number in his personal cell. Why would he? She always called him on their assigned MoTAF phones. When they first met, they exchanged numbers in their personal cells, but he deleted her number out of his phone when she joined MoTAF. He didn't want to confuse the two phones when trying to reach her. The MoTAF phone was his priority number.

He listened to all the messages. They were both from Megan and the missed calls were also from her personal number as well. He played each message twice. Taking deep breaths, he leaned his head back on the driver's seat headrest. He smirked wondering if it would be inappropriate to walk back into the school, sit down in the counselor's office and demand a personal one on one with the counselor. He unloaded on Liam some personal baggage. It was like self-medicating. Liam was all ears and the interaction between them was needed. But now he needed another ear. Megan's ear.

He pressed redial again and her voicemail responded immediately. He left a message previously and ended his call without leaving another. He heard the angst in the messages she left for him. It was time for a deep Kia detail and put all other to rest, if only for a little while.

He liked Kia. It didn't show the extravagance of the Lexus or Mercedes car emblems proudly displayed. The simple three letter brand name was all any intelligent consumer needed. The Telluride was sleek and attractive with bells and whistles coming as standard features. Although the same could be said for many sport utility high profile vehicles, Kia was in a class of their own. He chose Sangria for the color. It kept the men in blue from looking his direction while skirting above the maximum posted speed limit. The butter-scotch leather seats was an added touch. The HUD, heads up display, allowed him to keep his eyes on the road and glance at selective driving features reflecting onto the windshield. The reduced insurance premiums from the multitude of safety features was an added plus.

Chad never considered himself a ladies' man. He did like the various interior lighting features. It was fun to change the interior lighting during nighttime driving. Liam once told him "it was dope" and he had to borrow his car for a date after returning from a mentor's night out to one of his favorite Avengers movies. Chad told him no problem, once he had a girlfriend, and he got his learner's permit. It was after that night out, Chad brushed up on his slang terms. It was as if he was repeatedly asking Liam what he meant when Liam explained things about movies he liked.

While detailing his car, Chad recalled some personal reflections Megan told him regarding her parents. She mentioned the moments both parents mentored her on their values and what was important to them. During those talks she was able to speak to her parents about her struggles and how they helped her get through them, even though they were unaware of the specifics. There wasn't anything left unsaid in their relationship.

Chad sat behind the wheel with his door open and driver's window down. He opened the google app on his phone searching for the St. James winery website.

The winery brought memorable conversations between Chad and Megan about Megans mother. The drive was loads of fun which included intimate conversations between them. Soul-searching chats brought tears and laughter during their drive to and from the winery.

Wine tasting and tour was the reason for the day trips. Returning with several of their favorites kept the day trip memories alive. Although Megan's dad enjoyed an occasional glass of wine, sipping from chilled long stem crystal glasses was about mother and daughter reminiscing.

Chad dialed the winery. The message line offered options customers could select for the precise reason they called. He placed orders for three bottles of their favorites. The delivery would be within 10 business days. He would plan a special moment when he and Megan could talk about any misunderstanding they were having between them. He would apologize for whatever did or said. It would be a long wait for the delivery.

CHAPTER 24

Drake arrived in Olive Branch, a small quaint eccentric farming town. He surmised the description by a quick glance at the city highway sign listing its population. He missed reading the exact size but guessed it was about the same number of customers in a Target department store on any given Saturday afternoon. He need not ask for directions to the post office because he drove right by it. The signage and U.S. flag was a hint, requiring a quick U-turn. He slowed to the first four way stop sign intersection he came to. He could have run the stop sign or turned around in the intersection and not one person would have noticed. He drove a short distance and turned around in the first vacated driveway.

The grass was tall as if it hadn't been mowed since last fall. Leaves accumulated on the single step leading up to the weathered porch. Leaves cluttered the short driveway leading up to the single car garage. Newly sprouted weeds, not grass, found its way through the uneven severely cracked concrete single car driveway. The dented garage door needed replacing. A lot of things needed replacing or fixed on the home. There were empty lots across the street and either side of the house. The empty lots would be hard to sell if the dwelling remained among them. It was a perfect location for an annual October haunted house. The run-down dwelling could also serve as a safe haven for homeless meth users needing to get out of rainy weather or the winter windchill. Drake reversed from the driveway without looking behind him. There was no reason for concern, the sight distance allowed to ample view of the desolate street. The mailbox laid in the tall grass next to the wooded post to which it was once attached. The post leaned as if it would fall with the next strong breeze. As he backed out of the driveway, he wondered why someone would waste time hanging the lopsided no trespassing sign.

Drake retraced his path to the post office, stopping adjacent to the flagpole. The faded, tattered stars and stripes caused him to close his eyes and shake his head in disappointment. A single letter to the mayor, police chief, council member or Postmaster would garner a new US flag. The addressee would likely be the same person who performed each task. However, it would be anyone's guess if a struggling city budget would fund the replacement of Ole' Glory. Drake willed the door of the building to be unlocked. He grimaced outwardly at the possibility of a wasted trip.

The building was small as if it could double as a consignment store. He approached the double glass door and greeted his image in the reflection of the mirrored glass as he approached. He wondered how many eyes were upon him from inside when he reached for the handle. His query was immediately answered.

A gold name plate hung around her neck with one word in all caps, PATRIOT. Majestic she was, even before the taxidermist did his thing. The bald eagle perched high in the lobby corner on top of a tree limb staring at the entrance as if some weary unsuspecting meal prospect were in her sights.

Drake paused briefly and walked under the claws of the defender of democracy. He reminisced about the stretched-out wings of the same defender on the wall of Alec's apartment.

"Can I help you?" A gruff voice boomed from the receptionist counter across the small lobby startling Drake.

"Beautiful isn't she?" responded Drake nodding toward the eagle.

"My aforementioned question remains," the postal worker stared with piercing eyes.

"No, I'm good," Drake answered with his award-winning friendly tone and smile. He walked toward the combination mailboxes located at the back wall of the small post office.

"Hey!" boomed the voice coming from the only other person in the building. "I've worked here for nearly a decade. I've never seen that car before, and I know for a fact our paths have never crossed."

The man made a strong emphasis on the word "fact." Drake stood in front of box 21, the summation to the numbers of the year of the Declaration of Independence, 1-7-7-6.

Drake looked at his car. He didn't have any bumper stickers, notable dents, or anything to give reason for the man's rudeness. Drake hadn't given it any thought about his license plate. No reason a Missouri resident would have a small-town Illinois postal mailbox. Olive Branch wasn't far from the Mississippi River and the Missouri State line. It wasn't inconceivable someone unknown could visit the post office. However, it was a small town. The brute had a point, although he did not appreciate how he tried to make that point understood.

With his back to the man, he rolled his eyes and breathed in, but exhaling loudly in disgust. Drake was now caring less for the man and wanted to make sure he knew it.

He doubted the man would be impressed about his fathers' military service as a Marine. Nor would he applaud learning his engineering degree through the military. He was sure the man would have cared less learning about his mother born, lived, and educated in Manila, near Clark Air Base, in the Philippines. He would also care less to learn she obtained her PHD while raising a family. The postal employee was showing off his flag tat on his right forearm. That was obvious by the sleeveless t-shirt. If it weren't for the tattoo he'd probably have trouble spelling the word flag.

"Box 21 is what I'm looking for and where I'm standing," he said, "As if it's any of your business."

He slowly rolled the four numbered dial to 1, 7, 7, and held his breath as he rolled the tumbler to number 6. As Drake turned the small handle he closed his eyes in hopes the box would open. It did.

Opening the small brass door, he reached inside, and removed a manila envelope. It was the only item inside. Inside the envelope was a thumb drive and several typed pages. As he closed the box he rolled his right index finger over the numbers, scrambling them once again. The brute stared at him as he walked by.

"Close it out. Consider it paid in full," Drake grunted while returning the stare.

Drake ignored the man who attempted to murder him with his dagger sharp eyes. To announce his exit, Drake hit the push bar with enough force to break the door hinges. He slammed his car door with less of a public display.

The corners of Drake's mouth turned up into a full-face grin. He thought to himself, and he said out loud in a subtle laugh.

"I should have extended an Olive Branch."

Drake abruptly accelerated causing loose gravel from the aged asphalt to careen upon the one and only Post-Office step. There would be icicles in Hades before he would sit in front of the post office to read the contents of the envelope.

Drake easily surmised the postal employee was obviously bored and wanted to converse. It would have been a sad scene for him to break out his Bruce Lee imitation underneath the flagpole for all the towns folk to see. The carnival would have to wait for his next visit.

After driving a short 5 miles on Highway 3, toward Cape Girardeau, Drake succumbed to anxiety. He opened the envelope again pulled out the pages held together by one staple in the top left corner. He couldn't help but read the pages to understand why he made the trip.

The pages weren't numbered and there were too many to count while driving. He placed them on the armrest between the front bucket seats. He started reading the first page while steadying the steering wheel with his left thigh. He read exactly what he and Alec discussed. Alec finished the plan of events and his going to Olive Branch solidified the safeguards Alec put into place. Nobody outside designated confidants would be able to retrieve or remotely understand what had been agreed upon. He and Alec were the confidants. He, for the life of him, couldn't determine where Alia fit into the plan, if at all. But there it was, Alia was mentioned in detail in a plan. It wasn't anything they had discussed, but he read Alia's participation. If any data were lost or seized, he now held a printed hard copy. This was Alec's mindset and he agreed. A copy of information required safeguarding. That safeguard was now in his hands.

Rumble strips vibrated under the tires and through his body. He glanced up and quickly let go of the papers and grabbed the steering wheel. What he didn't realize, or notice was the abandoned vehicle parked on the shoulder next to a guardrail directly in front of him. The guardrail prevented vehicles from careening down a steep embankment and the awaiting culvert. The abandoned vehicle next to the guardrail left little to no margin of error beyond the rumble strips. The Illinois Department of Transportation had no statistics of probability relating to near mishaps. The rumble strips prevented or likely saved a number of lives. Drake could add the number one to a study.

He firmly grabbed the wheel with both hands and turned aggressively to the left. He barely missed sideswiping the mirror of the parked car. The oversteering caused Drake to nearly slide out of the driver's seat. He would have been in the front passenger seat if it weren't for the seatbelt doing its job. His eyes were the circumference of a coffee cup rim as his car now veered to the left into the opposing lane of traffic. In his favor, there was no oncoming traffic as he now careened onto the opposite roadway shoulder. Drake continued to overcompensate, steering his car back across the road toward the right shoulder guardrail.

It was the eye, hand, brain reactive phenomenon we're all familiar with. One can't help the urge to perform the often-mistakable response and uncontrollable desire to bring the car back to where it is supposed to be. Often, drivers cause unfortunate mishaps due to their own inattention. By not understanding the centrifugal force of a 3,300-pound vehicle they control, things quickly turn sour. It wasn't his time to meet his Maker.

Drake brought his car under control without soiling his pants. He slowed to a stop onto the shoulder beyond the guardrail he nearly obliterated. Drake's hands were visibly shaking. Inhaling through his nose and breathing out through his mouth barely staved off the nausea. He was sure he was going to faint and choke on his own vomit. With a shaky hand, he put his car in park, then pushed the on and off button to turn the engine off. He got out of his car and walked around the front to the passenger side. He kept his right hand touching the hood to assist his balance. He steadied himself placing both hands on the fender above the front wheel while leaning forward and taking in deep breaths. At that very moment he thought of Alec and the unfortunate wreck that caused his death.

"Nope. Not today Alec. I'm not coming to see ya today." With little warning, Drake revisited his breakfast and his lunch.

It seemed like eternity, though only moments later, the unfortunate roadside delay ended, and he was home. Immediately entering his single bedroom apartment, Drake threw himself into his ergonomic high back computer chair. It spun around bringing himself squarely in front of the screen. He wanted to shower and sleep. He wanted the day to repeat itself without the previous events having occurred.

Grabbing the manila envelope, he pushed his monitor keyboard aside and began reading the document that almost caused his demise. The thumb drive contained the same information he was reading. The previous brainstorming conversations from months on end were revisited, word for word. They were indeed surreal, but there it was. The cause and effect.

The cause was decided, the effect was yet to be. The epic scenario was simply that, a scenario. It was up to him to make it come to life, and he would. They would. They all would.

"They will know you were a patriot Alec. The world will know we all are."

CHAPTER 25

Tenor sat in his modest surroundings. He perused through the want ads wondering what cushy job he could find to improve his employment opportunities. What he really wanted were different surroundings, different coworkers and most important, an uptick in salary. He had the skillset, if only he could get rid of the ball and chain he acquired some years prior. Easy job, easy income, or at least a respectable income. Self-reflection had proven nothing came easy. He learned the hard way, if you play stupid games, you win stupid prizes.

He'd paid his dues and shown his loyalty. WITSEC wasn't the enemy. Although it took soul searching to understand, he was his own worst enemy. But not anymore. He couldn't be sure what their thoughts were of him, but he could make his case easily enough. There was not a single black eye from day one of his admission into The Program. How could there be? Every keystroke he made, on every device they gave him, revealed what little of his life belonged to him. At what point can anyone ever trust the unknown? The no name analyst was the governmental unknown. She was kind enough, or so she sounded. Who could really be certain from listening to a voice on the other end of a phone call? A little spunky for his taste, but he was once proud of his own shining moments.

He would hear from her soon enough. There were no misgivings about that. He'd been online searching tech jobs for much of the afternoon. He needn't remind himself, every questionable site visited, or any misstep would be brought to his attention. He was assured his conversations and anything that he would say to anyone in private or public was not recorded. It was because of them, that WITSEC was his life. One thing he knew for sure, being watched kept you honest. It didn't take much thought process for truism to be brought to the surface. He understood long ago he was where he was supposed to be.

After getting a call about another job contract being suspended, it was time to look for a better job. The union liaison explained jobs would be at a standstill in the near distant future. To put it bluntly, since he was the last one in, he could assume he would be the first to be let go if things didn't work themselves out. Tenor inquired about the specifics and why it affected their jobs. The answer resembled a longtime running daytime soap.

A county clerk, from two counties north of Laclede, was indicted for embezzling funds over a three-year period. This young lady was rewarded, by popular vote, to her third term serving the fine folks of Morgan county. Tenor asked what that had to do with their work. The answer was put in simplistic terms.

The county clerk built her campaign around truth, pride, confidence, and work ethic. She used her maiden name after her divorce. Her twin sister, who had not married, was her strongest supporter. That last name followed her sister all the way to Morgan county when the embezzlement charges were filed. The infamous campaigning twin sister was the CPA for the company their work was contracted with. The State of Missouri suspended the license of the twisted sister due to some hanky-panky that slithered into the books of the contracted construction company.

The 'follow the money' cliché got complicated. It trickled all the way to the trade school where graduates of the school were employed by construction companies. The ex-husband, of the twin, was an instructor at the trade school. Tenor had the union boss suspend with more explanations. He heard more than he wanted at that point and was sorry he asked why their jobs were at risk.

Work had been sustaining and surprisingly rewarding. He wasn't averse to manual labor. He enjoyed seeing work projects completed that he figuratively could put his name on. He intentionally avoided political discussion and discourse. It didn't interest him in the least. He couldn't put his real name on anything. Who was he anyway? Seven Up, Tenor Upshaw, or should he carry a notarized certificate proving his name was Brody? Thank you very much, WITSEC. The value of a legal piece of paper nowadays has proven that piece of paper worthless.

Timed perfectly and on cue, like a symphony conductor signaling the clash of symbols, the familiar chime from his cell broke the silence. It didn't startle him like before. Although the tone was no longer startling, it remained unwelcomed. What was more disturbing, it couldn't be changed or altered in any way. Other ring tones could be customized. The government had its rules and regs and this was one of the many annoying ones. The chime was to assure him the importance of the conversation and wasn't to be ignored. In simpler terms, answer the phone if it rings. It rang as if the ringer was turned up to drown out concentration. The million-dollar question to the elephant in the room would soon be answered.

The keystrokes prompted the howdy doody call. Concentrating on finding a job, Tenor understood the watchful eye of Uncle Sam. All he was trying to do was find a better job. He enjoyed making his own money.

"Tenor it's me. How are you doing?

The calming voice became an annoyance. Although they didn't talk often, it was an unsettling reminder when the chime occurred on his phone just how much of his life was not his. It was time again to charm her with his award-winning personality.

"Well, well, well. It's my favorite unnamed nemesis. I've been longing for your call to ruin my positively productive day.

"Seriously, are we going to do this again?"

"Yes we are until you give me a name," Tenor said.

The corners of his mouth turned up. He knew she didn't appreciate his humor. At least the part where the unknown person was reminded they didn't have a name. He couldn't understand, unless they were one day to meet, why it was he couldn't know her name.

"You sound like a Karen. I'll call you Karen. How's that? Ms. Karen it is."

"No Tenor. My name is not Karen," the calming voice put an emphasis on the word not.

"Well Karen, give me something to call you. It's not like we're going to meet one day. I'd really like to call the person I'm talking to by their real name."

"It's policy. By virtue of what I do, I'm prohibited from giving my birth name," there was a long pause in the conversation.

"Give me something," Tenor blurted with disgust in his voice. "I don't mean to sound ungrateful. You guys have given me my life back. It's just. It's kind of… It's… Well. It's -."

"Monique," my name is Monique," She spoke over his mumbling.

Tenor was taken by surprise by the interruption.

"Wow. Nice. I like it. That's a pretty name. Thank you for -"

Monique interrupted again. "Don't go around telling the people who pay me what I did. I like my job. I could get fired."

"Right. I'm not supposed to tell anyone that my name isn't what I've told people it is. And don't tell them, I get secret calls on a government encrypted phone informing me about extremist groups. By no means tell anyone--."

She interrupted, "OK, I get it. Seriously. It's against policy. I could get into trouble."

"Monique, I understand. I've got your back like you guys have mine. Now, tell me. Why have you called?"

"It's about the job inquiries you've been researching. I've pitched to the bosses about you potentially branching out with us on a matter that appears to be developing. However, it's not without risks."

"As you're aware, I'm accustomed to risk. What's the real catch?"

"No catch. The stipend you're familiar with will change. You'll be rewarded handsomely for your efforts."

"Cool. You had me at handsomely. What exactly are we talking about?"

"I'm sending you a word document. You will receive a case sensitive code within the subject line of the email. There will be an eleven-digit number in the attachment of the email. The Word document cannot be opened until the code in the subject line is sent by text to the eleven-digit number."

Tenor listened intently. It was straight forward and wasn't complicated. He hated complicity when it came to instructions. He already had a multitude of questions he knew he should ask but was confident he would get those questions answered before she was finished. The rest of his instructions came and clarified all his questions. He wasn't sure how she did it. He was beginning to like her.

"Easy peasy. No need to second guess," she assured Tenor.

"You have two attempts. There are no zeros or underscores for simplicity. If after the second attempt you're unsuccessful, the word document will have to be resent with a different unique code," she paused for Tenor to speak but he remained silent.

"That's it. You can make any notes of the email you want, but it will not print. If you attempt to take a screen shot or any electronic device is placed in front of the screen to take a photo of it, the document will be blurred beyond reading through the device for recollection."

"Dang. You guys really don't trust me do you?" Tenor exclaimed with slight sarcasm.

She responded with excitement in her voice, "Every document is forwarded in the field this way. There are programs we've created you won't see on the market. We try to develop new and exciting stuff like tech companies and hackers do. No offense."

"None taken," as he laughed into the phone.

"I'll be in touch. I want to know your thoughts on what is going on underground."

Tenor knew exactly what she was talking about. Extremists had gone deeper to keep the mainstream from infiltration, but they've become bolder than they ever were. They were brazening in their beliefs and actions. They weren't shying away from arrest as convictions and subsequent punishments had been lenient. Their beliefs were causing concerns to mainstream media as violence had become more common place.

Searching for jobs through Glassdoor web sites resulted in his receiving an uninvited phone call. Of course, all calls he received from his friend were unsolicited. Now, however, he had a name. A name he was surprised she relinquished. Not just a name, but an acquaintance he could admittingly say intrigued him. A name to the voice. Although he was not pleased with the phone call, he understood it. Once again, it was as if he couldn't be trusted. He had proven his worth ten times over. His mundane life needed purpose. He wanted a life he so deserved. He wanted associates he could call friends. Friends who knew his real name. Tenor wondered if that ship had already sailed.

He became accustomed to intrusive conversations and the mundane life he had created for himself, but no more. He had resources at his fingertips like any other warm-blooded American. He needed a job. He needed an unconditional release from prison and the only way to get it would be to obtain good paying sustainable employment.

Another well-known chirp sounded on his phone along with the vibration, as it rested on the wood veneer surface. The vibration continued for several seconds following the audible. His daydream became a quick nap before the interruption.

The tone accompanied by the vibration alerted him of an email received. If he chose not to look at his mail, a vibration would occur every time he picked up his phone alerting him of an awaiting email. It was one of many features he liked about his Android. He opened his email account which was linked through his laptop. There it was. An email from Monique. There was no name attached to the email. She was true to her word. She told him she would send it, why would he expect anything less?

Laying his phone aside, he opened his email on his laptop. The email subject line was as she told him it would be. Picking up his cell, he entered the eleven-digit number in the SMS message. He double checked the code to make sure each number was accurate. He didn't want to go through this sequence more than once. He pressed send as his newfound friend explained to him only moments earlier.

The word document sprang to life. He couldn't have been more surprised. A job offer. That's what it was, or at least that is what he was speed reading through. He slowed his visual scan and started reading from the beginning once again.

The following document is for approval. Upon agreement to the contents of this encrypted proposition, the recipient/s must respond without delay with an affirmative response. If the required timeframe is not adhered to, all offers become null and void, thus a negative response is forwarded electronically. All previous agreements shall remain in force, other than monetary compensation. If agreed upon, financial compensation will be extended to recipient/s beyond the current scope of said agreement. The recipient/s shall NOT close the browser or email until the document is read through in its entirety. Using the cursor, an "X" will be entered at the end of the third sentence of each document paragraph where a box is positioned. If the boxes are checked to quickly or slowly, the program will inadvertently sense the recipient/s are attempting to inconspicuously alter the document. The document will subsequently be voided as well as any current agreed upon compensation.

He uttered out loud as if he were talking to someone looking over his shoulder, "These guys are good. Damn good."

He read what appeared to be Old English script. Although it wasn't in medical terminology or thermonuclear physics jargon, it was clearly foreign. Barely understandable. It was judiciary legal jargon. One might want to first attend an FCCA, Federal Court Clerk Association, conference to decipher exactly what it meant. Thank goodness for smart phones and the Webster Dictionary app.

The room remained silent, but the voice in his head screamed at the limit of his larynx. His eyes were the size of saucers as he paused to go over the first few sentences of the first paragraph.

"Woah. These guys are serious."

And there it was. All his education and tech experience hadn't prepared him for what spun around the cortex of his brain.

CHAPTER 26

Megan got a good evenings rest. She faintly remembered leaving the library and going to bed. She awakened early and chose to get in her aerobics before starting her day. She would not to let the day pass her by. She showered had a light breakfast and worked through the normal lunch hour. Working remotely had more perks than she wanted to admit. Returning client and coworker emails at the law firm was invigorating. She liked what she did. She engaged feverously and was reworded knowing her clients were not mislead on what was occurring in their lives. Her coworkers were reminded she was earning her keep. Her day on the job would conclude early and she could rest easy. Rest was what came to mind as she thought of dialing back on her cardio routine. The protein snacks that followed her breakfast were fading.

The pace of her run was not the same. It felt good but her need for oxygen told a different story. Her mind cleared during her runs. This morning run was different due to her previous conversations with Chad. Nothing cleared from the previous day. She had friends and acquaintances but none like Chad. She needed to find a way through the fog. Dr. Morris, Ted as he preferred, was once her mentor in college and they remained close. They would talk often, and Megan needed that bond. Chad was different. He was her handler. It was odd for him not to remain in touch. More than odd, it was disappointing.

She glanced at the digital time display on her desk. There was never a remote chance it was inaccurate. Time always passed quickly when tending to office duties. It was midafternoon. The thought of closing out her workday was interrupted by the vibration of her cell on the desk.

There was no customary hello. She attempted to reach Chad after her run, and after breakfast. Nearly all fronts of disappointment had gone. Exercise works wonders for the soul.

"Chad? Where have you been?"

"Huh? What do you mean?"

The flowing lava would not return. She willed all things to pass and would not allow them return.

"I've been calling and calling! Why did you turn off your phone?

He wanted to call her by her preferred name, Meg. It wasn't in the cards, and he understood what hand was being played. She was going to win the hand, but he needed to lay down a card he knew would not get trumped.

"I tried to call but didn't want to leave a message. Something happened and I need to explain it all in person."

The volcano that erupted was not as Megan wanted. Her furry had not subsided as she believed. She wanted to call him out on his comment but there it was. As if the confirmation open handedly smacked her across one cheek and back across the other. He did attempt to call, not once, not twice. There were three different missed calls with time stamps. How had she missed those? She inhaled allowing her thoughts to smolder. Her phone was not silenced but on vibrate.

"Megan, are you there?"

"Yes, I'm here. I'm sorry I missed your calls. My phone was on vibrate while I was working and didn't notice you tried to reach me. You were saying you need to talk in person?"

She wanted her apology to extend but it would have been groveling. She swallowed her emotions as her mother would have wished. Every fiber of her soul expelled energy that erupted, but now was capped off. She wanted her apology to be accepted.

It was at this moment she missed both her parents. It was her mother who explained things thought to be incomprehensible. She wished for that gentle touch to the back of her hand while the ever so soft, soothing, and reassuring voice explained what she was experiencing and why.

"No need to apologize. We both missed each other's calls. It happens," Chad continued. "Can you meet me? I'll explain everything."

In her soft apologetic voice, "Absolutely. I'll meet you anywhere. Just name it."

A calm came over her as she reassured Chad, and her voice calmed lava of turmoil. Note to self, as her mother used to say. "Never answer an unsuspecting call when you're holding on to extreme anger. The recipient will not understand the fury."

Megan didn't need directions to Kickapoo High School. Springfield was her back yard. She did, however, need reasoning why they were to meet at the homefield football bleachers 35-yard line. She smiled. She wouldn't ask which 35-yard line. Students always sat on the nearest side to the stadium entrance. That was where she would find him.

The quick smile faded to a nondescriptive turn down of each corner of her mouth. She was harsh on the phone, so much so, she didn't even recognize herself. Her dad, without saying a word, would have given her the look which would shout disappointment.

Her mom would have said out loud, "Meg, you're doing it again."

With a multitude of things needing work, the understanding of her inner turmoil was one of them. This was not her. She was once again becoming somebody she didn't recognize. Not in all aspects of her life, but the relationship category was rapidly becoming a deep dark troubling abyss. She promised her mom posthumously to seek the help she admittedly needed.

As she pulled into the football field parking lot, there were more cars than anticipated. She found a location to park so he could easily locate her car if he hadn't already arrived. Without looking for his car, Megan headed for the closest 35-yard line to the gated zig-zag entrance.

A student practiced his hurdle techniques on the far straightaway and second curve of the polyurethane 9 lane track. There were older couples walking the outer lanes so not to interfere with the hurdles arranged on the curve and far straightaway. The occasional pre-summer breeze welcomed the anticipated mid-afternoon above average temperatures. The press box and high tiered seating cast an encompassing shadow over home field seating. She now realized why the 35-yard line was preferable. It was a perfect view of the field, at least where she sat. The 50-yard line was the obvious setting for perfect field viewing, but he mentioned the different location. "There's a reason for all things," she surmised to herself.

A couple, dressed nicely, appeared to be on their office break, however, there were no office buildings within walking distance from the school. Another couple sat visiting but didn't look cozy enough to be related or romantically involved. Two men, in their forties, sitting several rows to the front of her, could have passed for twins due to their short military style haircuts. The man on the right, in a stealth like move, slowly placed his left hand on top of the other man's right hand, leaving it there for an uncomfortable amount of time. Uncomfortable for her to witness.

Megan sat watching the multitude of stories unfold as she continued to people watch. Each storyline intertwined, weaving the peoples' lives together. Her imagination overflowed with the game her mother taught her. The ritual of people watching became a practice they thoroughly enjoyed when visiting parks and taking walks together. It was a customary tradition as they would intertwine the lives of people they passed on their walks.

Her mother would mention a lady who could easily be a grandmother walking alone. Megan would relate her thoughts of that person as they passed. She might observe someone on roller skates, and her mother would mention the young skater rehashing the answers to a final exam. It was an exercise in how everyone had a history and a story to tell. All too often, the game would turn into full blown laughter. A story of a man and women walking. They're holding hands but quickly relinquish their touch when approached by another couple who similarly did the same thing.

Mother and daughter would each describe the uncomfortable domestic scene as it would unfold. They would take turns inflaming the scene until neither one of them could stop laughing at the others take of the made-up chaos. Generally, when a SWAT team rappelled from a helicopter or the hair pulling brawl of the two women were separated by their male counterparts, the laughing ceased.

Megan's dreaming came back to reality when a hand gently touched her shoulder. She hadn't seen Chad come up from behind nor did she hear him announce his arrival. She blocked out all senses with fond remembrance of her mother. The touch, although harmless, was startling and unwelcomed.

Megan spun to her right with clinched fist to the touch on her shoulder. Enough force was expelled from the shoulder and seated position, to cause the intended result. Chad grabbed his left thigh as the pain, and the soon to be developing bruise formed.

"Oh my gosh! I am so sorry!" Megan apologetically screamed.

Chad limped three steps to his right, sat down without glancing at his assailant, and began rubbing his thigh.

"It's OK. I shouldn't have startled you."

The two men who were seated in front of Megan were now standing looking at them both. They started moving away from the bleachers and toward the stadium exit while holding their gaze on them. The work companions had already departed but the yoga class of a dozen or so had stopped their session. The instructor of the class had already reached the first level of seats before Megan waved her off.

"It's fine, I didn't see him coming."

The instructor smiled and said, "It looks like he may have learned his lesson," waving goodbye and returning to her class.

Chad looked down at Megan while he massaged his thigh. She stepped up to his row of seats. A smile slowly appeared on both their faces.

Chad uttered, "If you wanted to clear the show-me arena, you could've just yelled fire."

Megan looked at him massaging his thigh and realized how solid her strike was. She was almost certain she felt bone through the quad muscle when the hammer side of her fist connected.

"It appears my method of clearing the arena was more affective."

Megan couldn't help but smile. The smile turned into a near belly laugh. Chad looked at her in disbelief as she repositioned herself and sat next to him. Her infectious smile and laugh was all that was needed to turn lemons into the much-needed ceremonial lemonade. He cast a distasteful gaze but couldn't help finding some amusement in it all. Chad quickly became engulfed in her clowning as she playfully attempted to catch her breath and wiped the playful tear from her right eye. She placed the palm of her left hand on her chest as she leaned on his left shoulder for balance. He grinned and started laughing with her.

Chad leaned away from her and with both hands grabbed the shoulder that previously landed securely against his.

"Control yourself young lady. Your humor is no longer welcomed."

"Oh really," she responded between chuckles. "Shall I call someone to measure your height for the crutches you'll undoubtedly need?"

"Quit it already," he responded with a smile. "It's no longer funny."

Megan looked down at both his hands which remained securely locked to her shoulder. Her eyes focused on his hands, his forearm, elbow, biceps, and locked in on his sky-blue eyes. Chad quickly removed his hands from her shoulder, while his eyes simultaneously locked in on hers. He was transfixed to her crystal-clear hazel eyes. Both their smiles instantly became aloof, and postures straightened as if both were hit with ice water from the same bucket challenge.

Megan broke the uncomfortable silence and extended pause. "So. What did you want to explain and why are we sitting specifically here?"

"It's rather a long story, so bear with me."

Massaging his thigh, Chad began to explain. He reminded her of his adolescent years in the foster care program and started with a flashback of years prior. He mentioned some things he knew she recalled but included those episodes as well. He did so because they molded him into the person he was. He owned up to his past mistakes but painfully recalled the failures others had in his upbringing. It wasn't until he was old enough, did he recognize and understand the mistakes others maliciously made and were negligent in matters on his behalf. Since that time, he triumphed in matters only known to him and a few select others. Megan was among those few.

Chad continued his trip down memory lane to include an episode of which he was sure Megan was unaware. The incident was a precursor to the worst and most memorable day of his life. She interrupted, attempting to have him not relive the moments of that day, but he needed to set up the occasion. He continued explaining to how it related to why they were sitting on the bleachers.

He told her about being suspended from school for fighting. He was a well-mannered, honor roll student prior to that day. Some of the notorious annoyances would hang out in areas of the school, where others intentionally avoided. They called them bullies.

One of Chad's closest friends was tricked to walk through one of those areas everyone preferred to avoid. This friend was Black and failed to see the ill intent of others even if it were obvious to everyone else. Chad was with him when he walked into the group of bullies whose main intent was to steal his friend's backpack his parents recently bought him.

They picked a fight. Chad and his friend accommodated with the ringleader requiring stitches. While the rumble took place, his backpack was stolen. Chad and his friend were expelled. Chad was allowed to return after a week suspension, his friend who was also an honor student wasn't allowed to return the remainder of the school year. The family tried to litigate but the principal boldly intervened with the judiciary. His friend's family decided to move away, and he never saw or heard from his friend again.

When he returned to school after serving his suspension, Chad had to meet with the principal and school counselor. The principal explained to him that his family would experience the same fate if he didn't fall in line with other classmates.

Chad vividly recalled what the principal told him. "If he or his friends think they've been discriminated against, they should get over it and move on."

The principal called his dad at work and told his dad both parents had to come to the office to sign his readmittance papers to the school. His dad went home to get his stay-at-home mom. They were on their way to the school and a traffic light malfunctioned. Multiple vehicles were involved in the horrific crash. Counseling was the only way he got through those months following the death of his parents.

The subcontractor to the signal lighting company and the city paid out millions to the affected families. Chad being the sole survivor of his family. He was awarded one of the lump sum compensation. The funds went into guardianship until he graduated high school. Although the principal couldn't be blamed for his parents' death, he refused to forgive the principal for what Chad considered the direct cause and effect.

Megan listened as Chad relived memories. The 35-yard line is where his parents would sit to watch him play football. Some parents would sit in the same location behind the student body at every home game. If a parent couldn't be there, the seat remained vacant. It became customary, like reserved parking at NFL parking lot tailgating. Megan took the silence as a chance to speak.

"Violence never solves anything. I'm sorry you had to go through that."

"You're right, but it sure felt good to us both at that moment. The principal got his karma not long after that."

"What do you mean?" Megan asked.

Chad explained the parents had written correspondence to the school admin and met with the principal on more than one occasion about their son's harassment. When my friend was the only student expelled for the remainder of the year his parents decided to act. They took all their documented information to the prosecutor who refused to admonish the school or school district. My friend's mother was friends with the realtor who sold them their home. That realtor was in a tea club with the city prosecutor. The prosecutor was befriended by the realtor and when the dots were connected, heads rolled.

Chad explained, "The married principal was romantically involved with the married prosecutor. There was no question to why charges were never filed."

Megan closed one eye, and raised the other eyebrow indicating she still didn't understand. Chad continued telling his personal history lesson.

The tea club members had spouses on the school board. When a weekend party involving underage drinking became known, and the parents having the party were not prosecuted, the word got out.

"Comes to mind the slogans, pillow talk, and follow the money," Megan said.

Chad smirked. "The counselor who was in on that same meeting with the principal befriended me. Dr. Florra is now the Senior Director of the foster care program. She helped me when I was at my lowest when my parents passed away. I mentor for the program. She called me about a young man in the program a few years ago. We connected and kept in touch."

Chad continued with his story about meeting Liam at the 35-yard line. Megan understood the difficult circumstances she experienced losing her parents. Chad knew of those circumstances because her parents were members of MoTAF at the time of their deaths. It was because of their untimely deaths, MoTAF recruited Megan into their membership. When Chad explained he couldn't answer calls because of meeting Liam, Megan got the full picture. It was at that moment a warmth came over her.

Megan sensed her mother speaking to her, "Peace be still."

CHAPTER 27

Drake leaned on his high back fake leather cushioned chair. He was amazed as he read the document Alec planned for them to undertake. The only problem, Alec omitted the fine points of their plan. Those fine points gave Drake a unique perspective. What they joked about and discussed did not include what he was now reading. This part of the plan Drake didn't recognize. If Alec would have let on, he wasn't sure the discussion would have been jovial. They met for lunch, coffee breaks at work, and the occasional pizza get-togethers were something they both looked forward to. Now there was a void. There would be no retakes. No more dream building for the future. There was no longer a future with Alec. That ship had already left port. The finality of what he had read was beyond unique. This dream building was more of a nightmare unfolding right before his eyes. He wasn't sure the intended result was what Alec truly envisioned. He wasn't so sure it was what he would have come up with on his own. He liked his freedom. What Alec had envisioned, what he was reading, would impact his freedom or perhaps his sole existence.

Drake was exhausted. A long nap would be the only way to accomplish that. But who, vastly approaching age 30 take naps? He pushed away from the screen and rolled backwards to his quaint kitchen. He spun around, took a few short steps, and opened his refrigerator. He returned to his chair and repeated his familiar move, casting back to his desk while pulling a tab on the green 16 oz Monster energy drink. The cursory review of what he read was like taking an advanced post graduate course. His desire to stay focused would require him to quickly consume the cool refreshing drink and pop a cap on another one.

Drake tried to grasp the finality of their task. His task. A task he agreed to do with Alec, not without him. Every word, every syllable escaped from the screen in his head as if reading it aloud. The difference, the words were in a raspy, baritone voice. Alec's voice. It was as if sitting across the cafeteria lunch table, discussing another scenario of what could be. Only this time, there was no discussion. Drake was trying to understand how he got to where he was, and how he was going to proceed. It was resolute. There were no other options. He was willed to do what he had promised to do. To remain in their pact, to see things through, and fulfill the promise. His promise.

Drake didn't have total memory recall. What he did have was attention to detail. Taking notes from what he had read was junior high adolescence to him. He was amazed by all the theatrics thus far, but knew the crescendo was yet to come. Supervisors held disdain for subordinates who were righting the ship at their expense. Timing is everything. Alec failed to recognize it.

The scavenger hunt wasn't a game. It wasn't even a hunt by any stretch of anybody's imagination. He never thought he would have found himself in a small Illinois town looking for an item. It was as if it were a call to duty. His duty, his mission. Their mission.

Programing is not without the programmer physically allowing it to happen. This was not rocket science, Drake was good at programing. However, interlinking AI with unknown variable software defenses would make it impossible. Well, perhaps nearly impossible. This was Alec. Nothing was impossible in his upper cortex.

Drake surmised things were kept from him. He was unaware of more than he could fathom. It wasn't fair. It wasn't right. It wasn't what they had discussed. It was betrayal. He wasn't included in these resent steps until now.

The five step phases of grief and loss were right on schedule. Drake was in denial and simply refused to recognize the present tense. Most in his position wouldn't. Alec left him to solve the puzzle. A puzzle he didn't know existed. AI is a formidable ally. Or an opponent if one chooses to allow it.

The pause continued but only momentarily. The document was clear but the numerical countdown which appeared in the upper right corner of the page elicited concern. A dropdown bar under the numerical counter gave explicit bullet point explanations. It read:

Do nothing and the plan continues. Do as instructed and become part of the plan. Any attempt to interfere with the plan will be futile.

Drake understood Alec's mindset. He also understood he had to do more than think outside the box. It was more like thinking outside the universe, way beyond any Harvard and Smithsonian astronomer cosmic theoretic study. Alec was that kind of person. It was his mindset that solidified their friendship. He and Einstein would have been besties.

One day things were going to change. Theoretically, something was to happen, and it was to be sooner than later. Drake sat on a powder keg of undeniable intrigue to the what, when, and where. He hadn't envisioned lighting the fuse. He didn't have to, not with Alec being part one of the duo. The fuse was already lit.

CHAPTER 28

enor picked up his phone. This time without any delay and no smart butt comment. It was that unknown number to the ever so familiar ring tone. Monique deserved a normal friendly greeting. The last time they spoke, she was upfront and honest. She risked her job. It was time for him to reward her by showing his appreciation and respect.

"Hello," Tenor answered with the most uplifting tone for a single word greeting.

"Tenor! It's me, Monique. We got 'em. We know who they are!"

He wasn't used to watching TV game shows. The excitement in her voice was as if she spun the wheel and doubled her winnings. He had a multitude of comebacks but stayed true to the promise he made to himself.

"You got who and who are they?"

She stole his thunder. He wanted to tell her he was intrigued and interested in the position being offered. He wanted her to know it would be a pleasure to work with them, whomever they were. Still in her excited tone Monique continued.

"We couldn't understand why our programming didn't flag or locate anything for months. The programmers are good and were using a newly developed JavaScript in conjunction with an older language they must be redeveloping. The front-end coding which they were modifying faltered."

Tenor couldn't help himself. "Wow! Really? That is fantastic. Now tell me what that means."

He understood part of what she was telling him. He continued learning his trade because of the circumstances he found himself in. For him to play in the big boys' game, he would have to kick a few leaf piles to catch up to speed. The problem with that, programming gets changed faster than a baby's diaper.

Trying to understand new programming parameters would be as frustrating as trying to kill a swarm of murder hornets. Deadly frustrating.

"It means they screwed up. We can follow them and know what they're up to and if they're planning anything. We're back in the game."

"You guys are never out of the game," Tenor quickly responded before she could finish talking. "I'm in the game too. I sent the document back to you. I'm all in."

"Gotta go Tenor. Looks like I'm called into an urgent meeting, again."

She ended the call like so many times before. No goodbye, see ya, or talk to you later courtesy conclusion. He became used to it. Before it annoyed him, and it was well beyond rude. Tenor was also sure she hadn't heard what he said. He also knew he would get a call from her soon. She would learn he was on board and was to work alongside her, them, or whoever it was, and whatever it was they did. It was obvious she was excited about her work. Accomplishments are rewarding. What was also rewarding, being part of something larger than yourself. Tenor had become that person. The feeling was uplifting, invigorating, and absolutely wonderful. He wished he could celebrate and tell somebody about it. There was no one he could confide in.

There it was again, like he knew it would be. The ever-familiar tone of his cell. Their cell, the only phone he owned that meant anything to him. Tenor pressed the green answer button almost before the first ring ended.

"Hello!" Tenor was as excited as Monique was the last time they talked. It was his turn, and he looked forward to how things were going to transpire from this day forward.

"Hi, Tenor. We received your document affirming your participation in our program efforts."

Something was different, something was off. She was too business like, to official. The excitement in her voice was subdued. It wasn't like it should have sounded.

She continued. "Tenor, I want to welcome you to a group of dedicated employees whose sole purpose it to keep those residing or peaceably visiting the United States safe."

The respectful professional tone was different for a reason. It lacked one important feature. It wasn't Monique. She was definitely pleasant, but the voice was one octave higher than being computer animated. She was good, but a far stretch from being in Monique's league. There was something about her voice that made Tenor uncomfortable. A 39-year-old man would love to hear her voice. Especially during his weekly call while serving 5 to 10 in solitary confinement.

"Thank you," he responded. "I'm not sure what to expect but I'm eager to learn whatever you have in store for me."

The pleasant voice started with a litany of information. Not overwhelming by any means, though a little over the top for federal government indoctrination. It was the first of its kind. A barrage of thank you for wanting to do what's best for the country, your country appreciates you, you're now part of something bigger than yourself. Yada, yada, yada. He started to wonder how so many federal employees hadn't changed their minds and rescinded their acceptance and conditional offer of employment.

She was near the end of her scripted pleasantries. Tenor waited expectantly to ask the obvious. Maybe this was the norm of accepting new employees into the fold. This was painful to the point of requiring the downing of more Tylenol than safely prescribed. She explained the simple steps to DocuSign. He lost count of the times he was told to expect forthcoming emails explaining everything. He expected to be transferred, following the conclusion of the ongoing, never-ending, time-consuming phone call. That transfer would be to a therapist to help him navigate through the remainder of his day.

"Tenor, do you have any questions I might be able to answer for you?"

Without any forethought he replied in his best rehearsed Sylvester Stallone voice. "Adrian. Don't leave me Adrian."

"Excuse me. What did you say?"

"Nothing," Tenor quickly recovered. "I do have one question. I was expecting the other lady I always talked to."

It wasn't a question, but it was implied. He knew not to ask about her by name. It wasn't his first merry go round.

"We all are handlers assigned to specific cases," she responded. "I've concluded one case and have been reassigned. I'm happy to meet you Tenor."

"So, you're telling me I have to get used to another voice. You're voice? What happened to the other voice, I liked that other voice. Where'd she go?

"I'm sorry Tenor. I'm not at liberty to discuss it."

And there it was. The infamous, 'not at liberty to tell you the truth' statement. It brought back a flood of memories. Specifically, the time when he asked his supervisor why he wasn't considered for a promotion. He wasn't asking why the other person got the promotion, he wanted to know what criteria was utilized to make the decision. The cop-out answer brought a flood of reminders. Another catch all phrase of how people should 'just do their job' or be told by enablers 'get over it and move on.' Companies are flooded with like mind enablers who would sour the once bountiful fruit basket. The basket soon becomes overrun and takes on a sour odor. Employee attrition is no longer recognized by those retiring, but by those seeking other, more rewarding career opportunities.

"Of course, you're not," he responded with as much sarcasm as he could muster. "Thank you for the warm welcome to the U.S. government."

As he pressed the button, the abruptness to end the call couldn't have been more telling of his disappointment. Had he been played? He was just another case. That was all he was, a number. The other voice, his handler, whom he became accustomed to and admired, had been reassigned a number. He was no longer her case. What bothered him the most was the statement of not being able to convey what happened. Did Monique get fired for violating policy or get reassigned a number to 'handle' somebody else? Who was she? Was her name really Monique? Did she befriend him just to move on to another number?

The new employment build up diminished. Disappointment was front and center. He refreshed his mind of the warnings. The multiple-page document made several references to the danger he could face. The caution did bring intrigue to it all.

As confident as he was, he was aware there was fluff to his bark. He was witness to the most horrific political domestic terrorist event in Missouri. The nightmares had ceased but the memory would forever be seared in his mind. It was that burn which calmed the butterflies of excitement. He was optimistic.

CHAPTER 29

Chad and Megan glanced around the bleachers. During their conversation, seats were vacated that were once occupied. The track, however, was combing with people walking, jogging, and young kids riding bicycles. The student practicing his hurdles had left and was nowhere in sight. Two young girls about the same age as the previous hurdler were now practicing.

Chad was all talked out. The sun had changed its trajectory. There was calm in her voice and in her approach to what she wanted to say. The ongoing topic was heavy. She lightened the load.

"Both those girl hurdlers can take the guy hurdler, hands down."

Chad, in his soft dry humor remarked, "Without a doubt. Somebody should tell that young man to get some much-needed techniques from the girls' team."

They looked at each other and their smiles returned. The much-needed humor was welcomed. Megan changed her mind about confronting Chad. She let it go. It was her mom reminding her of the difference in the importance of the moment and the insignificance of any preconceived urgency. The missed connections with their phone calls made perfect sense once the cause was explained.

A sudden coolness came over them both. They weren't seated high in the stadium seats, but it was as if the breeze was meant for them and them only. Neither approached the topic of leaving. As if the final second ticked off the score board clock, people started filing toward the parking lot. Those circling the track turned and retraced their steps. Those who had made it midfield on the track, turned around and followed others as they made their way back to their vehicles. Most walked across the turf to shorten the walk. Chad stood and looked toward those leaving. The clouds had turned dark as expected and the slight breeze began to gust.

Megan stood, stepped onto the row of seats below where they were sitting. "That's our cue."

The wind picked up more as she gestured skyward. She turned and watched Chad as he too moved to exit the stadium. He walked to the center of the row of seats to start his descent. An intentional exaggerated limp favoring his left leg was readily apparent.

"Need a little help to your car Chad?"

"Not funny Madam Sherlock. Assistance to my chariot is warranted."

Megan took long strides stepping from row to row until she got to the walkway where she waited for him.

"Your chariot may be waiting, but your escort may kick you to the curb if you keep up this facade."

They exchanged huge grins when Chad reached the walkway. He put his left arm around her shoulder leaning slightly into her. She reached around his waist with her right arm bracing him as they synchronized their steps. His step became less exaggerated to the point his walk was near a normal stride. She calmly removed her arm from around his waist. He took the hint and let his arm slowly slide to his side.

As they approached his car, she noticed how polished it was. The rims were glistening even though it was overcast. The spray-on tire shine made it look as it his car was just driven off the showroom floor. The car wash was the cause of the dropped call. Chad leaving his phones in his car while talking to Liam was the reason for her calls going to voicemail. His explanation brought things into focus. She hadn't even realized she dialed his personal cell number. For Megan, things became much clearer.

"This is what you get for washing your car," Megan looked up scanning the clouds.

People were friendly and waiving as they pulled from their parking locations. Others glanced their way and gesturing goodbyes as each driver respectfully took their turn to follow the other out of the parking lot. They didn't recognize any of them. It was a friendly town. They both smiled and returned what seemed like an overabundance of friendly waves. People likely viewed them as a couple. Megan wanted to hate herself for all the missteps she experienced for not reaching Chad when she tried.

While standing next to Chads car, Megan took a step close invading personal space. He didn't retreat but looked directly into her eyes as she locked hers on his. Both hands glided over his shoulders. He gently placed his hands on her waist and around the small of her back. His fingertips clasped together as he pulled her close to him. Their torsos merged and she turned her head to lean into his chest. The hug was firm, and it lingered meaningfully long. She released only partially looking directly into his eyes. They stood there as if Christmas had come and gone without either realizing it.

"Thank you, Chad. Thank you for allowing me to get to know you when I thought I already did."

"No, I should thank you."

As soon as it came out of his mouth, he realized how lame it sounded. His brain screamed "Seriously, dude. Are you sixteen?"

They stood apart smiling at each other and Megan broke the laser locked eye contact.

"Go get some ice and put on that."

Smiling and pointing to his thigh, she turned and walked to her car without looking back. She willed herself not to turn around. She could feel his gaze with every step she took. She rounded her car to the driver's door. Looking over the top of her car confirmed her assumption. His eyes remained on her. She raised her right-hand above the roof, waving goodbye with her signature four finger wiggle. He hadn't moved from the spot she left him.

Sitting in his car, Chad whispered silently. "Did that just happen?"

His cell rang with an unmistakable tone. He looked at Megan backing up and pulling from the parking lot. It wasn't Megan calling, as she smiled at Chad and again waved. It was MoTAF. The ring tones were centuries apart in music genre. He only thought it was Meg because his mind hadn't ventured from their hug. He nearly suffocated in thought of their embrace. He pushed his dashboard onscreen answer button and turned up the audio volume.

"Hey Ted, how are you?"

"Hi Chad. I'm fine thank you. I've been contacted by MoTAF. We've been activated. We have info on you and Meg's phone breach."

Chad silently claimed Dr. Morris as his second father, his mentor. His favorite instructor didn't cut him any slack during exam or thesis time. The boundaries were never compromised. Chad got what he deserved, although there were times he resented the midnight study burn and multiple group study discussions that hadn't brought results.

It was Dr Morris who moved up the timeline to invite Megan into the MoTAF family. Although she was basically a member by proctor, nothing was formal until she agreed. Megan was also fond of Dr. Morris. Some of her classes overlapped with Chad. Most of her law courses did not. Megan favored class discussions with Dr. Morris. He would intentionally call on her, knowing she would unleash thoughts on whatever matter was being discussed. That knowledge was predicated by her upbringing. Both of Megan's parents were MU law school grads, as well as private practice attorneys. She often spoke to Dr. Morris about their dinner time law conversations. Both her parents would challenge Megan with their professional law experience. Those discussions brought the Swift household to life. It was as if mom, dad, and daughter were in the courtroom, each attempting to sway the other on the semantics of case law.

However, for Megan, the most memorable time with Dr. Morris was when she was called into his office. That interruption was Dr. Morris receiving an emergency phone call during class time. That break during class was all about Megan. The class was dismissed early, and Megan sat in his office and learned of a traffic crash resulting in the death of both her parents. It was after that moment he became her confidant and mentor.

Dr. Morris advised Chad he was going to send him an encrypted email at the conclusion of his call. He was to relay that information as soon as possible to Megan. While still parked, Chad looked and confirmed, Meg had already driven from the school campus. The call with Ted ended with normal pleasantries. He voice dialed Megan reciting her name into his cell.

Megan smiled big as she pulled from the lot and in line with other traffic. Several cars merged in the single lane, as if part of a motorcade following a high school pep rally. Her smile continued as she sang Bonnie Rait's 1991 hit song. "Let's Give Them Something to Talk About."

The lyrics were coming to her as she jubilantly sang. Her blue tooth activated, and she glanced at Chad's face on her car's touch screen. She immediately touched the green answer button.

"Was that hug a bit much or are you calling to ask me to pull over for a repeat?"

She almost couldn't speak the words through her laughter. It was her attempt to break the ice of the awkward embrace they shared moments earlier. It was a nervous laugh she was thankful he couldn't decipher.

"You're such a clown. Meet me at Panera," he didn't wait for her to respond. "The one on Sunshine. I got a call from Ted. MoTAF is being activated."

CHAPTER 30

Thinking outside the box was part of Drake's DNA. Thinking outside the universe was not. Sitting and waiting for the unknown was definitely not part of the fabric from which he was woven. After reading and understanding what he was faced with, a few questions needed answered.

He sat at his computer and considered turning it off. The numerical countdown was a distracting phenomenon. The purpose of the countdown was even more so. What was it for and to what end did it mean? To focus on the countdown was counter intuitive. Saying it out loud was something Alec would have done. Thoughts of his friend returned. He shook his head in disbelief of recent events.

What was to happen in the number of days of the countdown? Was the countdown even meant to be calculated in a 24-hour sequence?

Another alarm nearly caused his heart to stop. The volume on his computer was ear piercing. The collapsed drop-down box hiding the counter flashed red. The icon Windows Antivirus Protection icon was flashing as well.

The systems virus protection was topnotch. Windows Antivirus was good but what he and Alec had on their system was far better. They knew this because they created it themselves. They begged, borrowed, and stole from the best and created a seal proof defender system they talked about putting on the market. The stolen part of the beg and borrow was the problem. It would have had to be sold underground. The attorneys would have swarmed like honeybees searching for whomever disturbed their sleepy hive.

Drake clicked on both alarm notifications to no avail. The wireless mouse arrow froze on the screen. He was about to unplug the system but remembered the emergency automatic power battery source installed. Several features safeguarded their systems. His system. Drake stared at the screen as the audible sound ceased. The countdown and virus icon continued to flash. They were obvious warnings and Drake tried to understand what occurred and how he could circumvent the system to alter its current state. A few attempted keystrokes and he quickly learned nothing was halting the flashing icons. The keyboard was nonfunctional.

A dialog box appeared in the middle of his screen. It was not one of Microsoft's Windows notification scams. Those notifications had been uninstalled a long time ago and were not something he was concerned about. He didn't recognize this warning system, although annoying, it also required admiration. It was unique and well designed. Centered in the box was the U.S. government seal as a water mark. The coat of arms looked authentic. It contained an olive branch and thirteen arrows.

Centered on top of the water mark were the words: "To whom it may concern: Cease and Desist."

There was no control key function allowing the removal or altering of the dialog box. The wireless mouse turned into a paperweight. The dialog box became faint and each letter of the eight-word sentence faded away. The water mark changed from gray to bold black. The U. S. government seal, as quick as it appeared, shrank to the size of a pencil eraser. As expected, it too was gone.

He was disappointed, shocked, and amazed, but truly intrigued. The VPN, Virtual Privacy Network software Alec and Drake had paid for, downloaded, and upgraded from underground privacy sources failed. The online program was supposed to allow for online footprints to be hidden. He quickly grabbed his wireless mouse and pounded it several times, as if his computer malfunction were in the plastic worthless paperweight. The arrow on his screen moved responsibly to the pounding on the mouse pad. He was no longer locked out of his own computer. He moved the arrow on the screen and clicked on the system check icons. The system went through multiple scans that he and Alec designed.

All systems were functioning with zero malfunctions, malicious activity, or malware. The flashing countdown box, and the antivirus icon were no longer flashing. A cursory glance at the system check did show one addition. Not a virus but an add-on to his system. There were two dates on the addition. The date of the attachment and the date of an upgrade or alteration to the add-on. There was also an info dropdown box describing the upgrade.

There were programs that used others to function properly. For this reason, he had to err on the side of caution to prevent programs from freezing. The issue smartly found its way through every defense mode they created. He had to find out what it was and who it was that accomplished the impossible. Alec was the smart man who brought the gun to a knife fight. There undoubtedly was a third party who cared less and stepped forward with a hydrogen bomb. This was a challenge. A challenge he would except.

He clicked on the info box, and nothing happened. For nothing to happen meant there was no other solution. He had to find the attachment and find a way to remove it. He had to cut it out like a skilled surgeon leaving nothing behind to harm ever again.

The familiar watermark slowly reappeared, like before when his system became unresponsive. However, this time his mouse stilled functioned, and he was able to open and view other documents on his screen. There was one small difference. He could open anything he wanted, but those items found themselves behind the government mark. The mark was like a ghost. Slowly as before, melting to the forefront was wording he could not decipher. It slowly came into focus. He couldn't believe his eyes.

The audacity of the United States Government. Was this a challenge? This was not Alec playing a sick game from the grave. It would be like him, but this was starting to get personal. It was intrusive, and at the very least presumptuous.

The verbiage was straightforward albeit offensive. The numbers didn't mean anything of importance to him. It was not Mr. John Q Public, no sir. It was Mr. Big Brother himself, toying with him. This was a game grown men play, not a game for boys.

18 USC 2331 was the sequence anyone could Google. It wasn't foreign to him. He had heard about it and seen it before. He and Alec had jokingly talked about it. It was because of those conversations the US Patriot Act was of no importance to him. Uncle Sam had bigger fish to fry, such as a guy named Xi Jinping or Vladimir Putin. The Patriot Act was good for news segments and television ratings, but to John Q, such as himself, not so much.

But there it was in bold print. It was as if he conquered a level on a video game and was rewarded by advancing to the next level. But this wasn't a game. He and Alec didn't play games with their ideas. The words didn't fade away as with the previous watermark.

Violation of any part of the US Patriot Act, explicitly or implied, relating to section 802 of said Act, shall result in being held responsible for such act/s.

Drakes' eyes remained locked on his screen. Nothing had changed. Nothing happened. He had to find out who they were. A formidable friend, acquaintance, or foe. How could his system be breached without his knowledge? Whomever it was, a response was required. But first, he had to fix what was broken. He had to find out how the breach occurred, and subsequently find out who it was. They were surprisingly good. A false fail safe must have been uploaded for his virus scans to not recognize and reflect his system check was successful.

"Game on. Challenge accepted," he uttered.

CHAPTER 31

The path Tenor's life had taken over the last several years wasn't planned but he had become comfortable with how things turned. He instinctively traveled back down memory lane and the wrong fork in the road of his life journey. A sudden jerk on the shirt collar saved his life and he would be forever grateful to Chad and Megan.

Tenor thanked his friends for dragging him out of the tunnel of death. He often wondered how his life-saving friends were and if they thought about him. Not that he was able to tell anyone about his newfound life. That conversation would have found its way in the annals of Ripley's Believe It or Not.

The story would have begun by telling how he ended up in the witness protection program. The eyes would begin to role. As he would continue, they would hear how he became part of a plan to kidnap and assassinate the chief executive of Missouri. Tenor could tell all the specifics about planning and near execution of the failed plot. The eye rolling would have halted and there would be no one left listening to what actually happened in the halls of the Missouri state capitol.

The story would continue about being part of a clandestine organization financed by the U.S. government. He didn't believe it, and he lived it. Who would believe he was a willing participant of a clandestine group with purse strings from unknown places, run by unknown people.

Tenor came out of his daydream. He did what he had to do and had long reserved himself for continuing that path. His future was in his hands, mostly. He needed to forecast his future and solidify destiny. His purpose had been decided. His mission was laid out. His resolve was to follow the path like a destination programed into the Waze mapping system. There was always a choice. In his previous life, the choices he made resulted in a trajectory with no promise or future. Promises are not always fulfilled. Hope, however, always leads to better rewards. But it was the government, and with that in mind, the truth gets complicated.

He reviewed the information emailed to him. It was like agreeing to espionage. How can you infiltrate without being a spy? Whether it was electronic or cloak and dagger, it resembled an addictive substance. Preventing domestic terrorism in the Show Me State was not just rewarding but self-fulfilling. He could hold his head high. Money deposited by an unknown source was like nothing he had ever dreamed of until now.

A lot was left up to him. He was encouraged to keep the identity provided to him. Moving from the Midwest wasn't something he considered. He would prefer warmer climates but starting over far away from familiarity wasn't enticing. He didn't have many personal belongings. He hadn't come into their program with anything. WITSEC wasn't going to let go of all of their restrictions regardless of who was providing solace.

Without much forethought, Tenor opened his notebook. Semantics, the notebook wasn't his. Big Brother was never far away. His life was saved, and now it was time to pay it forward. Seldom do people get the opportunity for do-overs.

Digital technology had become invasive in other countries. The concern with the US government was that IP addresses could be vulnerable to hacking. In the instances of facial recognition and other advanced digital technology, foreign influences were constantly worming their way into governmental databases. Those intrusions were serious threats to national security.

He began reading encrypted email he was told to review. It came to his inbox sooner than expected. He realized full well at that point, he was predictable. How was it they knew he would agree to their terms in light of the potential dangers he was warned about? The excitement waned, but he was employed by one of the largest and arguably most sought-after employers. His talents would not go to waste.

There were threats of violence against governments all across the United States. He continued to read about the atrocities that previously occurred around the country. He was surprised, appalled, and became solemn all the while realizing he once empathized with what was now appalling. He made a promise to himself to make a difference. The opportunity was presented, and he would make the best of it. He was to make a name for himself. He would be a friend to strangers he hadn't yet met. His foe was his saving grace, and he was a silent contributor for others without fanfare.

The documents were without a doubt his bible of employment. They were rules and regs of his newfound claim to fame. He was never in the military, but he had been following orders as if from a Captain or General.

Although he would not question the whys of what he'd been told and learned, explanations were more than reasonable. He was never in a position to change his fate. Not until now. His future was never as bright, and he was grateful. It saddened him to not be able to tell anyone. Monique would have been his confidant. He missed her more than he thought was possible. Perhaps she had a hand with what transpired.

As he read the employment rules and regs, it became profoundly obvious. Paragraph after paragraph, situations and examples stipulating the same redundant warnings and prohibitive behavior. Had the government knowingly been sending a message to him using Monique as an example of what he was to expect if he violated the same regs? He finished off his energy drink. He had to power through the time sensitive document.

And there it was, right in front of him. His affairs were required to be in order. He was going in the field for clandestine activities. What he anticipated wasn't anything they hadn't already explained. Monique, however, gave him the only realization of what was to come.

Tenor unpacked a footlocker of emotions. He found himself caring about himself and others even more. His disdain for those who called themselves truth givers intensified. He was a naysayer by default. His concrete moral compass had been cracked. His turnaround wasn't something anticipated. It was easier to hate. It was easy to hate those who refused to wear the same shoes he was comfortable with. Not that those shoes fit, because they didn't at first. They were uncomfortable, but soon they became his normal footwear.

He had been kicked, knocked down, and stepped on so often, getting up never even crossed his mind. If stumbling was part of his journey, so be it. He would rise and forge on. Thanks to his second chance, he would make sure the opportunity was not wasted. Whatever wrongs he made were going to be made right. His foe was now his accomplice for the good. Uncle Sam could not have been all wrong.

CHAPTER 32

Megan uttered the words to herself. "Activated." She glanced up at the overcast cumulus fair weather clouds giving way to thunderstorms. There were no droplets falling, although the lady walking a fast gate, carrying the to-go meal to her car forecasted it.

After paying for her drink, filling her half and half tea, she positioned her seat exactly where Chad would have sat. She was going to enjoy the seating arrangement. Chad wouldn't sit with his back to any door if he could avoid it. His neck would be sore from watching every entry to the restaurant. She couldn't blame him. That was why they continued to patronize their favorite eatery.

The day would replay itself, but only in their memory. The day Chad handsomely, protected her from a gun wielding jealous madman. He covered her with his body as they exited the furthest door. He saw the man coming and she didn't. Chad watched the door as he had done many times prior when they dined.

Chad pulled into the lot to park. She parked her car like it was a fire engine red Chevy Corvette convertible, with elaborate custom pinstriping. It wasn't. It was, however, parked several spaces from the nearest vehicle. Door dings infuriated her.

Chad located Megan as he entered. Chad's gaze lingered longer than normal causing her to be self-conscious of her stare on him. She sat holding her half and half with a smirk which puzzled him from the start. He looked straight into her eyes and spoke like they visited for the first time in the day.

"Hi. Wanna grab a table by the window?" He tilted his head motioning toward his seating preference.

"Nah, I'm good," her grin nearly turned into a full-face opened mouth smile. He pulled out one of the two open chairs across from her. He angled his seat toward the foyer, receptionist, and bakery.

"Relax, Chad. I got this."

Her smile gave it away, although he wasn't readily willing to admit he'd been had. She wanted to show him she was capable of protection as well. It was the same Panera, but the seating arrangements had changed during the remodeling process. The floor to ceiling window arrangement provided ample view to all things outside. The crime scene from years passed caused the eatery to close for days. Management readily took advantage of the opportunity.

"Chad, I'm changing your name. I will no longer call you Mr. Cool, Calm and Collected."

Chad looked at her with a sheepish grin. Her eyes were smiling larger than a morning sun and her face glowed as well. She leaned with both elbows on the table, and both hands wrapped her glass of iced tea. Her eyes sparkled. Her smile told him not to doubt her abilities. She too could take care of herself as well as protect him.

"Chad, I said relax. I've got this," she repeated what she told him as if he hadn't heard it the first time.

"I sat here on purpose. We both know what happened before. You took care of me that day. I've thanked you and will never be able to appropriately repay you."

He tried to interrupt, but as he took a slight breath to speak, she released her folded right hand holding up her pointed finger to her lips. She didn't utter "Shhh," but he got the message.

"I've learned to keep my head on a swivel because of you. I got your 6."

She had softened her smile to a stern assurance stare. It was an understanding between them both, never to be revisited again.

His smile returned, "Thank you."

Her posture relaxed and she leaned back in a slumber as if she were seated in a recliner.

"So how is Ted and what's this about MoTAF being activated?"

Chad explained what was new in Ted's life, including his family and several things occurring in the lives of similar acquaintances to them both. He extended well wishes of which Megan was appreciative. MoTAF was the topic and explaining the encrypted email forwarded to him.

He was all business. He wasn't standing behind a lectern, but his delivery was not yielding to the atmosphere. Nobody sat close enough to overhear their conversation. His review of the crypted email was abbreviated but to the point. He promised Megan he would forward the email soon after they talked. The text message which prompted them to receive new cell phones wasn't a fluke. The message was traced to several unsuspecting data centers. The information elaborately and covertly wormed its way into a weak data center of a simi-large company. That company also utilized cloud storage. The worm laid dormant until an internal upgrade of the company's system occurred. That upgrade allowed the attachment affecting a shared cloud storage center utilized by several large companies.

Often large companies lack security safeguards or fail to monitor their centers as investors suspect. Those missteps allow breaches to occur. Once it was out of its slumber, the worm completed the task it was designed to perform. It melted into oblivion, deleting itself.

Chad never brought his tablet or laptop into Panera, or any public location he frequented. Neither of them trusted the sophisticated and unique abilities of nearby unsuspecting prying eyes. One keystroke or one person walking by with a handheld device or businesslike briefcase and one's identity or personal 401K is compromised.

Megan was not surprised to hear underground vises were at it again. They were not even called "sleepers" any longer. People who channel similar ideologies. Nothing was fundamentally wrong with the premise. The issue becomes problematic when like minds infringe on the welfare and peace of others. Freedom of expression and infringement tilted the scale of the blind folded lady. Chad continued with what the email explained and what Dr. Morris relayed to him.

"Ted said the frequency our cell numbers called each other, was reason the trojan used to attach itself to."

Megan said, "So I guess we shouldn't call each other so much."

"We have new numbers, and the cause has been rooted out. Ted said don't change our phone usage."

Chad had some unsuspecting news for Megan. She had already been registered to attend a one-week training course. She heard of the Federal Law Enforcement Training Center, FLETC, and of its location in Glynco, GA. She was pleased to know more training was in the works. Getting free from her job wasn't an issue. It never was.

Chad explained several MoTAF members from around the country were scheduled to attend. There would be no reason to bring a firearm to finetune shooting skills although the opportunity would be offered. The assigned training was for close encounter alternative defense and offensive techniques. It was aggressive and they encouraged the training for those who are not timid to cause others bodily harm. Megan had proven her talents in that department.

"So why this type of training, are we going to war?"

The look on his face told the story. The quizzical humor fell from Megan's face as she stared at him. He commenced to explain the DC analysts were not just ordered to find who sent us the messages, but why. They were not successful in that endeavor as of yet. They failed and those with purse strings weren't pleased. They did, however, find something interesting in the search. It temporarily satisfied bruised egos. The look on Megan's face was bewildered.

"I know what you're thinking, Meg. Remember, it is DC."

That statement cued the rolling of her pupils to where nothing but white was showing. It was an eerie view causing Chad to recall the St. Louis child star Linda Blair in the movie The Exorcist. There were some visuals that were hard to unsee.

"Do that again." he said grinning.

"Do what?"

"The thing you did with your eyes."

"What thing?" she said, knowing full well what he was referring to.

"Yeah, right. Never mind."

He refocused and continued to explain the analysts were impressed with the tech savvy of the unknown and probably unschooled foe. They were so careful and smart in the infrastructure of their craft, they failed to vet those who were mere novices. This left a sloppy footprint and the tracking of breadcrumbs throughout their mapping system. That roadmap had no destination, but it did leave an itinerary of sorts. Something was planned and it wasn't good. The activation was because of that roadmap. It laid out the who, what, and why. Hopefully more of the roadmap would be forthcoming and give MoTAF the remaining W's.

CHAPTER 33

Drake awakened refreshed and energized. He normally would stay up late into the night gaming. His past evening of running scan after scan was in hopes to solve the quiz. What happened to his system and who could have implanted unwanted malware as a joke? The alerts he received were of malicious malware. He, however, was aware any infiltration could send false messages to the recipient. Alec wasn't there to brainstorm, or trouble shoot. Solving problems alone was a paradigm shift he wasn't familiar with or comfortable without help. This was outside of any employment spectrum. He could troubleshoot with a team of coworkers. This was different.

Drake accepted any challenge. There was no choice but to follow the slogan of the tennis shoe company. The issue was the programs "what if" safeguard. All he had to do was perform the search with that the code word. It would not only search but activate the program that lay hidden. That was the sleeper.

Pushing back from the keyboard he placed both palms to the side of his temples while resting his elbows on his knees. He needed breakfast but he let that thought fade. Although he had an appetite, he knew full well nothing would stay down. His stomach churned and his palms were already sweaty.

"Relax Drake, you got this," he uttered the words again. "You've. Got. This."

He hit the enter key. Nothing. No alarms, no bells, no whistles telling him how stupid he was. Not even the skeletal cross bones skull he envisioned. He and Alec had laughed about several appropriate emojis appearing at a moment like this.

The system was still functioning. More emotions to unpack. Computer programing issues were never this complicated or concerning until now. He missed his friend who could explain things in a way he understood.

Drake flinched when the tethered 27-inch Microsoft Surface screens came to life. Not with an anticipated emoji but he was jolted just the same. No sound, although the rumble of a nuclear bomb in the far distance would have been well timed. Speaking from the grave, Alec's surprise filled both screens in bold font.

"Greetings my friend. Sorry for what you're going through."

Something heinous must have occurred for him to be reading the message. His youth staved off the shock that was sure to have caused myocardial infarction in any other person.

"Thank you, Patriot Partner, for taking up our challenge. I'd prefer to be there with you."

His eyes were the size of bowling balls as he continued reading. Patriot Partner was the name he gave Alec to call him, and it stuck. What a mastermind. It was at this moment Drake's mind started spinning thoughts of betrayal. Had he been set up for failure or success?

The document was brief but succinct in directions. Alec had entrusted him with the pact. It wasn't a contract but a friendship commitment. A pledge to carry through what they had started. The only concerning factor for Drake was much of what he witnessed thus far was foreign. Everything he'd experienced was not part of any pact they had discussed. This was as real as a Patriot Partner could be. It was his committal to their allegiance. Everyone has a choice to commit to something whether big or small. His choice was loyalty.

Drake finished reading the simple instructions. He could click on "forward" or "cancel." As explained, forwarding would start a chain of unknown reactions. The result of that acknowledgement was to be epic in proportion. That part was discussed a multitude of times. Armageddon was a concept neither one of them were prepared for. They also surmised things in jest. These scenarios were in their minds only. The manner to which they would accomplish those feats were mindful dreams. Now they were reality. A call to arms was in motion. He personally placed that call to action himself. The empowerment brought him back to brainstorming. Encrypted notices were sent to Patriot Partners all across the Midwest by the automatic program Alec installed.

The responsibility of the event organizer, at the Peabody Hotel in Memphis Tennessee, was to book reservations and market the hotel. A reservation was made only a week prior under a fictitious name. She asked the normal questions and forwarded required questionnaires for the reservation and venue record keeping. It was routine. The man making the reservation answered the prerequisite questions. He was just another client, but he had done his research. He'd done it before and offered a dollar amount above the venue price to secure a hold on the reservation. The company team building meeting was a ruse. She forwarded her questionnaire to the nontraceable email address. An attempt to track the email to its original source would be futile.

Hotels generally kept meeting rooms available in the off-chance clients needed a last-minute location to meet. The cost of doing said business under those circumstances and the inflated cost on short notice was never a concerning factor.

Team building. It was a believable concept and never doubted. The client nearly read from a script while answering event planner questions. The client was also a recipient of an email as were other Patriots. He too received correspondence from another nontraceable IP address. What wasn't known, the IP address was traceable and continued to be so. DC analysts had been high fiving each other for days. Unlike the IP info dump, Alec had programmed data to clog inquiry tech searches. This particular one didn't route to the Philippines or anywhere else across the pond. It should have.

The hotel event organizer moonlighted as a Patriot theorist. The questionnaire was returned within minutes and money transferred to secure the meeting room for a maximum of 20 participants. The meeting was scheduled for 3pm. All attendees knew each other by their screen names only. No name introductions were conducted.

The Peabody Hotel was an infamous location for visiting tourists. The hotel paraded ducks at designated times from the lobby fountain to a designated elevator. Ducks were viewed by the gusts behind a plexiglass petition. Families would take photos of the attraction. The lobby would be full of guest waiting for the next scheduled parade. The ducklings would step from the huge circular lobby fountain onto a ramp. They would then walk in file, one behind the other, on a rolled-out carpet to an elevator door which was held open for their arrival. The ducks rode the elevator to the top floor where they were bedded down to repeat the scene several times each day to the delight of all the guests.

The Patriots secured a room on the hotel's top floor. The room was only accessible by inserting a key card into the slot named Presidents Suite, labeled above the numbered floors of the hotel elevator. No more than a dozen members took turns looking over the side of the hotel roof top to the hotel circle drive below. Valet parking attendants were attempting to keep up with arrivals and departures. Nothing was discussed between attendees of the top floor meeting. The unspoken was apparent. There would be no disapproval of the meeting agenda. Any naysayer would likely meet the valet unannounced from the Presidents Suite roof top.

Similarly, another email was received. This recipient looked for a different venue location, unlike the one in Memphis. He sent his email to unique individuals. Within the forwarded message were directions to the Jones - Confluence Joint State Park. This park held a particular interest to the host for privacy reasons. It was where the Missouri and Mississippi rivers joined north of St. Louis, a mere 320 miles North of a similar meeting held in Memphis.

The park was well kept. A wide concrete walkway led visitors to the river convergence. The placement of large rock held the shores in place allowing the maintenance of the park to be completed with minimal effort following any river flooding. The park design allowed a unique view of both rivers from the center of the park.

Not by chance, eight people were contacted to meet the host at 3pm the same day as the Peabody Hotel in Memphis. Nine people arrived.

The introduction was provided by the man who provided him with transportation to the meeting. His name was not an email screen name but the man's birth name.

No agenda was reviewed, and no notes would be taken. Everyone but the new guest had heard the host speak to them all before. All other meetings were in a basement or backyard belonging to the host. The email received was to be discussed and what was to be accomplished by attending a rally at the Veteran's Memorial in Kansas City.

The host greeted the invited guests. "Welcome Patriots. It's good to be with you again. I must first ask for the introduction of a member I'm not acquainted with."

The Patriot member who gave him a ride to the park spoke with excitement in his voice.

"Absolutely. I invited my friend who understands what a patriot truly is. We were friends in college, and he was willing to come with me today."

The introduction was interrupted by a cell phone. The uninvited guest remained silent until he started to retrieve his cell which started playing a tone by Bon Jovi.

The host of the party held out his hand to the newly introduced guest and in a discussed tone warned the stranger.

"Don't answer that."

The only man with a phone in his hand said, "I've got to answer it, I'm expecting this call."

The host pulled a nickel-plated semi-automatic handgun from the small of his back. He pointed it at the stranger and said, "Not anymore."

The trigger was pulled, and the man fell from the boulders into the river on the Illinois side.

The horrified friend who brought the guest to the park yelled, "What are you doing!"

The host calmly answered, "Nobody brings a newbie to a Patriot meeting without first having him vetted. You and your friend are fish food."

The pistol was now pointed at the back of the man who stumbled in an attempt to run off the huge rocks that secured the erosion free elevated shoreline. The man fell following the loud crack of the pistol. The keys to the man's car were removed from his pocket and his body was carried the 30 feet from where he fell to the opposite side of the park. His body was rolled into the Missouri river. His car was driven onto the rocks, placed in drive with the engine running. The accelerator was depressed, and the car floated, then sank slowly as it moved downstream at the joint roaring waterway.

CHAPTER 34

Megan was ready to come home. The training she received was fun, rewarding and not what she envisioned. Chad explained to Megan all he experienced when he attended the course with a similar curriculum. What he failed to mention were particular sessions he wasn't sure she would be receptive to. Hand to hand combat was not like defending her team on the court and in the paint during her high school basketball play. It was physical. Learning how to disarm, maim, or permanently disable a person wasn't something she envisioned herself learning.

One day of recap and the class of 27 would be dismissed. They were from all over the country. The newfound friends would never admit they were part of any federal clandestine training. These same attendees could never acknowledge knowing each other in a public setting. Throughout the five-day course, instructors outlined the surprising insurgence of extremist ideology. Understandably, several class attendees were aware of critical incidents occurring in their states.

The instructor recapped the circumstances involving the anarchy in Missouri. Although Megan wasn't the only female in the class, she was the only person who was hailed as instrumental in halting a chain of events that would have reshaped history. As with military veterans not discussing horrifying experiences, Megan declined to elaborate on what the instructor had already discussed. He mentioned caparisons to Lincoln and Kennedy. In contrast to the names John Wilkes Booth and Lee Harvey Oswald, there would be no mention of her name saving the life of Missouri's chief executive.

There would be no final exam or ranking of scores posted by the last four digits of any social security number. MoTAF attendees were present and accounted for at the Federal Law Enforcement Training Center, FLETC. They didn't attend any classes like other attendees. There were no certificates of attendance or medals of accomplishments awarded. MoTAF attendees were secluded in a manner, they couldn't account for being on the campus themselves. In essence, they were clandestine. Those in attendance would have no record of ever being there.

Not as if there would have been any pomp and circumstance, the instructor called the training a success and complete. They were being released one day earlier than anticipated. He explained essential elements of online search parameters had prompted the class to return to their respective domiciles.

As if Megan was back in her advanced Constitutional Law class at the University of Missouri, she nearly interrupted the instructor to add her clarification to the class being dismissed.

"In other words, DC analyst have uncovered more hate and discontent and we're all in deep doo-doo."

The class erupted in applause and laughter. There was an extended uproar that didn't seem to end. She stood from her seat bowing as she turned around to acknowledge the class approval. The instructor roared in his loudest while applauding with the rest of them.

Those present hadn't worried about changing their return flights or any other travel complications. Most of them were on private chartered flights and those who were not had already received stipend compensation for their travel mile reimbursements. There were times the greased wheels of government were efficient.

Megan reached out to Chad regarding her return date and time change. He was already briefed on the update which was of no surprise to Megan. He was waiting at the Springfield Missouri International Signature hanger for her arrival. There were classmates from the training on her flight who lived in Kentucky and Illinois. The conversation topics were jovial. Nothing was said about the course curriculum which they attended. The chartered flight made the quick stops for the others before continuing to Springfield.

Chads arms were spread as wide as the Grand Canyon, and his smile was nearly as wide as he approached Megan on the tarmac. She guided her soft sided four wheeled Samsonite suitcase toward him while balancing a backpack over the other shoulder.

"Hey sharpshooter. How'd things go?"

"It was great!" she excitedly answered while handing Chad her backpack.

Smartly avoiding an awkward hug, she rolled her suitcase to the rear of his car. He didn't miss a step grabbing the backpack and unlocking the hatchback with his keyless remote. He lifted her suitcase while over emphasizing its weight. The painful look on his face, the holding of his lower back, and his knees folding like an accordion caused her to display the familiar eye role.

"Quit it already. I've watched you deadlift."

"What do you have in this, landscaping stones for a patio?"

Glancing over the roof of his car, Chad displayed his full-face grin. She returned his gaze by sticking out her tongue like a 16-year-old. The sharpshooter reference was the range practice he knew she participated in while at FLETC. He picked up the inquiry where she left it and asked about the toys of preference at the training range. She responded with smiles and unstoppable chatter about the new military prototype weaponry. They were able to test the accuracy of the Sig Sauer XM5 rifle. She explained within a couple of years the ammo manufacturer should be able to supply the new munitions for weaponry combat readiness.

Chad listened intently to the nonstop explanation of her learning environment. When she did take a breath, it was short lived as she continued to reminisce. She asked him if he knew where the ammo manufacturer was located. He surprised her to know the armament plant was near Kansas City. It caused her to pause and apologize for her rambling.

"You weren't rambling. I've been to FLETC, but the training you received has evolved since I attended."

Megan held up an Under Armor women's beanie skull cap she removed from her backpack. She continued about her training.

"Do you know what this is?"

Chad knew full well he had no choice but to play along.

"It's a stocking cap."

"Wrong my dear Watson," she exclaimed with enthusiasm. "It's not just a skull cap. It's a ring your bell skull cap."

Chad refrained asking what planet she came from or if her people were returning to claim her. She handed him the cap. Once grasping it, he could feel the rigid plastic surface under the Under Armor logo. On the underneath side was a thin foam cushion.

"I know, right," Megan retrieved the cap from him. "You always wear the cap with the logo to the front. You can headbutt somebody and it won't hurt your own head."

Megan explained she purchased the cap in the gift shop. They had several colors for women and men to choose from. A headbutt is a weapon an assailant would not expect in a close encounter. The padded underlayer prevents the person delivering the headbutt from injury.

Chad took the lull in conversation as an opportunity to mention they were headed to his place for a MoTAF meeting. It was to her disappointment she expressed not being able to go home first to freshen up.

Chad joked, "I'm fully aware of the long airport lines, exhausting TSA screening procedures, and cramped airline seating she endured on your return."

"You realize, you could have a rewarding career as a comedian. Will I be expected to recap my training?"

"Not at all," he responded. "The meeting was scheduled after you started training. When your class was cut short one day, it's good to brief everyone on what we have going on."

Megan shared a grim glance, "What's happening on the home front?"

Chad looked at her and with a grin replied, "At this point, we're all in deep doo-doo."

He couldn't help but laugh out loud and Megan did the same.

"I was told what happens at FLETC stays at FLETC."

CHAPTER 35

Already seated in the basement of Chad's home were Missouri's MoTAF members. Pleasantries were exchanged as Chad and Megan made their way to grab refreshments from the college dorm size refrigerator. The empty seats were customarily positions where Megan and Chad normally would sit during the infrequent meetings.

Chad began speaking as he normally would. This time there was no handout agenda to follow. He unzipped his tan leather binder, glanced down at what looked like a typed outline, and began the briefing. Megan looked across the conference table at Shirley McPherson, the administrative assistant for Dr. Morris. It had been a while since she had spoken to her and looked forward to some one-on-one woman to woman talk.

Dr. Morris never mentioned to Megan the day in his office that forever changed her future. They would forever be linked together by his delivering the devastating news of her parents' tragic accident. He was her professor, and she was without a doubt one of the brightest students he had ever taught. Megan's thoughts drifted to that day often. Way too often. Her blank gaze was likely noticeable. She refocused on what Chad said.

Chad's business manner was attractive. Not in a romantic sense. He was professional with a scholarly demeanor. There was a confidence about him. It was the poise and resolve that she liked. That's what was attractive. It was what brought her back from memory lane to the present.

Chad stood at the head of the conference table unlike other previous reunions. There were no blank pages of legal pads. Each attendee were frantically scribbling notes as if there would be a pass-fail exam at the conclusion. There was frankness, and grim demeanor permeating the room with no interruptions as Chad continued to speak. He too had a look of dismay as he brought his concerns to the group.

"There have been lone wolf incidents occurring across the country. The investigations into those incidents have not yielded concerns directed toward any governmental entity, or a specific cause."

Chad explained DC analysts were able to backdoor infiltrate security protocols of online enthusiasts. Their attachment finally wormed its way into its network. They were inside the extremist network and were taking precautionary measures making sure they didn't find themselves exposed in the same quandary. It was just like Washington, creating a group to find out what the other side was doing. They anticipated many of the unknowns would be determined rather quickly.

Chad continued. "They call themselves Patriot Partners. Their followers are stated in the thousands. Their numbers are more like the lower hundreds if grade school age grandsons and nephews were amongst the masses. The issue at hand, they've proven to be very capable enemies of the state. The question at hand is, what are they planning if anything, and when will they attempt their deed? That is what we're trying to determine, as well as to what purpose they hope to gain."

Chad painted a cautious summation of Missouri's state of affairs. Without overstating any political discourse, good would pound the head of evil doers. Chad reminded them all how deadly the game they were encountering. Adversaries now stand face to face in the light of day without fear of retribution.

Anniversary celebrations were occurring in metropolitan areas across the country. Those observances marked historical significance. Women suffrage, voting rights oppression, Vietnam war remembrances. The blistering July would mark the timing of celebrations. The precise moment of any celebration had not been confirmed and Chad refused to speculate. He gave no historical period mirroring the month of July. He apologized for not being thorough but assured members, analysts would be successful in finding out what if anything were on the horizon.

It was the moment of apology when Megan shyly raised her hand shoulder high. Chad looked to the opposite end of the conference table from where he stood. He grasped the back of the leather high back chair, smiled at her, and asked for her input. He knew full well the raising of hands to speak was not necessary.

"There are a few things which could presumably cause disapproval. The signing of the Civil Rights Act of 1964. Independence Day is unlikely a day of disappointment."

Heads nodded in agreement. They all looked toward Megan for more occurrences to which they assumed she would be familiar with.

"There's Sandra Day O'Connor. She was the first female nominated to the U.S. Supreme Court."

Chad with a grin looked at Megan, and said, "We all applaud her contribution to the highest court."

At that moment, a member offered his tid-bit of knowledge. "In July OJ Simpson was officially charged with murder."

"Congress created the U.S. Marine Corps. Oorah, Semper fi," another member proudly exclaimed.

Chad held up both hands as in surrender, "OK, those with birthdays in July will now cease all notable remembrances."

The chuckles diminished and sheepish grins remained as everyone looked at each other in amusement. Chad gained minimal attention as he continued with his summation of what the DC analysts were able to determine from their own hack. Everything was speculative, but the summations were right in line with what had been previously experienced.

The bomb shell was detonated. Everyone was informed of a vetted associate being utilized to help thwart any threat occurring. Skepticism rose again like a sleeping volcano. Megan voiced her approval and reminded everyone how their foe was saved by their actions and since proved himself while under WITSEC. She reiterated how she vouched for this person. It sounded odd even to her as the words come from her mouth.

"Let me put it this way, my friends," she steadied herself for debate. "Brody, Tenor or whatever name he is going by nowadays, understands his past and realizes we have given him a future."

When she concluded her critique in his defense, they all remained silent. Seemingly unaware, Chad was no longer standing. It wasn't clear to anyone if he relinquished the floor to Megan, or he preferred to sit. She came to the young man's defense all the while understanding he was a novice, except for his computer tech skills. Everyone was captivated by her insistence. As if pleading, she reminded them, she too was naive as well.

Chad decided reinforcing the inevitable was at play, "DC informed me his participation would be limited and it's unknown in what capacity. The decision of his assisting us was not decided by anyone sitting at this table."

As if on cue, Dr. Morris spoke to eased the atmosphere strangling everyone in the room.

"Nobody is suggesting this young man is out of his league. He has fully agreed to and acknowledges any and all dangers. He signed, as we all did, the proverbial dotted line."

Megan piped up to fill the room with the air that got sucked out when she first started speaking.

"Am I the only one in the room who just found themselves back in the professor's Political Science Theoretical Debate class?"

The room erupted in laughter. After a pause, and the humor began to diminish, Dr. Morris replied.

"I'm appreciative of those of you who failed some of my courses to fondly remember the ones you finally did pass."

The smiles turned into faded smirks. They glanced across the table and around at each other. Nothing more was said. There was now a pink elephant in the room that nobody dared to mention.

Chad broke the silence, "It's time to pack a bag people. We've been called upon and I have no doubt we'll be successful. The next time we meet, we may all wonder what the fuss was about."

CHAPTER 36

Tenor couldn't help but miss his friend. Monique became an important part of his life. How could he have let her go? As if he had a choice. But that was how it was presented. He'd undoubtedly would lose sleep. Insomnia was something he hadn't experienced in a long while. After his admittance into their program, sleeping became a hit and miss proposition.

He was in a safe place although the intermittent late-night restlessness consumed him. He understood and agreed to the consequences of his actions. It took forever to accept, but no other choices were presented to him. None were available.

As time passed, the insomnia diminished, and sleep patterns returned to normal. He was encouraged to obtain employment and he found it rewarding. He picked up the phone he was given to use when he needed assistance or in an emergency of any kind. He pressed three keys. The asterisk, pound, and the answer/call key. It rang once. Tenor wasn't at all surprised by the not so warm and fuzzy voice. The automated service line responded after a long, extended lull. Once confident he had been disconnected, a voice responded.

"Thank you for calling. Please stand by for your call to be returned," the line disconnected.

"Well of course. As if I could talk to a real person."

Tenor launched hard in the computer chair. The chair nearly toppled with his weight. His arms flailed like a swimmer's backstroke before gaining balance thwarting the fall. He needed to talk to somebody. He needed clarification, answers, and now he needed to wait. The hurry up and wait game was not something he was accustomed to.

The cell rang at its maximum volume. Not recalling ever changing the setting, he hit the answer key and put it on speaker.

"Hello."

The familiar sound of keystrokes could be heard in the background. Someone was quickly logging information which undoubtedly gave reason to the delayed response of his answering the call.

"Hello Tenor. Sorry for the delay in returning your call. What can we help you with?"

He stood up immediately, grabbed the phone and started walking the first of several circles in his modest living quarters. He recognized the voice. He couldn't believe his ears. He lost all sense of rationale to why he called.

"Monique, is that you? What happened? Where have you been?"

She deflected the questions, as if staying on script, "Tenor, we received your request to speak to us. What can we do for you?"

He didn't understand her awkwardness or her avoidance. He understood, after all this time, how the system worked. During his acceptance into WITSEC, Tenor saw no need or desire to reach out to anyone. If he called, the system would create an automated notification for those responsible for getting in touch with him. In retrospect to how it was explained, their job was to keep him safe. Someone would reach out to him immediately to assist with any concerns he had. Those concerns could be as simple as counseling, or an emergency relocation.

Because he repeatedly asked about why she hadn't been the one contacting him, she was tasked with explaining.

"I've been assigned to acquaint you with more of our program," she continued. "You've read and signed our agreement and we acknowledge your willingness to assist."

"Yes," Tenor responded. "But what I really want to know is why someone else and not you started contacting me."

"I will answer any and all your questions. But first, let's get to what's threatening the heartland."

She was diplomatic and persuasive in keeping with what she needed for him to understand. He was enlightened well beyond what he expected. The who were the Patriot Partners. The why was the all familiar don't tread on me ideology. The question of when was yet to be determined. The calendar was open. It could be anytime or any place. A list of probabilities had to be formulated. What was certain, Missouri would definitely be ground zero. The magnitude of the threat was also unknown. Similarly, the method in which to halt all probable threats would be daunting. Nothing noteworthy in law enforcement intel caused alarm or alerts to be issued statewide. The information DC analysts obtained was because of their stealth-like companions across the U S doing what they did best, infiltrate and analyze.

Tenor understood the concept all too well. His willingness to pay it forward was his way of saying thank you. Saying thank you to Uncle Sam took a little getting used to. Being part of something much larger than himself felt good. He couldn't shout it from any mountain top, but the self-worth was just as exhilarating. No trophy, no badge, no pendant, no T-shirt. Nothing. He would perhaps embrace a well-placed tattoo in the not-so-distant future.

He was being asked to infiltrate his previous counterparts. The same partnership that got him in WITSEC in the first place. What he wasn't aware of, a ruse was already in place. Uncle Sam had been playing sidekick ever since the backdoor virus wormed its way into the Patriots' playground. The playground had a different name, but the game and the players were the same. Some new classmates had joined the games, but the rules were still in place. The language became unfamiliar and that was where Tenor came into play. He knew the language and previously played the game. Uncle Sam, aka, DC analysts, were wary to not cause the game and its players to go further underground.

What concerned Tenor, who was playing whom? What did they know and were not telling him? How much of the Patriot's network had they uncovered and why wouldn't they let him in on it so he could help? He would log in, acquire as much knowledge as possible to help in their endeavor. He was given all the information needed to assume the Patriot Partners role. He assumed the online identity the DC analysts created. Tenor stepped right into the shoes as if he had always been there. He also understood that he may never leave WITSEC because of it. He already accepted the task, he wasn't backing out.

MIAC, Missouri Information Analysis Center, was at the epicenter gathering catalysts. The agency was responsible for analyzing potential terrorist activity within the state. That information was disseminated under the state's homeland security umbrella to other responsible counterparts. Information would be forwarded to state, local, and federal authorities to thwart those threats. Private entities would also be brought in the fold to battle any lurking evils. MoTAF was not public or private. They were federal, but they also didn't exist. It was one of the intriguing elements for its members.

MoTAF received training alongside federal counterparts. Numerous acronyms of the English alphabet attended training at the federal training center. The FBI, ATF, and DEA, among others attended. If there was a federal agency with law enforcement or investigative responsibilities of any sort, the government created them, and representatives were in attendance. Every state had similar homeland security responsibilities which mirrored Missouri. Their duty was similar to their federal counterpart. To locate, inform, and dismantle threats of terrorism.

After talking to the DC analyst, Tenor was energized. No longer pacing, he sat relaxed and eager to know more about what his duties would be. The same repetitive answer was the response to most of his inquiries.

"It's fluid, Tenor. We can only surmise so much," Monique answered. "You will be a crucial element of our work in DC."

He knew the possibility of being shoulder to shoulder in the fracas. What was explained and reiterated multiple times, he would be a silent combatant on the government's digital front line. It was where he was most comfortable and more than capable.

"Monique, can you do me a favor?" Tenor asked with reservation nearly stuttering his words. He continued forcing the words to escape his lips.

"Please tell those who saved my life that I'm going to help them any way I can."

"I can relay your sentiments. I'm sure they'll be appreciative. We'll talk soon."

The line went dead. There were some things that seemed to never change. There was no goodbye. There was no polite customary conclusion of the call. Tenor chose to change that very thing. It would be something he could control and inadvertently be to the positive.

CHAPTER 37

Tenor sat comfortably staring at his 27" screen. It was different this time. He gazed at the walls of the open concept floorplan, smiling. Nothing literally had changed. There were no new paintings or accent decorative wall sculptures. He was lucky enough to low ball the previous tenants out of a photograph he became accustomed to. They were tired of looking at it and planned to discard it once they moved into their new home. A Rembrandt it was not but might as well have been. It wasn't a painting but a well captured photograph of a majestic Bald Eagle.

The seemingly 3D creature rested on its perch high above the waterway. He glanced at the framed 3D photography Pulitzer as it stared back. No matter where in the room he stood, the eagle looked directly at him.

The chat room was lively and exhilarating. Excitement filled the screen as if reading snippets of War and Peace. He found himself energized. It was mesmerizing as well as engaging. There was a call to arms and everyone in attendance concurred the time was now.

Tenor couldn't restrain himself. As a rule, he would become empowered by what he read. This time, he could barely keep up with comments as they filled the screen. It was easy to follow, although it was as if everyone were talking over one another and not allowing the other to finish their thought. Speed reading would be beneficial to keep up with it all. He also understood to get his ideas known, he must be concise when he engaged.

He leaned forward, wringing his fingers and hands as if rubbing lotion in preparation for taking a typing test where speed and accuracy were the focus.

"My bags are packed. I just need to know when and where," he hit the send key.

It was apparent there were no speed readers in the room. Either that, or he was being ignored. The rules of engagement were always followed. He needn't read them again. It was like a beginner's course of etiquette. You knew what was and wasn't acceptable. He hadn't infringed upon any rule.

Without forewarning, the delayed understanding of what was communicated earlier was repeated. As frustrating as it was, Tenor knew not to express disappointment. They were all adults, or so it was understood. It was if kindergarteners were translating to classmates. His patience grew thin until he read an expected response.

"Mine are as well. I'll drive or catch a plane. Just say when and where."

"Mine have been packed for several weeks."

"I'm between jobs so I'm right there with ya."

"How ya gonna get past TSA?"

"Read three pages ago. It's in JC."

"I mean KC. Not JC."

"I'm packed too."

A picture instead of a screen name appeared and all correspondence paused. The unwritten rule was adhered to. Nobody responded to the picture. Nobody dared breach the name or gender inquiry nor did they need to. Women were amongst the ranks and most had their spouse injecting their beliefs. It was the spouse who caused the membership to multiply.

Women were steadfast in weaving the threads holding the Patriot fabric together. It was like the bake sale, the garage sale, the welcome mat to the new neighbor, or the comfort dish for the scorned friend. They came to each other's aid. A call was made, and they came again, and again. They could be and were an unsung driving force.

The picture of an eagle stared back from the screen. It was majestic in its appearance. Not a full-bodied eagle. The white capped head centered on the screen down to the top of the folded wings resting against its body. When the eagle appeared, the chat room chatter paused. It was as if those in attendance were all in the same logistical presence to each other. As if all breathing could have paused when he or she stepped to the dais. Applause would erupt and all would remain standing until told by the person behind the dais to be seated.

"My Patriot Partners, you are correct in your timing. Your conjecture is on point. The heartland is where our country's stronghold stands. Your timing is forthcoming."

The eagle faded and a QR code appeared as the eagle faded away. The code came into focus. It stayed for only a few seconds and faded away just as it appeared. It was the understanding of all those in the chat room, the self-proclaimed, and agreed upon shepherd had left the room when the QR code faded. Other screen name participants left the room as well, one by one. No other comments were conveyed.

The cell phone sounded, and Tenor reached to retrieve his text message. He left the chat room after the last participant was announced to be leaving. He expected to hear from his DC friends. His new employer. If they hadn't reached out, he would have initiated the conversation by calling them as he previously had done.

He refrained from over communicating to the online chat. He was more than amused to understand he was in the room reading. He successfully infiltrated their room, their sacred safe haven. He understood all too well what they were capable of.

He read his message. "Congratulations. We successfully infiltrated the chat room. They were aware of you participating and engaged with you. We'll chat soon. Contact us at will. M."

Tenor stood and pumped his fist in achievement. It worked and he was more than relieved his identity wasn't compromised. Computer techs are diligent in their craft. He of all people were cognizant of that it was real. He wouldn't have been comfortable returning to the Capitol city. What happened in Missouri could happen anywhere.

The thought of returning would have been surreal. A slight chill ran up his arms as he remembered being surrounded by officers in a secure location, while witnessing death and destruction right in front of him. All because he believed rhetoric and philosophy was true.

She signed her text "M." That in and of itself caused the chill to return. He didn't want to be a bore, but questions still loomed. It could wait, but how long should he wait for answers to the unknown? Packing a bag for a cause is part of the equation needing clarification. He understood the cause, but how was he to prepare? Self-doubt started to loom, and uncertainty began to rise in his very core. He picked up his cell and dialed the number with the hope of reaching "M."

The automated response to his call brought an unexpected groan. He had not appreciated the system refusing his call only to return the favor. He waited.

During the first ring he answered, "Monique, is that you?"

There was a pause. The all familiar and unexpected pause. It occurred the last time he got a return call, and it still bothered him. Frustration filled his veins. Anxiety wasn't taking a back seat. Tenor revisited calling her out by name when he answered his phone.

"Hello Tenor. How are you? How can we help you?"

He took a deep breath and exhaled. Repeated the sequence.

"Tenor? Hello, are you there?"

"Hi Monique, I'm fine thank you. I have a list of questions but haven't written any of them down. I'm not sure where to start."

There was no need to write them down. He started in with the when. The answer was expected. It remained an unknown. He continued to ask but got many of all the W questions out of the way from viewing those in the earlier chat room. Most of the anxiety which rose was minimized. The calm to his temperament and his ever-rising anxiety diminished. It was her voice. She possessed the soft, gentle, and most soothing articulative tone he had ever heard.

After his questions, she asked one, "Is there anything else I can clarify for you?"

It was the skillful and polished way she concluded the call. He could only come up with a three-word response.

"No, thank you."

"You're very welcome. So, Tenor, tell me. How have you been?"

He couldn't believe it. She engaged Tenor and wanted to talk. She actually asked how he was and was interested in his wellbeing. The conversation took a different turn. They conversed as if they had known each other for a long time. What was not known, because they were literally strangers, became known. They were becoming friends. In her own words, they were coworkers. A sense of calm relieved all his concerns. She even enlightened him on the 401K program he could contribute if he so chose.

His life had changed, and he could not believe what had already occurred. In a rather short time, there were life altering incidents. Her soothing calm brought back memories of his past. A tumultuous childhood turned promising, and then turned hellish.

Memories of Christmas at his grandmother's return. Presents were in abundance. What wasn't visible under the tree miraculously appeared at every turn throughout the day. He was spoiled throughout the year by her, but especially during his favorite holiday. It was when he turned 16, his grandmother turned ill, and his favorite holiday ceased to exist. He learned in his adolescent years how special his grandmother was. She instilled in him the importance of education and she became his confidant.

She never spoke poorly about his mom, her daughter. Nor did she mention the creep who left them both when he was four. He refused to call him dad because his grandma refused to talk about him. She would just say he played foolish games.

He didn't blame his mom for working as hard as she did. He did resent not being able to sleep in his own bed. His grandma's house became his second home, his only home. His mom brought the guys home from work, and she started yelling a lot at his grandma. His grandma explained how his mom and her agreed that he could stay at her house as long as he wanted. It wasn't until he was older when he understood what that meant. He had classmates with the same kind of grandma.

They learned a lot together about computers. She was excited as he was about the games he played. She learned the educational tool he fell in love with. It was fun for her as well. The learning continued at his grandma's after classes were dismissed. She alone taught him things his teacher didn't. It was when he turned 17 that his life changed dramatically.

He was mad at his grandma for a while until a school counselor explained how her dying wasn't her leaving him. He was old enough to leave his mom and live at a friend's house until he graduated high school. He fell down the rabbit hole and played the same foolish games he grew up witnessing. He was a quick learner in his brief college years. His bad company and know-it-all attitude ended the educational experience.

Tenor thought about his grandma often. Monique's voice brought back the understanding of meaningful games he was willing to play. Games he was compelled to succeed at. Games that had meaning.

His conversation with Monique was educational to the point his grandma's life lessons were coming full circle. Tenor told Monique how his grandmother was like hers. She took that as a compliment, and he assured her it was. What surprised him was that she mentioned she had a grandmother who was her second mom. Monique wished he could have met her and how a wonderful life teacher she was to her.

Monique concluded their chat by reiterating he could call anytime he had any more questions. He sensed she reverted back to work mode. She voiced words he wasn't expecting. He was taken off guard. Speechless.

"Have a good day, Tenor. We'll chat soon. Hopefully real soon. Goodbye."

It was his turn to implement the all-familiar conversation pause. Without any similar sentiment, the call ended. He became her, at least at that moment. He could only smile and smile big he did.

CHAPTER 38

Megan picked up her cell and sat it back down on the kitchen counter. She knew better than to call him. Why would she. There would be no reason to talk about nothing. Besides, the cobbler was ready to come out of the oven. Talking on the phone would only delay the delicious reward. The perfected abbreviated recipe was her favorite. She watched her mother make the dessert over and over, until her mom assured Megan, she mastered it as well.

A perfected measure of cinnamon topped the apple filled favorite. On occasion and for variety, peaches replaced the favorite. The white cake mix, and butter completed the recipe perfected for two. A third helping could generally be manufactured from the recipe and was always better right out of the oven or reheated, topped with ice cream. The dessert brought back a flood of memories of happier times.

This time, as with recent previous baking episodes, the sadness escaped her. The smile would remained throughout the last spoonful. Megan was light footed around the kitchen humming along with her favorite tunes coming from her Alexa playlist. There were no regrets. She didn't concern herself with the amount of sugar intake. She was in her best physical shape. The sampling of her mother's favorite recipes were of no concern.

She hadn't experienced this frame of mind for some time. There was no question why butterflies fluttered. There was no sitting down with her mom to comprehend and understand all the emotions accompanying them. Those talks did clarified everyday simplicity. A larger smile followed a muffled chuckle as thoughts careened of her dad rolling his eyes. He would exaggerate the cupping of both hands over his ears while grunting to discussions of a new Clark Kent she had seen or met on campus. Those happy thoughts were more comforting than in recent months as well.

She barely heard her cell. The vibration hummed through the sparkling marble countertop and the ring interrupted her playlist of jubilant times.

"Alexa, stop!" Megan raised her voice above Whitney Houston's booming vibrato.

She picked up her cell while glancing at the phone screen. She smiled knowing full well her voice would emulate her mood. In a joyful and exuberant tone, she answered.

"Hey Chad. How's the leg?"

"You just won't let it go, will you?"

"Not a chance," she retorted.

"Hope I didn't interrupt anything special," he waited beyond the awkward silence. "Well, that answers that question."

Megan cuffed a hand over her mouth. She put her phone on speaker and grabbed her dessert bowl with ice cream.

"I'm sorry, my mouth was full of a delicious treat."

Chad quipped like a scolding dietician, "You know you're cheating on what's supposed to matter the most."

"My waistline won't suffer today, or any day soon for that matter."

"Thanks to me," Chad returned with a chuckle.

"I'd ask if I could join you, but I doubt you're having my favorite Oreo Thin Mint cookies."

"You would gladly give up your cookies for my mom's favorite apple cobbler."

"My dear, are you offering up treats?"

Megan was taken back by the nonchalant comment. She had never recalled any term of endearment. She knew she had to let it slide knowing full well he hadn't realized what he had said.

"Nope," her stern rebuke hit its mark. Another awkward pause before she continued.

"My mom taught me how to make a recipe for up to three and I'm not sharing. Sorry."

He defended his turf. "I can find my way around the kitchen just fine. We should have a cook off.

Megan didn't let it slide. "Maybe in your kitchen. You're off limits to mine."

"I've never been past your living room. I'd say its past time you offer up a guided tour."

"Perhaps in the not-so-distant future, it's a date."

Megan lowered her bowl to the counter, resting both elbows, and planted her face in both hands. She wanted to slap herself, but the sting would be heard through the phone, even if it were muted.

Another pause filled the air. This time the air was heavy as if driving in a fog at night, with only one headlight. She couldn't believe she said what she did. Attempting to take it back like a10-year-old would make matters worse. She wanted to scream but hoped he would rescue her. He did.

"Hold on Meg, I'm getting a text."

Megan felt the vibration of her phone as he spoke the words.

"Chad. I'm getting one too. Please tell me this isn't happening again. Could somebody be sending us both another malicious text?"

"Let me read mine and we'll see if yours is the same," Chad responded.

The awkward pause lingered, and lingered. Megan's mind drifted to driving a mile long scenic mountain highway, downhill with no brakes. A crash was imminent. Chad interrupted her nightmare.

"Megan, you still there? It's MoTAF."

She couldn't let go of the probability of their identity being compromised. She turned up the volume on the speaker phone and read her text as well. He chose to look at his text before her which solidified her assumption he was concerned as well. She would call him out on his façade. That's what friends do for each other. Keeping it real, at all times. Any compromise to their identity put both their lives in danger. The thought of looking over her shoulder wasn't inviting. Living in fear wasn't living.

While reading the message, memories came rushing back. Excitement or anxiety. It was a thin line between the two, a slippery slope which required constant monitoring.

"I was afraid it was another warning," She said.

"I'm not saying it was a fluke, Megan. We've been assured measures were taken. There's no need to worry about it happening again."

"You do realize you're pulling back on what you said before about not worrying," Megan sharply recounted.

"I'm saying there are those who are capable of making sure we stay under the radar."

"You're an analyst, Chad. You know how dangerous this could be for us."

"The tech world is large. I'm not oblivious to the possibility of identities being compromised."

She quickly replied, almost interrupting. "I'm not losing sleep over it. But I sense I'm alone performing a death-defying high wire act. It's a long fall to the concrete below."

Chad replied, "If you look past that wire you're balancing on, you'll see me. I'm that safety net."

She was strong, confident, and with few regrets in life. She was taught self-reliance. He suggested she lean on him for safe keeping. She didn't need him for safekeeping, but the thought and the way he explained it, was without a doubt comforting.

"Thank you for saying that."

She pushed the thought aside to what she wanted to say. She was not so sure his ego could handle it.

The MoTAF development would have prepared them more when they met earlier. They could have discussed in detail the odds of preventing another tragedy. Missouri was again the focal point. The reasoning at this point was anyone's guess. What they did have for certain was the answer to one of the remaining W's. A zoom meeting was scheduled for late in the afternoon. Missouri would once again be the target of history making proportions.

Patriot Partners were focused on making themselves a household name. The who was determined from online chat room rhetoric. What couldn't be determined was the number of followers as only a few were boisterous in their allegiance. A respectable number were present and accounted for but not active participants in the chat room. There was a single figurehead who was feared and respected. Whoever it was had a command to be reckoned with and pledged to stand tall or fall with them.

Chad removed a receipt from a magnet on his refrigerator. He logged into the winery web site and entered the code for the order he placed. It had been shipped. Nothing was put in motion, but the planning could now begin. He would bring her favorite wine. He would ask her to make the dessert she bragged about.

CHAPTER 39

The zoom meeting was attended by each MoTAF member. The backdrop for each member was scripted as bookshelves lined the wall behind the participants. Each zoom view had the same pull-down bookshelf backdrop. Below each member were initials, not names to go with the faces. There were a select few who took the effort to purchase voice altering devices for the meetings. Voices were altered allowing them to emulate a familiar person when and if they spoke. It became humorous when those attendees would speak unexpectedly using their altered voice.

Dr. Morris never changed his voice's adaptation. He became accustomed to Darth Vader and always seemed to lighten the mood at the right time. Faces would appear on screen when the allotted scheduled meeting would begin. He would appear on screen and greet everyone. Every attendee couldn't help but laugh when Darth Vader spoke. Once the meeting began, matters were discussed with serious intent.

Missouri was again the focal point of potential domestic terrorism. Intel gained from the so called, brotherhood of patriotism could not be overstated. Although the name had changed, the cloak that covered those who harbored similar ideology hadn't. The cancer metastasized and continued to grow. Progress, however, was made to thwart and eliminate hatred. At least that was their hope.

Dr. Morris summarized what was learned by the chat room infiltration. Emphasis was made regarding how sleek the techies were in their field. The DC analysts were aware the talent for evil were capable of going dark again if it were learned they were infiltrated. It was their only way to stop them.

The looming question remained. When and where would the devastation be attempted and how would they pull off whatever it was they dedicated themselves to do? What or who was the target of their plan?

The meeting became more of a think tank. The seriousness of the moment remained evident. There were various views and a multitude of probabilities, none of which could be verified or eliminated. The task was fast becoming improbable. They needed assistance and the obvious solution would be those who lived and worked in the areas of concern. Preliminary footwork was needed to secure the answers.

The playbook was written for this purpose. No need to reinvent the wheel. Counterparts in major cities would step up and come through as they had previously done. This was no different. Failure was not an option.

Dr. Morris tasked Chad with reaching out to his DC counterparts to get the inquiries started. He also suggested Megan assist. Following her training, this would be another area to hone skills recently acquired.

The meeting was near conclusion. A solemn tone came over each screen as Dr. Morris continued to hold participants' attention. He was compelled to reiterate each one's safety to successfully defend democracy. He reinforced MoTAF was the silent majority of unsung heroes. Their clandestine force must continue to defend what was sacred to the majority. Hatred has no foothold, and it was up to them to make sure it never found solace in Missouri's backyard.

Dr. Morris continued, "Things got dicey the last time we confronted evil. We succeeded before, we will once again."

With precise timing Dr. Morris activated his voice enhancement device. Darth Vader entered the room unannounced.

"May the force be with you all."

The screen erupted with laughter. Chad activated his voice enhancement device and in the cartoon voice of Porky Pig, he interjected.

"That's all folks."

Dr. Morris rose, leaving his chair and his view on screen for the others. He returned seconds later to his seat and in zoom view to others wearing a Darth Vader mask.

He didn't speak. He didn't need to. Leaning close to his computer camera, fully aware those watching were seeing him zoom in and out of their view. He waved and closed his zoom connection. Others followed while continuing to laugh, some still uncontrollably.

Megan picked up her cell and called Chad. She was still laughing but muffled her enthusiasm waiting for him to pick up.

"Hey Megan, what's on your mind?

"Well, Mr. Porky, let me begin by saying you broke character by not wearing your pig face."

"I still can't believe all that happened," he continued, "Particularly after what we'd just been briefed on."

"It's your fault. All on you Chad."

"Don't blame me."

"I just did, so own it," she smirked.

Megan couldn't contain her humor and laughed loud and intentionally into her phone. The zoom gathering brought things into focus even though it concluded jovial. They were once again in a place to thwart terrorism.

The inquiry reached out like an octopus searching the oceans floor. The ruse was a visitor coming to tour their city with infrastructure as the focus of interest. City tourism was front and center and more than accommodating to showcase the finer points and secure potential federal aid to refurbish impoverished areas. No promises were ever made, however, the mention of the all-mighty dollar supplementing dwindling budgets opened endless possibilities.

With the sweltering summer temperatures approaching, community calendars were full of tourism magnets. Patriot Partners were drawn to highlight their cause and recruit members. That was their focus. It was always their focus to find those vulnerable to similar ideologies. MoTAF hoped nothing more heinous was afoot. Finding those who would follow through on heinous acts was a serious obstacle.

Defending Missouri was MoTAF's calling. They didn't want to be a catalyst for any national trend. The nation witnessed the cause and effect that rippled from the city of Ferguson. It was a different beast, but a beast, nonetheless.

Megan asked the optimal question nobody asked in the zoom meeting.

"How are any of us going to recognize who we're up against?"

"That's the question we're unable to answer," Chad replied. His cell lost connection but immediately returned to full strength. "There's something Dr. Morris didn't want to mention in the meeting."

"That's so unlike him to hold out on us," Megan replied. "What didn't he tell us?"

Chad said, "The DC analysts were able to infiltrate their software and find out a lot of intel. They weren't able to decipher a QR code that appeared in the chat room. It didn't show on any of the DC analysts' screens. There were a few letters and a number but no picture of what was displayed."

Megan understood Chad may not have any answers to her questions, but she was determined to ask anyway.

"So, what do you think was in the QR code? Are they going to be able to decipher it and let us know?"

"Hold on Meg, I don't have all the answers either," her enflamed tone spewed her frustration. He was perplexed by the same things she wrestled with.

"We can't sit and wait for the unknown to happen," she continued. "What if the target is a family with kids, or what if it's a day care or high school? What if it's us? What if it's me?"

"Megan, you're right. Recruiting may not be it."

He continued, "What we can surmise, the QR code linked a location and perhaps an event taking place in the near future. We have to be ready."

"We can't be ready if we don't know what we're up against," her frustration boiled.

"I agree totally, Megan. We'll figure it out."

"And where do you get your confidence? I'm on the same team you are and I'm not seeing what you're seeing."

"Let's brainstorm. Come over, we'll chart out some possibilities with what we know so far."

"Sounds good to me. In case you forgot, we both received threatening messages."

"I haven't forgot, and I doubt you will neither."

Although it was business, he wasn't so sure the invitation to brainstorm was a good idea.

Megan changed and grabbed her purse. She walked briskly toward the foyer and retraced a step glancing back to the hallway mirror. Her hastened glance lingered. She stared at herself, laid her purse next to the antique vase underneath the mirror, and calmly retraced her steps to her bedroom.

She sat in front of her dresser mirror and said, "He will not see me like this."

CHAPTER 40

Tenor failed to scan the QR code that appeared in the chat room. The code was designed to fade from the screen seconds after it appeared. The QR code revealed what was missed or at least answered a few questions to the puzzle. The Eagle was an unexpected touch to the onscreen rhetoric. He hadn't seen anything other than an emoji and an occasional meme normally viewed in social media platforms to ingest humor. What Tenor witnessed was far from anything associated with social media.

The QR code caught him off guard. Before he could react, it was gone. He momentarily thought about doing what he did best and insert his skills to searching the chat room for what was previously embedded. He also knew it was already being done. If there was a way to view what others saw in the chat room, the DC analysts were capable of recreating it. He was painfully aware of being out of his league after so many months. Techniques changed quickly, as did protocols to hide hacker deceptions. If he were to remain faithful to his new employer, he would leave it to those who were constantly learning their craft. What he didn't want to experience was an unwelcome knock on his door accompanied by men in dark suits and sunglasses.

Tenor's vivid imagination began to run its course. Could it have been a test? Would those who he trusted test his loyalty? If it were a game, what choice would he have but to play? Thoughts drifted to Monique. It was she who brought him into the fold, and it was she who he believed in. She was honest to a fault. She risked it all for him. The same vivid imagination brought him back to reality.

All was not lost. He could ask her anything. Although the lines of communication were open, he long ago decided not to breach the restrictions previously placed on him. He understood things were getting complicated and he accepted it. He owed a lot to those who came to his defense when he was unaware of what he needed. A debt he could only attempt to repay.

Moments later Megan rang Chad's doorbell. She always marveled at the ranch style brick veneer. It looked pricey because it was.

Chad was a tenant in his own place. It was explained to Megan not long after they got to know each other, and her trust was solidified. The federal government owned the land and the dwelling that sat on it. Any open record search would show his paying an extravagant tax. Megan joked about herself making payments through her tax dollars, and not being able to live there. Chad's defense to it all was the same analogy for the city streets and interstate highways. He was losing the debate and they jovially agreed to change the subject and never to return to the topic, until it was brought up again.

Although there were no neighbors in any close proximity, the grounds were electronically secured. Warning signs were posted. The signs weren't those one could purchase at a Menard's or Lowe's home improvements franchise. The small print was illegible, but one reading the keep out signs would relate the same signage to that of Nevada's Area 57.

Chad never experienced unsolicited visitors. Those who arrived at his doorstep were observed well before their arrival. MoTAF members had access to the secure confines. Gate remotes were installed on vehicles for clearance to his property. Vehicles could approach between designated speeds and the entrance gate would open to allow passage. It was a well-designed system.

Upon entering, Megan couldn't help but marvel at the surroundings. It wasn't the design or the decor, it was how immaculate he kept the place. She wasn't sure why. It wasn't as if he had visitors arriving unannounced. Perhaps it was his upbringing. She understood that concept, although she couldn't honestly call herself a neat freak. If something weren't done, there was only one person who would do it.

"I'm impressed," she said. "You were quick to pick up the place."

He looked directly at her and smiled knowing full well there was no picking things up in anticipation of her arrival.

"The cleaning lady already left," he uttered as he turned and walked into his study.

His smile remained as he sat at his desk. She followed, making herself comfortable in a soft cloth recliner. It was the seat he offered to her the first time she came to his place. She was made welcome, and the familiarity never escaped her. She was offered something to drink, which she declined. She was as comfortable in his home and would have helped herself to his refrigerator if she had the urge.

Inside the hallway coat closet, was the entranceway to the basement conference room. An elaborate set up to what he called "the cave." It was where MoTAF members met to discuss terrorist infiltrations or potential threats from ill doers. There was no need to enter the cave. What they planned to discuss could also be accomplished in his study. The conference room setting was too formal.

"I waited till you got here to let you know I heard from a DC analyst. They couldn't view the QR code but something revealing did show up."

His computer screen was turned to a viewable angle. A tap on the space bar on the wireless keyboard brought the screen to life. Megan leaned from the edge of the recliner toward his computer. She took his unspoken offer and rose from being comfortable to see what he was pointing at. She placed her right hand on the back of his chair and leaned forward balancing her left hand on his desk to get a closer look.

Chad pointed at the email he opened, making particular emphasis on the bolded wording in a specific paragraph. She leaned closer causing his chair to give a little to the weight of her focus over his left shoulder.

"Is that saying what I think it means?" She stood erect taking a step back for his response.

Chad wanted to comment on how she looked. Although nothing extravagant, she looked nice. He noticed the soft aroma, the faint whiff of an expensive scent surrounding her when she walked into his foyer. He hadn't said anything when he welcomed her in. He now regretted that misstep as the opportunity had long since passed. Any reflection now would be awkward. His failure to not comment on her looks and her fragrance slapped him across both cheeks. She took the time to look the way she did. He kicked himself for not making the effort assuring her that he noticed. She expected it – maybe. She was often oblivious to the obvious. An attractive trait which weakened him.

"Yep. There's no other way to interpret it."

"It's obvious, is it not?" she replied. "Without saying where or what they are planning, it's an obvious clue to the where."

"Exactly," Chad quickly retorted. "Our friend Tenor has been researching for us. He likes being able to do something worthwhile for a change."

The bolded text appeared to caption the QR code as if giving it a title of what would be the result of the scan. Chad explained the analyst couldn't view the code but what remained was the caption to the code. It was thought to be a statue of Greek mythology embedded in the code. The name of the Greek god accompanied the image. The image wasn't visible, but the name was.

"But what could 'fountains of all stations' mean?" Megan turned up both palms of her hands.

"Tenor researched images of fountains all over the country. Most of those images were at parks and train stations. All he had to do was narrow down images in Missouri. There were few in the St. Louis area."

Megan said, "I'm afraid to ask how many in the rest of the state."

"Too many to mention, but a smaller number of them were near train stations in the Kansas City area," Chad replied. "We're better off now than yesterday. We're getting close."

Chad explained what Tenor learned from his search. The online messages gave clues to what could be forthcoming. Those clues were like pieces of a puzzle yet to be put into place. Previous online messages weren't retrievable, however, there were repetitive dialogues which gave meaning to everything talked about. The wording was matched within specific search criteria. The result of that search gave them what they were looking for.

Within the Patriots chat room, the dialog was about patriotism and the future. There were several repetitive mentions of fountains. All those comments resembled blowhard rhetoric. To Patriot members, it was as if a sporting event was taking place, and they were cheering themselves on to victory. It resembled a call to arms.

In theory, the location was Kansas City, the self-proclaimed city of fountains. The future of the Patriots was also narrowed down to the same city location. There were statues at the World Warr II museum called Guardian Spirits. There are four spirits, Honor, Courage, Patriotism, and Sacrifice. There were two Assyrian Sphinx statues in Kansas City. Memory and Future. All the rhetoric kept referring to those items.

Megan listened intently as Chad paused. "This is all in theory," she said cautiously. "How can we be sure Kansas City is where this all is to take place?"

"We don't exactly," Chad answered. "It's all we've got to go on and it's solid information. I'm removing all doubts. It's going down in Kansas City."

CHAPTER 41

Patriot Partners were organized. Diligent in their pursuit and passionate about their cause. The questions remained, what were they pursuing and what cause were they advocating? Other than strong divisive rhetoric, it was anybody's guess. They were dedicated in their belief system. The serpent's head resurfaced once again and was more lethal than ever before.

Three weeks passed, and the Patriot site was boisterous again. The screen rhetoric welcomed those arriving in the secured chat room. Although unbeknownst to any of them, it was no longer secure.

Three weeks to the noon hour time frame and the online site was once again thriving. It wasn't a secret to the hardliners how they communicated. They called each online chat a "conference" for believers. The time was determined long ago and was disseminated by invitation only. The numbers 1776 were added individually, with the summation totaling 21. Twenty-one days and at the noon hour a conference would convene. The chat group grew in numbers.

There were strict guidelines adhered to. Over the top violent rhetoric would find members banned from online chat. You could participate in any violent act, you couldn't boast or admit to such acts for other members to become aware of. The constitution was their foundation. Those who would admonish the Patriots belief system, were banned from membership, as well as the person who invited the new member. It was an enforced contract.

Tenor became reindoctrinated into the tech world and was thoroughly enjoying his new tech friends. Monique was his favorite. He hadn't shied away from asking about her or contacting her directly for any advice. He hadn't been interviewed for his newfound job. He was simply hired.

He answered a call expecting Monique but noticed it wasn't her direct line.

"Hello, it's Tenor."

"Hi Tenor, glad you're available and I hope you're at home."

The female voice was kind, warm and inviting. He was beginning to think it was a prerequisite for the job.

"Yes, I'm home. What's up?"

"The Patriots have started another online chat," the DC analyst continued. "We want you to join in and entice the membership. Monique will contact you after you've concluded your group chat."

"Will, do. Tell Monique I look forward to hearing from her."

Tenor signed into the Patriot Partnership chat room and immediately gained a welcome from those already in the room. He noticed a side bar window of an invitation to join a chat. Immediately clicking on the green bar to join the chat, he read reference to 1776 and holding closed meetings every 21 days. Today was the 21st day. The countdown box indicated as such and was flashing red.

The rhetoric was normal and was boisterous. A call to arms had not gone unnoticed, however, there was no mention of what exactly that meant. It was understood Patriot Partners would not be denied their voice. They again denounced evil worshipers. Patriots would not allow the country to fall into the hands of the devil.

Tenor was silent. He removed his fingers from the keys. Beyond his hello and glad to be with you again chat room greeting, he remained silent although affixed to the screen. He continued watching and reading about the ongoing transformation of a new dominance. It was definitely new but also familiar.

In a not-so-distant past, he was a vital part of the all-familiar evil. He didn't adhere to the characterization, nor the labeling of anarchist authoritarians. Reading what he was now, Tenor began soul searching. It was as if a magnifying glass was hovering over his soul revealing ideology he no longer believed and now denounced. He was playing a role. It was if he was born again. He heard about it, read about it, but hadn't believed he would again be part of anything resembling it.

He smiled at what he had become. He was part of a sting. At least that's what was depicted in the movies. Trying not to attach to much of what he was seeing, he continued to read. He was a newcomer to the scene, his place in the scene was profound enough to land him squarely in the thick of it all. It happened quickly, and in truth, it didn't hold any importance to him. He was where he wanted to be. He was going to make a difference and would prove to himself and others he was not the same person.

"Where will we meet?"

"At the future, of course."

"Or at the past."

"The past and future will meet for sure."

Online comments were rolling on the screen. Tenor recalled a previous chat dialog he participated in. These people had aligned themselves with the unknown. In theory, he was aligning himself with the same. They knew where they would be, they understood their mission, or so it seemed. It hadn't been revealed to him what it was they were going to accomplish or what they attempted to bring to light for the world to see. What was apparent, he had aligned himself with the devil.

As he delved into the mindset, there was more to it. He was now an arm of the government, but he was not the arm of the leftist, or devil. Arguable as the point could be made, he recalled nothing in any previous chat rooms of politics.

There had not been any mention of political right or wrong. The left and right were not an issue until now. You were either right or wrong, left or right. There was only one side and you better be correct. There was no hint of division or opposition.

The polarization is what stood out on both sides of any issue. Do not compromise. Stand tall, hold your ground, do not conform. Hold steadfast to the truth and what is self-evident. It would be a simple concept of what some people would call division.

"The rails will come off the track."

"No tooting of the horn arriving at the station. Not this time."

"All points from East to West will form."

"The devil will die."

"The right will defeat the left once and for all."

"The left was never in the fight."

"Exactly, what fight?"

Rhetoric was more profound than previous online appearance antics. Tenor knew full well it was time to enter the fray. No longer a bystander, the time was right to become one of the hated. In all historical fronts, it was exactly what he became. He didn't like being told who he was or should become. He had disdain for the proclaimed nay sayers who liked to stand on their pedestal proclaiming so. As a kid, he recalled the phrase, 'because I said so.' Every kid did. As a young adult, that same phrase continued to haunt him. It was repeated over and over by professors in his short collegiate life.

Déjà vu. He was reading but not believing there was even a slight chance of aligning himself with the philosophy he was now witnessing. He was steadfast to his belief system. He only had one issue that bothered him and he long since refused to dwell on it. The question remained. At what point in his young life had he aligned himself on the side of evil?

A small percentage of society were antisocial. Few retained personalities one would characterize as sociopaths. As Tenor read the onscreen conversations in front of him, he quickly came to a different mindset. The percentages were larger than any professor of ideology would ever consider. He was now tasked to become one of them if not only in falsehood. The task would be easy. It was another mindset that troubled him to the core. He was to become what he once was. What he now thought was vial, he signed on to fight against.

By hitting near bottom, Tenor pulled himself from the bowels of evil. He was told by one of his befriended construction coworkers to grab hold of his coat tail for a bumpy ride. He would show him what life had waiting for him. He learned the upside of the internet and social media. The up and down of information afforded choices. It was the ability to decipher what kind of information and from which groups or causes they adhered to. It all came down to choices. Tenor hung on for dear life.

His coworker opened up about his young life. What this friend didn't realize was that it mirrored Tenor's own in some respects. No family to call his own. The coworker's grandfather was his father figure. He along with his grandmother raised him. His friend made a choice following a life altering bad one. It was his grandparents who kept him from living the life of his only brother and two of his cousins. Their life choices resulted in a shortened life span. He reluctantly made the right choice and only looked in the rearview mirror to remind him how that choice changed his life for the better. Tenor was witnessing how one person found the positive side of life.

Tenor couldn't elaborate on their similar upbringing. He understood he made the wrong choices which landed him in WITSEC. It was because of his coworker, he found laughter and positive thinking. He heard all the cliches, but never knew anyone who lived by them. It was no surprise to his friend, the struggles Tenor would complain about paled in comparison to his own.

When Tenor would talk about a difficult time as a teenager, his friend would respond with something so troubling, Tenor couldn't believe what he was hearing. He wanted to tell his friend how his choices were forced on him but like his job, he couldn't be forthcoming.

The story of how he came to live in Missouri's Bootheel is what gave Tenor pause. His friend never knew his father. His mother tried to hold down two jobs while living with his grandparents. His only brother dropped out of school to get a job which was a bone of contention with his mom and grandparents. He got in good with so-called friends who schooled him in the way of making easy money. That easy money was the problem. He was found on a street corner wearing the wrong colors on the wrong side of town. Two of his cousins had similar life ending experiences.

His friend's grandfather retired from the Alabama Railroad with a substantial pension. He was frugal and saved his money. A church parishioner suggested him to invest and invest wisely. When his mom left him with his grandparents, never to see or speak to him again, his grandparents decided to move to Missouri when a community church burned. The truth to that dark part of history was kept from him. It wasn't until years later he learned about other church burnings and why. His friend still owned property in the Bootheel and traveled to where the jobs took him.

When his grandmother passed, he earned enough money to learn the craft of construction in trade schools with his grandfather's help. He also acquired lessons in investments from his grandfather. He was old enough to care for his grandfather until his passing. His upbringing taught him the meaning of living frugal and happy.

Tenor's cell phone chimed. It startled him to the point where he noticed he missed several comments in the chat room. He read his text from Monique.

"Where are you? Engage in the chat! You're going to miss a golden opportunity for us."

Tenor started reading the one liner conversations. Much of the chat, as if it were in code, didn't make much sense to anyone who didn't understand the mindset. A near act of congress was the only way he found himself reading what his eyes looked upon. One could easily surmise what was being said. A third grader could come up with the same understanding an adult would.

After catching himself up to speed of what he wasn't following, there was no question looming. The train station in Kansas City would be ground zero.

Union Station was a beautiful place to dine, to visit with families and friends. He needed to engage and find out more. He was given orders to engage. Orders. He was being told what to do, again. He was at work, albeit this work was different. He was ordered to do something. He wasn't sleeping but he might as well have. He must be the best Patriot Partner he could be. He typed what came to mind.

"Your friends will believe in your potential; your enemies will make you live up to it." (T. Fargo)

CHAPTER 42

Patriot Partners went berserk. It was obvious those in the room believed somebody gave their first initial and last name. A heinous felony had been committed in their presence.

"WTF"

"What are you doing?"

"Are you CRAZY?"

"Who are you…. nvm."

"I would say you're stupid, but. Oh wait…"

The firestorm continued and soon became relentless in vulgarity. It wasn't the comments they were reading, it was the name attached to it. Tenor watched the mud wrestling contest. He was the obvious champion, hands down. He won the contest without a single toenail touching the pit. His grin turned into the largest smile he displayed in recent months. Well, not exactly. He recalled a joke at work several months prior. The laughter halted work to the point the day supervisor decided to call it break-time because resuming work at would have been futile.

Tenor surmised those in the chat room held the same intellect of red and black ants in a jar. Nothing happens until somebody shakes the jar. All the ants get mad at each other except whoever shook the jar.

What he read became mundane, tiresome, and childish. A tone was heard from the system speakers. It was faint but noticeable, nonetheless. The silence in the chat room was also noticeable. Nothing happened, not a comment uttered.

A faint watermark came into focus. It was an eagle perched on a limb, looking to one side. Hanging around the neck of the eagle was a chain displaying one word. Patriot.

The eagle watermark faded as quick as it appeared, leaving the one word in bolded elaborate script font. The chat room remained silent as if rules were being adhered to or the boss stepped into the room demanding respect once again. The eagle along with the dangling word faded just in time for a QR code to appear.

He opened his cell phone camera app to scan the code and waited. A nano second passed, and his phone came to life. The showcasing of Kansas City's south side extravaganza appeared.

The familiar ringtone sounded. Tenor was already crossing his fingers, wishing the person calling to be Monique. He glanced down at his cell knowing full well it was the ringtone of her direct line. He couldn't hold his breath and speak at the same time. Not thinking about how to answer, he went with his gut, and kept his fingers crossed.

"Hello beautiful."

"Very funny Tenor. We have never met, so you don't know what I look like. Especially, to answer in such a flirtatious way."

"We haven't met but I'm a good judge of character."

"My voice says nothing about my character, but you're the one with wishful expectations. Dream on if you so choose."

"Monique, are you saying your character is not up to my expectations?"

"My character is above reproach. I'm saying I could have the skin tone and texture of a ninja turtle and the face to match."

Monique wasn't sure where he was steering the conversation. She applied the brakes and brought things back into focus. There were unknowns yet to be discovered. A breach in the cell phones had not happened before and hadn't been resolved. The wireless network was less than forthcoming with required information relating to the hack. The finger pointing continued between the facet of government that didn't exist and the mega cellular network. An impasse was inevitable.

An informative briefing gave Tenor the degree of interacting with the public he would participate in. He would never leave his handler's side. This wasn't the first of its kind and he was a vital part to its success. The work he agreed to was potentially dangerous and why he was placed in WITSEC. There was no misunderstanding of the stakes involved.

Being able to give back to those who gave him a second chance was something he looked forward to. The Patriots didn't just play in his back yard, they were at one time guests in his house. Not literally, but figuratively.

Monique needn't remind him of the two main players in his success story. Chad and Megan went to bat for him when the decision was approached about him infiltrating the Patriot network. The goal was to eliminate the online hatred and division that continued to nurture the seeds of young likeminded souls.

Tenor was the mind and soul of what he believed in. That belief was ill served. He reminisced about interrogations and mind-altering exercises he was put through. Forced injections and admitting to things no one would believe. This was different. Understanding the Patriot Act brought pause.

He admitted his wrongdoings even though it was coerced or under duress. It was hard for him to believe his life as he was living it. There wasn't a comfortable leather couch in any office that would allow him to unpack all he had been put through. That comfortable surrounding didn't exist. He was giving back to those who were convinced of his loyalty. It was the only way.

Moments later, the briefing concluded. The chat room had already ceased. Monique assured him things were going to conclude as they always did. The good guys win. Those were her exact words. Nothing was scripted.

This recurring endeavor was charting new waters. It ask all to board a lifeboat with no motor, one oar, and at night with no horizon to view. She wasn't convinced things would end well. Her assurance didn't ring true with Tenor either. As convincing as her tone, the silence between them told the truth to the unwritten storyline. There was no hiding it, although her attempt was an award-winning performance.

Tenor didn't know what to expect and the learning curve was steep. He was sure of one thing. He would not be uprooted again. He wasn't changing his name, moving to a new place, and starting his life over. Tenor was done not being in control of his life. If it were offered, with all the diplomacy he could muster, he would decline. He owed it to himself to be in control of his life.

Monique liked him. She wasn't sure why, but the young man was bright, witty, and confident. She couldn't put her finger on what pulled her to him. She was four years and six months older than Tenor. Age was the only thing she was certain of. There were a quadrillion differences between them. Nonetheless, she was drawn like a magnet, like a bee to honey.

She checked all the boxes, but there were some points of concern she couldn't define. They weren't on the debrief list to check off. There was no square box for intuition, gut, or feelings. Factual conclusions didn't allow for broad brush summations. She had been at her job a decade longer than she thought she would have. It was to be a steppingstone on a path upward to anywhere she chose. That was why she stayed. It wasn't climbing the corporate ladder which pulled her toward a rewarding career. She found what she was looking for. She hadn't realized it until she witnessed the fruit of her labor. Lives saved, purpose, and fulfillment. No dollar amount could be attached to being a part of something positive, even though she couldn't brag of those achievements to anyone. Her assignment to this case was different.

There was nothing she learned in all those years depicting what was going on with her now. She was assigned individual cases before and all of them were rewarding. Other team members were exuberant of success stories as well. This story was still being written and she didn't paint with broad brushes. She would protect him as well. She owed it to herself.

Tenor was apprehensive about what he was undertaking. History need not repeat itself, not this time. He was a good guy, and he was assured all would be protected by the same forces who placed him in the bubble he was currently in. He also understood he was stepping outside the safe haven where he was placed. He hadn't looked over his shoulder before. He hadn't any reason to be cautious. He was entrusting his wellbeing to the same people who placed him in The Program. They were to be trusted and he had no cause to believe otherwise.

The anxiety he was experiencing after talking to Monique was understandable. It was exactly what she told him would happen. A handful of people were afforded the opportunity he was given. She alone could have changed the minds of those who suggested he help in their endeavor. People were placing faith in his abilities. His tech skills opened the door, but his playing by the rules kept him safe.

Tenor would leave in one week from his humble abode for a drive to the Downtown Kansas City airport. There he would meet his unsung heroes. They were the two people who saved his life and backed his support for good against evil. Being able to see and thank them in person meant the world to him. He enjoyed the antics of becoming one of the bad guys all the while being on the side of good. Besides, being good paid much better.

CHAPTER 43

Thanks to Covid, Chad and Megan were able to work remotely for their normal jobs. Chad reveled as a consulting family law attorney specializing in the foster care systems. Megan accepted an internship after receiving her law degree. That internship solidified employment at a large affirmative legal defense law firm in Springfield. Much of their work didn't require face to face consulting. When in-person consultations were preferred, they were happy to accommodate the clients and the firms flourished from their budding expertise. Virtual consultations were becoming the norm with most legal proceedings. Times changed from the days of boardroom meetings. Paperless functionality became common in judiciary proceedings.

Cloud storage and eSignature software were becoming prevalent as well. Baby boomer workforces were becoming prehistoric. Employers offering 401 retirement options were becoming a thing of the past as millennial generation were opting for lucrative investment incentives. The transfer of funds to handle business contracts were commonplace as well. DC analysts made all the arrangements for the upper meeting room at the opulent centrally located airport. The conference room would be easily converted into a real-time command post.

Zoom meetings were conducted and all players were virtually greeting each other sooner than any had anticipated. Depending on the protocol within each respected domicile, some birth names were utilized. There were no Darth Vader voice overs. Each screen box had the word "host" under each MoTAF member residing in Missouri. All other zoom participants utilized their state initials and their first name if they chose to include it.

DC analysts were among the zoom attendees. Some analysts were to accompany others on streets in the city of fountains. The traveling analysts had the term 'On Assignment' under their virtual picture. The command post would exceed the capacity limit. Some participants were jovial and excited about seeing the famous city. Some referred to the gathering as the party not to miss. The business meeting was quickly getting out of control. Jokes began about attending the Sprint Center concert to the mention of Pink, Usher, Sting, and Eminem appearing together.

The only person not on screen was Missouri's liaison, Dr. "Ted" Morris. Several MoTAF members were texting each other exuberant about Ted's appearance. He was online but not in view. The fun continued but quickly came under control when Dr. Morris took his seat and welcomed everyone. He got a warm response from attendees and the sound of silence took command of the room. A dog barked, not once but twice. It wasn't a meek Chiwawa. The bark resembled that of an English Mastiff. There were smiles on every face in the zoom view. When the barking ceased, silence returned like the hush of a stealth bomber flyover from Whiteman Airforce Base. Dr. Morris was the proud owner of the bark. He returned to sit in front of his screen view after securing his pet companion to a different room.

Dr. Morris took his seat and broke the silence. "Regarding the concert at the Sprint Center," Dr. Morris said, "it's a sold-out venue for anyone wanting to see *pink* M & M's being *ushered* into a place to get *stung*."

Some attendees stared with quizzical dismay at their screen. Some began speaking simultaneously as others shook their heads in disbelief. Some placed their heads on their desks, others swiveled in chairs turning their backs to the screen. Two attendees wrote the number 10 on paper and held up their score to the camera view.

At the meeting's conclusion, members joked about running out of ink from notes they had taken. Someone mentioned Amazon delivering spiral notebooks and another admitted celebrating more than one birthday before the meeting ended. It had been a while since a multi-state alliance meeting. The tone was the same. Excitement to participate prevailed in thwarting terrorism.

Members closest to Kansas City from the 8 contiguous states were driving. Chartered flights were secured for analysts traveling the furthest from ground zero. Prior conversations with friends from the east resulted in their bowing from the party. Although they assisted in years prior, only a few Illinois protectors could assist in the Missouri's endeavor. Gun violence in the Chicago area caused regrettable concern and current solutions were far from curtailing the problem.

The sleek multi-passenger Learjet retained the tail number 779MLT for Missouri's MoTAF members. A block of rooms were reserved at the opulent Intercontinental Hotel. A small conference room to hold a dozen people was also reserved for any overflow of the Downtown Airport. All networks were interlinked between both reserved conference rooms. No admittance was authorized once the rooms became functionable. The hotel was walking distance from the infamous Ward Parkway shopping district. Individual room invoices were nonexistent. The U S government didn't bring attention to ghost personnel who may overnight and were part of the package deal invoice.

All the planning was as if a business conference was taking place. It was a party but there were no handouts or schedule of events for attendees. There were no pens, pencils, frisbees, or grab bags with company logo on tables. Those were toys generally found at conferences. Not that there weren't any toys brought to the anticipated party, because there were. That was the main reason for the chartered flights. The Kevlar vest would have raised enough eyebrows and the items accompanying the vest would have caused airport lockdowns. The boy scout motto was adhered to.

The mandatory zoom meeting benefited everyone. There was only so much preparation one could make within the parameters they had to work with. The unknowns remained. The element of surprise was in the favor of the devil. One could argue the devil never wins and crime doesn't pay. The debate would intensify depending on the number of victims who weighted the balance of the blind folded lady.

Every tomorrow quickly turned into yesterday as days were crossed off the calendar since the festival weekend arrived. Law enforcement counterparts were already geared up. An unexpected federal funded request for increased LE support garnered extra volunteers from surrounding cities. Overtime incentives brought a more than expected willingness to work the scheduled long hours. Rumor was, uniformed officers were offered free drinks and meals from the venders parked in the Union Station courtyard. Venders long since understood, from similar events, officers donated the dollar amount of their meal and accepted the gratuity drink. Officers freely filled vendor tip jars knowing each paid a large sum for rental space for the two-day event. It was a win-win.

The chartered flight brought analysts Friday afternoon to set up the conference room at the Downtown Airport and Intercontinental Hotel. Rental cars were loaded with printers, tablets, monitors, and enough interface USB and ethernet cables to rewire Kansas City's Power and Light District. The Presidential White House war room would be impressed with the set up. The circuitry required room ventilation to prevent monitors from overheating. Portable fans circulated air around the conference rooms. Portable battery units were kept charged in event of power outages. This wasn't their first rodeo. Years prior, similar hardware was said to have brought down an aging transformer of a hotel they prepared under similar circumstances. The boy scout motto was again adhered to. By days end, everyone was ready as could be for whatever the was to be.

Saturday morning arrived with an anticipated upper 80's mid-July temperature for the day. The analysts prayed for rain although they preferred calm air travel. Foul weather always dampened plans of evil doers. Bad guys were fair weather predictors. They didn't appreciate mother nature foiling plans they counted on to bring name recognition to whatever cause they were to promote.

Connectivity was flawless between the setup war rooms. Analysts updated MoTAF members with any info received before they were wheels down. The briefed members on the flight were perplexed with one discovery.

LPR's, license plate readers, and FLOCK camera systems were utilized specifically for the event in Kansas City. Readers were placed strategically in traffic locations within the city limits. The technology was generally utilized for tracking criminal activity. Stolen vehicles were the main search, although warrant and wanted searches linked to license plates have been utilized.

The tracking of registered vehicles linked to the Patriot Partner chat room unlocked IP addresses which were logged into the database LPR's utilized. If readers picked up the same plate numbers with in the Kansas City metro area, law enforcement on scene would be notified and could respond near or at the event. Thus far, three vehicles had been linked to the chat room and were being tracked within the KC area. It was an all bark and no bite buildup.

Of the three vehicles being tracked, none were stolen. There was no way to determine if the occupants of the tracked vehicles were participants in the chat rooms. If the registered owner of the car were one of the occupants, it could be thoroughly investigated further, if a violation had been witnessed. No arbitrary traffic stop could be initiated. No threats of illegal activity were retrieved in any of the online verbiage.

Analysts notified members of a vehicle identified by the camera system. The license and vehicle identification was listed, and images were forwarded to law enforcement as well as MoTAF personnel on assignment. The vehicle of interest was flagged for several reasons. Information linked the owner to an Illinois Patriot Partner. The owner of the vehicle was linked to a missing person investigation. The investigation involved a vehicle that surfaced with submerged trees and entangled debris along the Missouri Illinois floodplain. The car surfaced a short distance north of St. Louis. The owner of the vehicle and a friend were reported missing. The submerged vehicle pulled from the river was confirmed to be owned by a member of the Patriot Partners.

The Lear cruised at 30,000 feet after making two stops and taking on six MoTAF members. A short time later the party commenced. Analysts at the Intercontinental finished the conference room set up and joined the others by speaker phone from the Downtown Airport. Members while in the sky joined by speaker phone as well. The connection was superb. Dr. Morris was jovial and socialized with those in the room as if he were hosting a dinner party at his residence. He welcomed those in the air and joked about how he had the power to increase or diminish the turbulence they might experience. After his formal welcome to Kansas City, and those still enroute, he made a request to all players to stay connected with the command post. The Downtown Airport conference room was designated as the primary Command Post.

Dr. Morris spoke directly to members on the plane and asked if they had any questions from the briefing folder they all had been reviewing. He asked the same to those listening in at the Intercontinental. Chad and Megan were nearing Kansas City via Interstate 70 and were in on the conference call. Everyone understood Megan was the handler to their newly employed intern. He had not arrived in the city and wasn't expected for another two hours. The electronics he was currently using had the tracking and mapping app showing exactly where he was and his speed.

Chad and Megan hadn't seen Tenor for several years and they were to rendezvous at the airport. He would be briefed and join others at the venue site.

Before the conference call concluded, Dr. Morris informed members about a Patriot Partner who was a person of interest in the missing person investigation. The license plate reader system identified a vehicle, and it was located at a restaurant east of Kansas City adjacent to I-70. Local law enforcement decided to arrest the owner on a warrant for questioning relating to the FBI investigation. The driver left the restaurant and stopped at QuikTrip for fuel. Several plain clothes officers and others in uniform convinced the man to join them without incident.

CHAPTER 44

ach MoTAF member with boots on the ground were issued baseball caps. Each ballcap bore the front logo of the Kansas City Royals. It was summer and baseball, as the saying goes, was in full swing. The bill of the cap was red, unlike any other. It wasn't exactly a fashion statement but rather ugly in comparison to sanctioned MLB apparel. The caps would be easily identifiable in a crowd of hundreds, if not thousands. That was precisely the idea to go along with the color coordinated lightweight backpack. The backpacks were lined with Kevlar. Similar to the insert panels issued to the parents of grade school kids of inner-city low-income families.

The crowd increased in size. Barricades blocked the traffic lanes of Pershing Road in front of Union Station. People were roaming, taking in all the festivities. There were face painting locations and balloon twisters were making wrist bands, animals, and head bands for kids and adults. Food trucks were changing their breakfast menus to lunch selections. Live musicians were performing around the grounds below the Liberty Memorial. The acoustics were of no concern for the saxophone, guitars, or harmonica players. They too had rented space and the guarded tip jars were near to overflowing.

MoTAF members careened to the southern part of the city taking in the sights and blended with the masses. They were enjoying the city and acclimating themselves to their assignment. It was going to be a long day. Members donned appropriate footwear and were well versed in the briefing notes issued to them days prior. The briefs included an arial mapping of Union Station as well as the grounds of the Liberty Memorial Mall.

The stairwell and elevator locations were easily marked of the parking garage and other public areas. Union Station required an in-depth study. There were several floors and businesses within the structure. Exquisite dining, a movie theater, escalators, stairs, as well as the walkway leading to and from Crown Center's hotel and Shopping Center. The law enforcement counterpoints came through quickly with all requested mapping areas.

Members were small in number compared to the area of concern. Specific assignments were required, and those assignments were further broken down into quadrants. Each member became familiar with the complete coverage area. In the event one or all of them were to convene in an area, they would be familiar with the most expedient way to assist each other.

The encrypted frequency was not without dead spots. Communication between members were a concerned especially between the command posts. The CP was vital for the success of all operations. The lower levels of the parking garage, as with the lower level of Union Station, presented limited radio coverage. A temporary solar powered repeater antenna, with battery backup, was erected at the War Museum. It was paramount to avoid communication dead spots at or near the venue. Small antennas linking to the solar repeater were placed in areas were radio coverage were of concern.

Cellular coverage were assessed between members and the CP without issues or failures. They were ready as ready as could be. The unknown remained and it was never far from everyone's mind. The solemn expressions spoke volumes to everyone. Averted eyes gave way to unspoken truisms. Each member checked their backpacks without uttering a word. They would see each other on the main stage although no embrace would occur. They had been on the front lines before.

Traveling from the downtown airport to where they termed ground zero created unexpected issues. Drivers maneuvered around overpass construction on Rt 169 over the Missouri River. The detour signs funneled driver destinations with minimal inconvenience. Another inconvenience near Union Station caused mayhem. Lane closures with workers holding traffic control signs created another unexpected annoyance.

It was a caravan of MoTAF members with other slow-moving traffic. There were no vehicles driven by team members that looked alike. There were small, compact sedans, others were midsize as well as SUV's. Humor replaced the seriousness of the moment when a member sounded off in his radio mic to the others.

"If we were in black limousines with U S flags on our front fenders, we could get through this a lot quicker."

The comment was right on point but received no reply. Political overtures were always a touchy issue. As the traffic slowly careened through the delay, each driver and passengers observed the reason. A backhoe bucket was deep into a hole and the machine operator at the controls remained focused on his task. A pile of dirt covered the roped off sidewalk warning pedestrians to avoid the area. Not even a person with a red tipped walking stick with an assisted canine could miss what took place. Five men with orange hard hats were staring into a hole. Two were smoking cigarettes, two were holding shovels. One man was animated with his arms and hands. He angrily pointed into the hole discussing the issue which caused them all to be at work on a Saturday. The animated observer was the apparent unhappy on duty supervisor.

Another comment came soon after the first. She giggled as her question came through for all to hear. "How many guys does it take to dig a hole in the ground?"

"The same as it takes to screw in a light bulb," came a quick response.

The CP notified team members of assisting flights that were soon to land at the downtown airport. All MoTAF members would soon be on the ground and familiar with their sector areas.

Within the hour, members were combing the grounds. Union Station as well as the World War II Museum were targets for potential disruptions. None were yet observed.

Chad and Megan completed their alternate memory lane course of travel and were on their last leg to Kansas City. They stopped first at Panera Bread on Missouri Boulevard in Jefferson City. It was the first of two stops on their memory lane itinerary. The ambiance had changed. Nothing resembled what they recalled years prior. Remodeling does change one's memory, but the warm friendly atmosphere remained. The closed off concept, which resembled many late seventy's residential living rooms, no longer existed. They sat next to the floor to ceiling windows covered by solar, light filtering blinds.

Chad and Megan had an early lunch to avoid the bumper cars of the noon hour four lane chaos. That part of the city hadn't changed. Their second and final stop was the granite fortress. The Missouri Capitol was rebuilt in 1840 after being destroyed by fire three years earlier. Not much changed from when they were last there. State House security protocols did change. Gone were the days where someone declaring a defender of democracy could carry their lawful owned AR into the halls of a Capitol and stand in front of the Governor's welcoming reception area. Missouri would not resemble the open carry gun law protests as experienced in other states.

Chad and Megan made their way through security finding their way to Senator Truman's office. The office was where the last steps of the late intern began. The fatal last step was in the basement parking garage. Chad asked Megan to join him for a self-tour in remembrance of that dreadful day. Autopsy revealed the young victim succumbed to a single gunshot wound. The caliber was not from any firearm belonging to a MoTAF member. Chad recalled the intern falling after he fired a round from his handgun in the smoke-filled garage. His attempt to stop the assailants was not before a ricochet struck the victim. Chad continued to blame himself for not bringing the assault to successful end before the loss of innocent life. Those demons kept him from sleeping for months. He often traveled down the straight and narrow one-way road of blame.

Chad was glad he and Megan were riding together to Kansas City. Walking the halls of the State Capitol brought similar reflection for Megan as well. The two-and-a-half-hour drive to Kansas City was solemn. There was minimal conversation about what they remembered about that day. Neither needed reminding what the other experienced.

Chad received a forward from a DC analyst who identified herself as Monique. The text came through the Bluetooth connection configured to Chad's car. He pressed receive and both listened. Their WITSEC intern whom Megan was to mentor and ultimately become his handler, would arrive at the Kansas City CP location earlier than anticipated. The timing was going to be tight, but Chad and Megan would arrive shortly before Tenor. Although no briefing with him was needed, a clarification of responsibilities was preferable for Megan. She not only had to watch out for herself and possible evil doers, but also had to keep a mothering shield over someone else as well. Another message sounded but this time was on Megans cell. It was a JPEG image from Monigue. The requested photo of Tenor was welcomed. He changed from when she and Chad remembered him.

There was more than usual LE assistance and comrades than ever assigned to any city celebration in recent memory. DC records indicated this event surpassed Presidential events outside of the capitol city. Chad was not impressed. Be it those in the political climate who kept records that meant so little to so many. The day was already becoming long for them. They hadn't even arrived at their destination.

CHAPTER 45

Tenor arrived at the Downtown Kansas City Airport ahead of schedule. His travel was monitored. He entered the reception area and took a comfortable seat in the spacious lobby. Although a few of employees ask if they could help him in any way, he declined and kept repeating the answer of waiting for friends to arrive.

Chad and Megan walked into the lobby a short time later. Tenor missed the couple entering the airport as they started climbing the stairs to the conference room. They were the only people he witnessed take the stairs. It was the climbing the stairs that caused Tenor to notice them. No one, including employees, followed the sign pointing upstairs to the conference room. They looked the same as they had years prior. Tenor was surprised they didn't notice him seated. He watched them climb the stairs and it occurred to him, he was the one who changed. His hair was blond, and he put on a few pounds from his construction job.

Tenor stood and quickly closed the distance from his seated position. He started the climb, and with excitement, he called out her name.

"Megan! It's me, Brody. Brody Wesson!"

Megan nearly bumped into Chad who stopped abruptly and stood in the breached door entrance to the CP. She didn't respond to her name being called. She knew the name of the person who called her out but didn't recognize the face. Neither did Chad. It wasn't the face. It was the straight shoulder length blonde hair and the near complete tattooed sleeve on the left and right arm. Tenor had changed. He wasn't the same person they released into WITSEC. The jpeg photo didn't do him justice. He was still unrecognizable.

Chad stood tall, rigid, and military straight as he pushed closed the door he just unlocked. It was a defensive stance Megan had not seen coming. Another protective gesture she appreciated more than she was willing to admit. This was a stance of a father protecting his child from harm. A stern glance one would view of a mother shielding her baby. A silent warning from a fierce defiant stare.

"Oh my, hello Tenor! I didn't recognize you."

Megan didn't try to hide her surprise or amazement. Chad's reserve stare wasn't as forthcoming and hadn't faded. His fixed gaze was not welcoming. Remaining laser focused, he softened his body language.

"Hi Tenor. It's been a while. Good to see you."

Tenor didn't skip a beat and continued his greet and meet. The excitement overflowed about seeing the two of them. Tenor knew both Chad and Megan were to meet him at the airport. Everyone expected the reunion albeit under different circumstances than years prior.

He was early, at least 20 minutes early. Megan kept her right arm holding her backpack waist high. Tenor stepped toward her invading personal space, as if expecting an embrace. The backpack placement served its purpose. With impeccable timing, Chad extended his hand and with a firm grip, shook the hand of the man who he barely recognized and hadn't seen in years. He was now less confident and more uncomfortable with their reacquaintance. The man, he was willing to sponsor, who he wanted to reward with an offering of a second chance, would be tethered to Megan for as long as the assignment warranted.

Both read their brief about Tenor. Their new confidant had also been briefed and read every protocol document before e-signing them back to Monique. They were all on the same page. Chad would not let his reluctance show. Now wasn't the time. Chad and Megan had talked in length about Tenor's name change. They agreed to not to use his birth name as well. Brody was used to his new name and there would be no reason to change. MoTAF members knew him as Tenor, there would be no cause for confusing the already uncomfortable.

Tenor kept his tone upbeat. He was almost giddy as if it were a college homecoming having not seen classmates for a decade. For Chad and Megan, the resemblance couldn't have been truer. In comparison, much had changed but there would be no standing in front of hanging banners for photo ops.

Chad commented on Tenor's prompt arrival and mentioned they might as well get started on how the next couple days would likely transpire. Because there were unknowns, everyone would have to be diligent in preventing a catastrophe. Both Chad and Megan congratulated Tenor on his willingness to assist MoTAF and his efforts in infiltrating the Patriot's network. Megan was careful not to broach the topic of him once being on the side of evil. Tenor still considered himself an unwilling participant, but a participant, nonetheless.

"Tenor, you're about to meet our underboss, Dr. Morris," Chad said with a serious tone. "He is the liaison with our DC counterparts."

Tenor wanted to comment on his conversations with Monique. There was a lot he wanted to say. Being referred to by his real name was on the top of his list. The business tone was a signal for him to only speak when spoken to. Chad punched in the code to the makeshift CP. Tenor was surprised how a 3-year-old could enter the room with the numbers one through four entry code. Chad opened the door, entered, and held the door for Tenor. Megan gestured for him to enter before her.

Dr. Morris was hidden behind a large 27-inch HP screen with his back to the tinted windows. The tapping of a keyboard could be heard and continued even as he spoke.

"Give me a sec, I'll be right with you," without looking up or around the terminal. He was well aware of those walking in the room.

Dr. Morris stepped around Chad reaching out his hand to Tenor. With reluctance, he reached out to grasp yet another firm grip. He was relieved the shake was more welcoming and not part of a strong man finalist competition. Megan in a subdued tone explained to her understudy several things occurring in front of them. Dr. Morris contacted MoTAF members by their assigned sector and was requesting sit rep. She only paused to allow Ted to mention accolades of her and Chad.

"You must be Mr. Tenor Wesson. Welcome to Kansas City and thank you for your willingness to assist us."

"Please sir, call me Brody. I'm more than happy to help you guys anyway I can."

Dr. Morris looked toward Chad and Megan.

"Sorry young man. We know you as Tenor. We will not confuse ourselves or you about your identity."

Chad quickly joked about how he and Megan both owed Dr. Morris money for his unsolicited flattering comments about them. Dr. Morris offered them the chance to remain in the CP for as long as they wanted. He was going to drive to the south side and take in the sights. Chad and Megan both responded suggesting him to be safe and they would see him shortly. Dr. Morris thanked Tenor again for his assistance before leaving the conference room.

Megan offered Tenor a seat and she reached into her backpack pulling out a three-ring binder. Chad removed an identical binder from a briefcase he put on the floor.

He opened the binder, looked at Tenor and said, "Let's get down to business."

Moments later, the impromptu briefing concluded. Tenor was tag teamed on things he had already read or heard from Monique. He understood the dangers. The redundancy of the information was brutal. Government red tape reared its ugly head.

Megan pushed back from the conference table, as did Chad, and Tenor.

Megan grabbed her backpack and said, "I'm going to change clothes before we go to the south side. Be right back."

Megan quickly descended the stairs and found the women's restroom. She changed into comfortable afternoon attire. The custom backpack was light in weight, carrying only necessary essentials. It wasn't efficient for her firearm to be zipped in its lining, but she had practiced the quick removal for potential emergencies. She braided her hair and slid on the custom baseball cap pulling it low over her forehead resting just above her brows.

With ease, she slung on the near empty backpack and adjusted the ballcap one last time before exiting the bathroom. Casting her eyes downward to avoid unwanted traveler conversation, she climbed the stairs to the conference room CP.

The trio left the CP pulling the door closed behind them. Tenor sat comfortably in the front seat of Megan's car. They began their commute but not before she tapped the avoid delay feature in her car's GPS mapping system. The mapping system warned of an unavoidable traffic delay. Dr. Morris, as if on cue, radioed to MoTAF members he was not joining the festivities but returning to the CP. The traffic delay was more than his temperament could endure. When Dr. Morris returned to the airport, he contacted the Intercontinental CP and requested updates. There were none.

Several members were responding with the airport CP of potential nonfriendly combatants circulating at the war memorial museum. At the entrance to the lookout point over Union Station, there were two statues. A group of people were mingling around one of the statues. Dr. Morris reminded the members by radio the intel gave credence to the Patriot group joining at the Memory Sphinx Statue. Identified by red armbands, there were only a handful of men standing and conversing at the statue. The statue to the east was identified as the Future Statue. It was at this location a large group of at least ten men, all wearing red armbands, were talking to each other in various joint conversations.

A female MoTAF member brought the group to the attention of the command posts.

She announced, "It's a club who obviously doesn't adhere to equality."

There was no response to the comment. She came through the airways again. This time in an apologetic tone.

"I am so sorry. I was mistaken. There is one female with the group at the Memory Statue. Her red armband is on the left arm."

Assumptions were plentiful of why an armband placement would be cause to separate by gender. The reason probably could be located somewhere in their bylaws if anyone cared or was interested enough to do a deep dive looking for one.

Dr. Morris added, "I've made LE contacts. If the group isn't causing a disturbance or no complaint has been received, there's not much they can do. They're going to send a few uniforms to that location."

"Copy that," the female MoTAF member responded.

There was an undetermined number of officers in civilian clothing looking for all sorts of rude, crude, socially unaccepted, illicit and without question dirty deeds. There wasn't much of a thrill to ruin someone's weekend if it could be avoided. However, a safe and festive family gathering was the emphasis. A few badly bruised apples would not ruin the overflowing bountiful basket of fruit.

Tenor watched and listened to all that was happening. The tide slowly turned as Tenor was second guessing his predicament. His drive to Kansas City was as if he was released from decades of incarceration. He was introduced to the person who turned the tide of his hate and discontent. He point blank ask Chad about mind altering programs he was a party to before his admittance into WITSEC. Chad mentioned the program was pulled because a small percentage of mice didn't survive tests under their laboratory-controlled environment. Tenor couldn't determine if he were serious or not. It was one of many defining moments. He was fully aware of the unique perspective of his expendability. He couldn't hide and he couldn't run. Besides, where could he go? Starting life over was not a welcoming juncture.

There was little conversation as Megan drove the three of them to the venue location. Chad sat in the rear seat. Time seemed to stand still before Megan pulled into the parking garage entrance. She pushed the green button and took the time stamped parking tab. The bar raised allowing entrance to the garage. As luck would have it, a lower-level parking spot became available. Brody's gaze lingered at several vacant handicap parking locations. Chad noticed and without hesitation quizzed him.

"Tell me you didn't expect her to park in one of those spots?"

Tenor didn't respond and Chad didn't need to rephrase the question. A red flag went up the staff for Chad. It was going to be a long day.

CHAPTER 46

The renowned Plaza shopping district was booming. Traffic was at the speed of a turtle marathon. Foot traffic resembled mid-season tailgating following a Superbowl Championship. It was the weekend. Parking on the city's south side resembled Walmart on payday Friday. Money was to be spent.

Mic checks were again tested after Chad and Brody parked. The repeater system worked flawlessly. A vender was financially rewarded at his booth location at the War Memorial wall towering over Union Station. If not for the crowd, it would be a snipers paradise. The vender was asked to make sure the Royals banner remained upright against the wall. The repeater antenna holding the Royals flag kept MoTAF analog connection crisp and uninterrupted.

As a crowd formed at both sphinx statues, law enforcement were making their presence known. The mere sight of police in tactical gear caused more than usual interest. When joined by other defenders of peace, revelers started to disperse. Those who were drawn in by the abundance of force were between the ages of four and eight. The dogs on a leash were favorites. The revelers with armbands were less enthused. The handlers extended the length of their leash as the canines were enticed to linger between the east and west statues.

A tall, lanky, frail arm bander raised his voice to anyone who would listen. Several peacekeepers came to his side and started listening intently.

One of the canine officers asked the boisterous man, barely past twenty-one years of maturity, "May I see a copy of your vendor permit?"

The young man was drawing an audience. It was exactly what he was hoping for. To show the men in uniform a thing or two, or three. A young lady noticed the abundance of uniform officers converging around the armband group. She jockeyed for position to capture a video sure to be uploaded to her favorite media page. Another held his cell parallel to get the perfect wide angle, as did another, and another.

The armband genius took one step too many toward the officer and responded to the permit request. "I don't have to show you any stinking...."

The requesting officer removed an item from his service uniform belt before the young man finished his sentence. Another officer removed an identical item from his belt and stepped close to the genius. A third officer removed his extended steel police baton. The same type of baton the other officers were holding. The sound of the club locking into place caused those with cellphones to immediately become entrepreneur paparazzi.

An armband rescuer stepped forward. He looked at all of the close proximity men in blue, calmly stated, "We didn't realize we needed a permit to hand out educational literature."

Another officer interjected, "It's only a couple hundred bucks, and you'd have to have paid days in advance of the weekend festivities. Can I see the educational pamphlets you're handing out?"

The armband rescuer handed him a business card. "This is all we were handing out."

As he looked around gesturing to the people still holding cell phones, he was glad some had gone about their business.

"You're handing out business cards?" the officer said as he looked at one of the cards. "It's not educational, but hey, it's your card."

The officer continued to explain, the time had passed for them to participate by renting vendor space, but they were welcome to join other revelers, take in the sights, and sounds of the weekend. He didn't stop there. Being one of the city's finest community betterment officers, he took the opportunity to inquire about the armbands. It was at that moment Mr. Genius got stupid.

What caused the young man to step nose to nose with the first officer inquiring about their permit is anyone's guess. There were video footage playback of what would happen next. Cell phones appeared from every possible angle. Genius misjudged the distance at the end of his pointing finger as it made a slight indentation on the officers uniform shirt pocket. Officers standing at each of the man's arms firmly held his wrist lifting the 5'6" giant to where his toes barely brushed the concrete surface. He was quickly cuffed and walked from his armband friends toward the reserved parking area for police vehicles. A fully marked police van with no windows waited for a new passenger.

A member of the group stepped forward offering his apology for his friend's behavior. There were eight armband participants engrossed in their surroundings. Several city ordinances with numbers were quoted. The group were strongly encouraged to refrain from handing out business cards due to them not obtaining the proper vendor permit. It was explained how they could appear and join their friend who would need a ride from the courthouse after arraignment in a couple of days. A judge wouldn't hear a not guilty plea until Monday morning or possibly Tuesday depending on the docket number. By then, the alcohol would be out of his system.

One officer couldn't hold his grin, turned, and walked away so not to laugh in front of the videos being recorded. They stuck together like glue. Not one of them came up with the rehearsed strategy because there wasn't one. A lady with an ugly Royals ball cap and long lens camera stood alone reviewing her photos taken. She apologized for her interruption and greeted the woman in the group who handed her a business card.

Other officers recognized the ball cap as their unofficial LE assistance and wanted to see the cards as well. Several of the group produced business cards and with renewed enthusiasm handed them to the officers and the lady with the camera. The card displayed no name or phone number. On the front side of the card was an eagle with extended wings. The words Patriot Partners were under both wings of the eagle. On the reverse side of the card was a QR code with the letters EGOL under the box.

The MoTAF photographer took more photos of the armband group and walked a few paces to the solar charge repeater antenna box. Away from prying eyes, she photographed both sides of the card.

She relayed information that the sole female of the group wore her armband on her left arm while the males wore theirs on the right. Also conveyed, none of the armband visitors used their cell phones. A photo of the card was emailed directly from the camera to both CP locations. Photos of the armband participants were also emailed directly to Dr. Morris at the airport CP.

Ted radioed the members, "I received the photos of the armband group and the business card. I'll upload and forward the pics to DC."

The photographer relayed to the members, the business card is identical to the one they were briefed on. The QR code on the back of the card would identify the armband patriots' ideology platform.

The officer who approached and spoke to the Patriot bystanders addressed the group with a suggestive tone.

"Your friend will have to ride comfortably in one of our windowless vans to our station. You're all invited to support him and wait for his release."

The only female of the group shook hands with the officer who spoke and said, "Our friend has bad history with police, so he's a little opinionated."

They looked at their spokesperson with puzzlement. No other Patriot member uttered a word. The arm bandits spoke in whispers to each other as the cell phone paparazzi dispersed without anyone noticing.

The only woman of the group looked at all the officers and expressed appreciation for their service. She reached out her fist and was met with responding fist bumps from the other officers who had arrived. She walked away from the officers as well as her armband friends for privacy. Her thumbs were moving with lightning speed on her cell.

The only lady with the armband placed her phone to her ear.

"I got your text and I just responded to it. Yes, I'll meet you in a few minutes."

"Thanks. I thought it was easier to just call. I'll see you in a bit," Drake ended his call.

Things were back to normal at the Veterans Memorial. The sights and sounds of the city's celebration had not missed a beat.

What sounded like a sonic boom vibrated through the open air. It wasn't a military fighter jet, although Whiteman Airforce Base was a stone's throw away. The sound echoed off window glass and tall brick buildings. Sightseers peered over the memorial wall looking for where the sound originated. The landscape hadn't changed although the focus of the celebration had taken a notable detour. Another large explosion reverberated and caused finger pointing in a direction over the memorial wall.

Uniformed officers refocused their attention and moved to the finger pointers. Onlookers were already five rows deep. Officers excused themselves to the front of the growing crowd looking over the wall. An officer at the wall radioed to any responding officers on the ground where the noise likely came from. Officers were already requesting support from other officers near the large churning smoke funneling upward from nearby buildings.

Sirens were bellowing off concrete office buildings and adjoining structures. KCPD contacted both MoTAF temporary command posts. Airport CP director Dr. Morris radioed his members in the city requesting confirmation of the possible explosion. He contacted his sector members at the Hallmark shopping district. Their response was negative to the cause of what sounded like an explosion. They also responded by not seeing anyone sporting red armbands. Dr. Morris contacted the Veterans Memorial sector.

"KCPD have dispersed the armband visitors. They are now with the large crowd and can't be distinguished from other event patrons. The elevated vantage point at the memorial gave credence to the location of the explosions. People were quickly moving toward smoke coming from the east side of Union Station."

"Copy that," Dr. Morris responded. "Union Station sector can you copy airport CP."

"I copy," Chad said.

"I copy as well," said Megan. "Although Brody has moved away from me."

"We're trying to get through all these people. Everyone is moving toward the explosion and smoke," Chad replied.

Dr. Morris without calling out a specific team member, "All sectors keep me apprised."

Each sector replied, there was no coincidence in the idea the Patriots had struck. Sirens continued as EMS maneuvered around barricaded streets. There were reasons for barricades. As expected, pedestrian traffic increased from the excitement. People moved through streets without concern of vehicle traffic. Golf carts manned by two police officers moved slowly trying to maneuver through the chaos. The golf carts were of no use without sirens. Officers were using their whistles to part the crowd. Much of the crowd wanted to see what the explosions were all about as well.

Ted alerted the team members, "All sectors be advised. I have confirmation. The explosions are at the site of the road construction. A ruptured gas line at the dig site caused the first and subsequent explosion. There are fatalities and multiple injuries. Avoid the area, remain in your sector. Airport CP out."

Each sector responded back to Dr. Morris affirming the information given.

Chad still couldn't locate Tenor by radio. All sectors heard Chad call with no response.

Megan called Chad on the radio, "Chad, I haven't seen him either. I'll meet you at the Union Station fountain on Pershing Road."

"Copy that. I'll keep calling his cell."

It didn't take long. Chad saw Megan's ball cap about the same time she saw his. They smiled at each other as they approached, knowing full well the caps were a good idea in the huge crowd.

Chad said, "We have a problem."

"I know, I tried to call him too. I'll go inside the station and try to spot him," Megan said in a frustrating tone.

"Works for me. I'll walk to the courtyard where we were last. Meet you back here in 15."

Megan took fast strides into Union Station. Looking amidst the mass of people, it was a task of impossible proportion. Too many people, and not enough personnel to help look. If he didn't want to be found, he literally could be in Kansas within minutes.

Inside Union Station, Megan failed to see a man in front of her. Her forward momentum struck the man with such force it shocked them both. She immediately apologized, locking her eyes with his to solidify her honest apology. He graciously accepted her clumsiness but gave her a crude gaze casting from her eyes down to her feet and slowly back up.

As she continued walking away from the man, he called out to her asking what her name was. Megan didn't turn around but kept walking toward the down escalators. Megan theorized, Tenor may have walked inside the station to utilize the restroom. He was to have notified Megan or other team members if he separated. While moving down the escalator, Megan kept scanning the crowd and noticed the Neanderthal of a man she bumped into had his eyes on her and was moving in her direction.

She spotted the women's restroom and cringed when noticing the out of order placards at the entrance. Poor timing for bathrooms not to be working. Not for the crowds in the station, but mainly for her safe haven away from the no neck knucklehead. He was as big as a coke machine and the man's neck was nonexistent. His arms were huge, resembling potato sacks stuffed with miniature footballs. The only thing not so odd about the man was his hair. Expensively cut and trimmed as if he was Bernie Madoff's tax attorney.

Megan ignored the signage and walked into the restroom. There was a near echo to the emptiness of her surroundings. The only working items were likely the music coming from the speakers in the ceiling. There was a near echo to the volume of the music. She was the only person there. The signs outside the entry way were not lying. Megan was soon no longer alone in the nonfunctioning surroundings.

In a firm assertive voice Megan said to the man, "Sir, you can't come in here. Leave!"

Mr. No Neck stood in the entrance way blocking Megan's exit. He had a creepy look on his face. Creepy was the only way she could describe the man other than his size. Megan wasn't overly concerned. A 3-year-old could pick the man out in any police lineup.

"The signs say I can come in."

"No sir. They say women's restroom and they're out of order."

"So young lady, why did you come in?"

"Maybe I wanted to change clothes and it is a women's bathroom. Sir, please leave. You're making me nervous," She lied.

Megan took off her ballcap and retrieved her FLETC skull cap from her backpack and placed it on her head with the emblem centered on her forehead. She planned on schooling the man on what a mistake he was now making. He was big. No, he was huge. She could only assume he was as quick as paint drying in a cold moist laundry room. She could not match his strength. The man looked as if he could bench press an Abrams tank.

"Why am I making you nervous? I haven't said or done anything to scare you."

"You're in a women's bathroom. You're not a woman. Please leave."

The man stepped toward Megan. She retreated to the metal divider for toilet privacy. There were no toilets, just holes in the floor where toilets once were. She backed into the metal dividing wall on purpose for support. A no telegraphed, unannounced head butt was an effective defense. Everyone has a plan until someone gets punched in the face.

Mr. No Neck extended both hands and grabbed Megan by her shoulders. She didn't see that coming. He didn't either. Springing her body from the metal divider, she forced her forehead into his face. The metal plate in her skull cap made the sound of a baseball bat hitting a ball over a fence for a home run. The foam pad on the inside of the stocking cap cushioned her forehead as designed.

Before the man could regain his composure, she moved eloquently as a ballerina creating a safe distance. She decided not to leave the bathroom with the possibility of being in a foot chase up the escalator. She had to end any potential foot pursuit. He was bent over at the waist, still moaning, staggering, and holding his nose. Megan stood at the side of the man when he began to curse and explain what he was going to do to her.

"Sir, you learned the alphabet at a young age. There are three letters you should concern yourself with right now."

The man regained his footing and stood upright. Megan took a nano second to regret conversing with the man. She pivoted in a designed choreograph move she learned while at FLETC repositioning herself at a 45-degree angle. The instep of her right foot struck the man's left knee with the force of a Clydesdale rear hoof kick. The decibels of his yell likely echoed to the upper floor of the station to be drowned out by the scurry of the crowd. The man folded to the floor like an empty wrinkled 3-piece suit.

Leaving the man in extreme discomfort, she said, "The three letters of the alphabet are, A – C – L. You might want to get that looked at."

Megan exited the front doors of Union Station and radioed Chad. "I'm almost to the fountain. No luck locating Tenor."

Chad replied. "No luck for me either. I thought you found him. You took long enough."

"I got delayed by a guy needing to learn the alphabet. I'll tell you about it. Let's regroup and find Tenor."

CHAPTER 47

Tenor looked at his cell to read his text message. He was already waiting in the parking garage adjacent to Union Station where he was told to be. Lower level near the exit. It was a simple request, and he was anxious to meet a new friend. A Patriot. As the newcomer to the chat room, he was surprised, yet humbled, being contacted by someone who said they conversed with him there. Tenor was cautious meeting anyone from the dark web. It would take some getting used to meeting somebody who said they became acquainted without messaging them directly or knowing anything about them. It was the only way of braking free of the ball and chain. Too late to turn back, the wheels were set in motion.

Several people were in cars leaving, others were in a rush to destinations unknown. Curious people rushed to the cause of the explosion instead of avoiding it. Tenor wasn't one of them. His transportation was nearing.

An older black escalade moved frantically through the garage. The driver was noticeably annoyed as he drove the wrong direction of other exiting vehicles. The older luxury SUV would have been cherished by a previous owner. The current owner likely refused to obtain insurance as noted by the severely cracked windshield and missing headlamp, front grill, bumper, and other notable body missteps. The expired registration was another tell-tale sign. The frustrated driver rolled down his window and displayed the offensive hand gesture to another driver vacating a parking location. The annoyed, anointed driver was going the opposite way of the directional arrows. It occurs in every Cosco or Walmart parking lot in every city. Drivers ignoring the directional arrows for parking causing other drivers to move out of their way. The entitled driver pulled into the vacated parking location.

Tenor's attention was alerted to the commotion and wanted to side with either driver. He discarded the ballcap he was ask to wear and sheepishly looked around for the same discarded item donned by anyone else near him. A white four-door hybrid was backed in a parking spot near the exit. The driver waved other cars to pass him to exit. There was evidence of good over evil. The driver of the hybrid flashed the cars headlights. It was the signal messaged to him by text to look for. Tenor could see the front seat passenger visor turned downward with a placard attached. The placard had a red border with a white background. Blue lettering could be seen from a considerable distance. The letters E G O L caused a smile to form on his previous nondescriptive stare. An obvious true Patriot displaying the red, white, and blue signature. Tenor was the only pedestrian not walking but standing as if waiting for a ride.

The driver pulled to a stop and lowered his window. "You must be Tenor. Get in."

Tenor knew he would count on them to help start a life of freedom. A woman got out of the front passenger seat as Tenor approached.

"Hello, my name is Alia. This is Drake, he is who you've been messaging. He will drive you to the airport."

"Nice to meet you, Alia. Drake told me about your loss. He was a true Patriot."

Tenor walked around the front of the car, opened the passenger door, and got in.

Drake reached in front of Alia and turned the visor upward so not to obscure his vision. He drove to the garage attendant and handed the parking tab he had acquired earlier at the electronic pull tab machine.

"Keep the change," Drake said as he paid the attendant. The white and red striped arm bar was raised, and Drake pulled in line with others.

Several minutes passed before they could navigate away from the city celebration. Foot traffic had increased as well as vehicles causing delays for blocks. No conversation between the new acquaintances were exchanged. Plenty was shared during previous online and private chat room conversations. Things became much clearer after putting a face to text messages and remembered screen conversations.

Chad and Megan stood taking in the crowd in hopes of seeing Tenor amongst them. The unspoken words between them were detailed on their faces.

"I can't believe I've been duped. He gave us so much promise after all these years," Megan spoke in a disgusted tone.

"Not you, we. We all missed cues somewhere. I'm not blaming myself for this and you shouldn't either."

Megan didn't want to overstate her disappointment. "Who else is to blame for it. We allowed a man under the watchful eye of WITSEC to get lost in a city of 500 thousand people. I should have kept a closer eye on him."

Chad was not letting her displeasure slide. "Unless you got a mouse in your pocket, there's no we to this equation. He has gone rogue on his own. Plain and simple."

"Easy for you to say."

"Yep, it is, that's why I said it," Chad replied in a failed attempt to explain his point of view.

Traffic on Broadway resembled a parking lot as they crept toward the shortest route to the Downtown Airport. It was jacked with drivers navigating around the gas line explosion chaos. Nobody adhered to the do not block intersection signage.

Drake leaned forward to both passengers in the front seat, "Did you bring the package I mentioned."

Alia turned to him and sternly said, "We understood your request. I wasn't going to allow any Patriot under me put themselves in jeopardy and link themselves to the item you foolishly requested."

Drake looked in the rear view as he spoke. "Tenor, it's nice to meet a new Patriot member. You just met our General. She is the one who has put together what we fondly refer as General Orders. Stay in your lane and you will become revered as other members are."

Alia handed Tenor a small plastic bag. "You'll need this. You'll want to dump the one you have and purchase another one once you get to where you plan to go."

Tenor opened the bag and pulled out a small box. A burner cell phone was something he hadn't thought about. He leaned back in his seat and with a newfound purpose.

"This is definitely happening."

"Perhaps. We will see," Alia replied.

The trip took as long as expected. Drake knew not to inquire about his new friend's plan. The phone was the first step to his new friend's freedom.

"The burner is an alteration of your request. No Patriot will be associated with any intention of violence," Drake bluntly informed him.

"Thanks for the phone. I was thinking I may need something to protect myself."

"I made an executive decision to keep us all out of jail," Alia said.

"You act like you don't trust me," Tenor interjected.

"Would you trust me if the table were turned? Rhetorical. You don't have to answer," Alia replied. "Besides, what made you think we would give you a handgun because you say you're a true Patriot?"

"That's fair. Thanks for your help, *Patriots*," Tenor said with a hint of sarcasm to the term.

Not another word was spoken until they approached Hanger 10. The erratic driving with the stalled traffic caused road rage to reach the boiling point. Drake cautiously pulled into the airport parking lot entrance. He didn't put the car in park. He and Alia were not entering the airport with Tenor.

"How will we keep in touch? I'd like to repay your kindness," Tenor said.

"Our online site and chat room will not change entry protocols. We can be reached that way, and once you have obtained a new phone, you're welcome to give us your contact information," Alia informed.

Alia handed him a stun gun. "This is the only gun I could get on short notice that can't be traced back to any Patriot. Adapt and improvise your plan."

Drake pulled from the circle drive parking, and into an adjacent parking area.

"He's a loose cannon. I'm not so sure we shouldn't hang around and see what he's planning," Drake looked over at Alia waiting for her thoughts.

"He's talented, but so far out of his league it's not only frightening, it's dangerous. We will change our chat entry protocols to our web site and chat rooms. We will not inform him of our new numbers. He is naive to assume his messages were private."

Drake replied, "You're right. He's been out of the loop so long he's complacent to what is going on around him. He's a liability."

Tenor walked from the circle drive to sit in his car. He looked around for Drake and Alia and was sure they had already left. Retribution was his new plan. Sure, he was offered a new beginning. It was offered by the same people who imprisoned him. He was tricked. His own blood tricked him. He was betrayed and lied to. Enough was enough. He was free from the chains placed on him.

The government was also stifling the Patriots' freedom recruiting efforts as well. Recruiting was all they were doing, which wasn't a crime of interest to Uncle Sam. It was time to fully extend his wings and soar with other true Patriots. He had to make a clean break.

Tenor did not miss the vibrations his cell emitted during his separation from Union Station. Continuous vibrations nearly caused his jean pocket fabric to weaken. He hadn't officially gone rogue. He was still in Kansas City. Every missed message was from his so-called handler or her MoTAF sidekick. He liked Megan, but he made his decision. His freedom was more important than repaying a debt they say he owed.

He would listen to the missed phone calls messages if any were left. He would ditch his phone. Alia was right, his phone was a chain he must break free from and soon. He saw an open bed pickup truck. A phone in the truck bed would not be found for days if not weeks. He would not be chained to a phone any longer. The battery was at 90 percent. They could track it for hours, but nobody would answer. His anger dissipated and his infamous smirk returned.

The truck where he planned to dump his phone sat in an area painted yellow and labeled no parking. It would not be there long, and neither would the ball and chain he's been attached to. Brody walked to the truck and the cell vibrated again. He glanced down at it and altered his steps to the shaded circle drive of the airport entrance. It was Monique. He needed to talk to her. Adapt and improvise.

"Hi Monique, I've been meaning to call you."

"Hey Tenor, I've been meaning to call you as well. I got busy and haven't been able to reach out."

Her voice was upbeat. She responded with the same excitement. Now was the time. It was perfect.

"Busy doing what?" Tenor ask.

"Seriously, Tenor. I can't inform you what we do. Besides, you might tell your buddies all about it."

"OK, I see what you just did. I can't tell anyone anything, and they wouldn't believe it if I did. We've been through this."

"Yes we have Tenor, so don't ask. How are things in Kansas City?"

Monique left the Intercontinental CP moments after Megan radioed she was no longer with Tenor. They were never to be separated. Tenor was being tracked through his cell and Ted called Monique to see if additional resources were needed if tracking couldn't be maintained. Monique didn't want to lose connectivity with the repeater link. The app link got stronger when she got closer to the museum. She guessed correctly, assuming Tenor could be located at the Union Station parking garage. What she didn't anticipate was the quick movement from the garage. He was on the move. With all the talents Tenor had acquired, she was sure he was able to steal a car and be on the run. He was only a short distance ahead of her in the slow-moving traffic.

With almost 100 percent accuracy, Monique glared at the vehicle she was sure he was in. The percentage lowered when she noticed it was a woman with short hair and a child seat in the rear. The tracking app was extremely accurate, but with the volume of vehicles a precise location was mere speculation. Another vehicle ahead of her location was observed three people in the car. A flag attached to the window garnered her focus. The yellow, Don't Tread On Me, Gadsden flag flopped in the breeze, as traffic halted at a green traffic signal. A violent road rage was imminent if a human traffic controller didn't intervene soon. It would be a sure suicide assignment whoever drew that short straw.

Don't tread on me wording circled the snake flag trademark. Her focus was now on the flag and the passengers. A flashing neon sign asking police to take notice might as well have been affixed to the roof. The locater app was accurate within a few feet of her location. The red dot continued to blink near the blue triangle depicting her location. The red dot blinked faster. What seemed like forever, they exited Rt. 169 for the downtown airport, other cars did not. What she didn't anticipate was the stalled traffic at the roundabout to the airport main terminal. The targeted driver drove the wrong direction of the roundabout, nearly striking a minivan. She saw the target vehicle driving past cars on a narrow shoulder.

The blinking red dot was as accurate as a center mass group of two rounds to a target silhouette, from her Glock 27 Gen4 at 10 yards. An undeniable personal preference of concealment.

Obeying the signage to the roundabout, Megan aligned with the traffic lazily maneuvering the circle without drawing the single fingered gestures and blaring horns the blinking red dot received. There was no longer an app needed to determine where Tenor was. Out of sight but not out of range. Monique opened her phone address favorites and dialed the top number again.

"Ted, it's me, he's coming to you."

Dr. Morris' response answered jovially. "I'm glad you got me on speed dial. With the number of calls I'm getting from you, people will wonder about your intentions."

Monique didn't respond as expected. "I think he's going rogue. Can you get to his car and stop him? He's making a big mistake."

"I'm on it," Ted replied, "I'll notify Intercontinental CP I'm vacating post for a while."

Dr. Morris radioed the secondary CP. Each MoTAF sector also responded with confirmation. He shut down his computer monitor with the mapping of each sector involving the city celebration and gas leak explosion. He rose from his chair and heard the CP electronic door lock chirp. The door opened and in walked Tenor.

CHAPTER 48

Monique called Megan and enlightened her on Tenor's innovative problem-solving abilities. She was not pleased to hear he was likely on his way to the airport but relieved to know Ted was there to intervene. Chad was not convinced Ted could stop him from leaving. Both were relieved Monique was on her way as well.

In a disappointing tone, Megan said to Monique, "Ted may not be able to stop him. It's the U. S. Marshalls and WITSEC's problem now. They didn't have to sign off on his working with us."

"You're wrong Megan. DC agreed all the way up the ladder. It was MoTAF's recommendation for his success in their program. You concurred and so did I."

"It was his decision to bolt," Megan said, "let him run. He'll be spinning the hamster wheel until he gets free room and board and three meals a day if he lives that long."

There was no conversation between Megan and Chad for a couple agonizing miles. An occasional warning from Chad about an overly aggressive driver was all that was said. Their revolving red Kojak light was not going to assist in their commute. Chad pulled the plug and the light stopped spinning long ago. Repeated calls to Ted were not answered. They called Monique and suspended any idol chat.

"It's Megan, we can't reach Ted. Have you reached the airport?"

"I've tried to call as well, with no luck. I'm almost there. Tenor is still at the airport," Monique continued, "that tells me Ted was able to stop him from running."

Monique could hear the angst in Megan's voice, so she explained a tracker was uploaded to Brody's phone when it was cloned. An intense stare between Chad and Megan would have caused the Statue of Liberty lady to lower her arm. They didn't ask Monique any questions, but the silence between them told of a plot to a movie they had both seen. Monique continued with what they learned from the cloning of his cell. They learned the Patriots were planning a recruiting effort at a large venue. That venue was the Kansas City celebration.

She further explained they found a bigger fish to fry. That fish was an ugly faction of the Patriots. End to end encryption on burner phone communications created an investigation which they had called: Fishing Expedition. It was a federal investigation involving a double homicide. The murders occurred near the Missouri and Illinois state line. The witnesses were holding out for a plea deal and not being specific of the exact location of the murders. There was a discrepancy as to whether the crime occurred in Missouri or Illinois. It became a federal investigation due to the jurisdiction issue. There was more information learned from the cloned cell phone which Monigue didn't provide.

"Somebody's been holding out on us, and I'm not happy about it," Megan said staring at the snarled traffic ahead of them.

Chad looked at her, "Well look who's coming around."

"If they've cloned his phone, they know who he's been talking to and how long he's been planning this," Megan's face soured as if sipping a warm diet soda.

"Exactly." Chad said, "Our DC analysts have known he was talking to somebody. That somebody met Tenor and got a ride to the airport."

"Right under our noses," Megan said.

She pushed hard on the center steering wheel column. The horn blared longer than Chad would have preferred. The traffic was a problem but encountering road rage was a problem they didn't need. Chad held his tongue and brought up a different subject matter.

"So, tell me why it took so long to rejoin me at Union Station?"

After Megan explained her delay, he understood and was thankful she was able to remove herself from the incident safely. Chad dialed again and put his phone on speaker. The sound of the connected call could be heard. The recorded message began after several rings and Chad ended the call.

Megan looked at Chad with concern in her eyes. It would be a while before they could clear traffic to expedite their drive to the airport. Her tapping of the steering wheel was bothersome, but he understood. It was a waiting game they weren't accustomed to. The horns blaring from frustrated drivers wasn't helping either. Chad dialed his phone again and the ringing could be heard through the speaker. Not realizing he dialed Monique, Megan was surprised to hear her voice. Megan spoke loudly to make sure Monique could hear her speak above the blaring horns.

"Sit rep, what's going on?"

Monique calmly responded. "Hi Megan, hello Chad. I'm almost at the airport. I'm still trying to reach Ted, but he hasn't answered. He's aware of Tenor catching a ride. We only assumed it was a ride back to his car at the airport, so he was alerted."

Chad didn't mince words. "Monique, I'm not pleased being left in the dark. We could have talked to him before any of this happened."

It was Megan's turn, "We recommended him to assist us outside of WITSEC. We should have been briefed, if not out of professional courtesy, out of respect."

The phone became silent. Chad turned up the phone volume to not miss anything she would say. They heard what they both expected.

"I'm sorry. It's above my pay grade," She continued, "I'm approaching the airport now. I'll keep you guys informed."

"But you haven't Monique. There's a lot -" The call disconnected before Chad could finish talking.

Megan looked at her passenger's stern scowl. He looked from Megan and out his passenger window. She watched him inhale slowly, then exhale. Chad turned, looking again at the snail-paced traffic jam before speaking.

"DC is the head of the octopus. Like it or not, we are one of the many arms. We won't always know what the other arm is being told to do."

There was another awkward silence. Megan responded with the familiar smirk on her face. "Really? An arm of an octopus. That's all you could come up with?"

Monique wasn't pleased having to deceive their own players, but she had a job to do. The more who were in on the cloning of Tenor's cell, the probability of something uncontrollable occurring. In furtherance of the plan, it was decided MoTAF be kept in the dark. Monique had seen it before. Probable deniability was alive and well. If something terribly wrong occurred, the blame only went so far up the ladder.

Nothing could be revealed regarding the email correspondence between

Alia and Drake. DC analysts were able to mirror what Drake and Alec accomplished with developing AI technology. They could clone emails but didn't want to encourage any wrongdoing. That was a slippery slope nobody wanted to climb.

Alia, still distraught from her loss, was an active player with her brother. Drake was unaware of the scope of her involvement until his receiving an unsolicited email from her. He agreed to fulfilling her brother's wish. Although at first feeling duped, he was again intrigued by Alec's intellect in furtherance of a plan. A plan all three of them were a part of.

DC analysts were letting it play out to get the big fish. A witness to the two murders didn't want to sing in the choir he unwillingly found himself in. He wanted to go solo. The interrogation revealed the answer to the remaining W's.

At the Downtown Airport, Tenor graciously greeted Ted and started his recitation he practiced for circumstances like he was now encountering. Tenor didn't have a chance to embellish his lie.

Ted interjected and explained to Tenor WITSEC was fully aware of what he was doing. Everyone wanted to see if he was serious about leaving the program and forfeit what was offered. Ted tried to explain things, but the logic wasn't resonating. He was a young man who had proven he could contribute but was misled.

Tenor laughed at what he was told and said, "Dr. Morris, I've been lied to all my life. You're part of that lie. I've been a puppet for the government. They have tugged on my strings long enough. I'm cutting the chords. I'm leaving. Period."

Monique slowed not finding suitable parking and pulled adjacent to a chain link fence. She took quick strides while walking the length of the asphalt lot. Ted looked out the reflective tinted solar windows to the parking lot below. Tenor looked and saw a lady walking to the hanger lobby entrance and noticed the smile on Dr. Morris' face.

Ted said, "Tenor, you haven't met that lady, but you've talked to her several times. That's Monique."

Tenor looked at the lady then back at Dr. Morris. Ted reached for the holstered handgun on the table next to his laptop. Tenor pulled the stun gun from his left pants pocket. With his right hand, he gripped both of Ted's hands firmly on the gun and holster. The thumb release on the holster had been pushed and the gun was nearly free.

A short bolt of energy from the stun gun went through the jeans of Ted's right thigh. He stumbled back, losing his grip on the holster, falling against the conference room windows. Tenor released the trigger as quickly as he pushed it. He easily gained control of Ted's loaded Glock. The stun gun caused numbness in Ted's toes and right leg, but he was able to stand as he leaned on the window frame.

"What are you doing!" Ted shouted, "Just leave, don't make things worse for yourself!"

"So that's why you were reaching for your gun, to ask me to leave?"

"I knew you were coming and so did Monique. That's why she's here. She's here to see you."

Ted continued to massage his leg regaining strength to stand without assistance.

"If I were concerned, you would have met the business end of my Glock when you opened the door."

Tenor looked out the window not seeing Monique any longer. It was only seconds before she would enter the room. He hadn't formed a plan, but he remained calm under the circumstances. He wanted to talk to Monique. He was looking forward to meeting her, but not this way.

The conference room keypad chirped. The attractive brunette stepped in and looked directly at Tenor.

"Hi Tenor, I'm Monique. Nice to finally meet you."

CHAPTER 49

Chad dialed Ted's cell number, and again it went to voicemail. Hearing the recorded message produced sour, distasteful scenario thoughts to Megan's frontal lobe. Chad didn't burry his thoughts. He was an open book to those close to him and once in a while, to those he didn't know or asked for his opinion.

"Something's wrong," he said. "We don't try multiple times and not reach who we're calling."

"At least the traffic is moving," she replied, "it shouldn't take long now."

Monique looked at Tenor and at the cell phone that kept interrupting their conversation. The ringing was bothersome. Tenor hadn't come up with a viable solution to his predicament and the lady of his dreams was not part of any plan he envisioned. The gun captivated her attention. It wasn't of any importance to inquire how he got it. She remained calm as if holding a winning hand in a poker game. No stress, no problem. Her focus was on Tenor.

"Tenor, I'm sorry we're meeting under these circumstances. Do you prefer I call you Tenor or Brody? Why are you wanting to leave the program?"

Her second question was rhetorical. She knew what the answer was. The conversations from the cloned cell as well as his choice to sink all his electronics opened the window to everything he had done. What was surprising to the DC analysts, was that their software wasn't recognized by his system as an intrusion. They should have left the software firewalls to professionals.

"I prefer Tenor. When I think about it, it probably doesn't matter what you call me. I'm done with being played like I'm the toy."

Tenor began his rhetoric. He was no longer going to be a puppet for a tyrant government. Patriots were being recruited across the country. The world would learn the truth and not the lies told by television networks. The

Midwest would fan out and teach the rest world what was happening right under their noses. Monique let him continue until he turned the rhetoric toward Dr. Morris.

Dr. Morris' discomfort was an issue. Ted looked at Monique although nothing registered in his expression. His eyes were on her, but they weren't focused. It were as if he didn't see her standing at the other end of the room.

The look on his face was blank, as if he were in a daydream. Monigue quickly surmised everyone in the room were in trouble, including Tenor. He was a problem to himself.

Ted wasn't a young man. He stood from his leaning position, and without warning, he was on the floor. The sound was that of a 50-pound bag of sand being dropped on concrete. Tenor stepped and looked down at him. Monique closed the distance between them without Tenor noticing. Tenor focused on Ted's position and appearance. Monigue was now only a few feet from him but not close enough to attempt grabbing the gun. She needed another diversion.

"It's his fault as well as others," Tenor said, pointing Ted's gun down at him. He's a puppet master and he's no longer pulling my string or anyone else's."

"Tenor, look at me!" Monigue shouted.

Tenor looked at her and his face softened. His eyes watered at the plan which had not yet materialized. Monique tilted her head to the left, flicking the curls from her face. She pulled the curls behind her right ear so she could see him clearly. It was a move she practiced on her dad as a senior in high school. She would ask for gas money after he relinquished the car keys to her on a Friday night out with her girlfriends. The car always had plenty of gas, but he gave her money anyway. It always worked.

"Where did you shoot him? He needs medical attention."

"I didn't shoot him!" He shouted and picked up the stun gun off the table next to the closed laptop. "He grabbed the gun to shoot me, and I hit him in the leg with this."

"Tenor, I know you're upset. This isn't how we were going to meet. It's not how I envisioned seeing you. Let's not ruin our getting to know each other."

Monique could see the little boy on the playground in his face. He was conflicted and it wasn't a good place for him to be. She attended federal training and case studies were replayed over and over again. It was time to reason with a person who couldn't distinguish deep fake from reality.

"Tenor, he's in defib," Monique pulled one from an old playbook. It was tried and truly tested. There was no medical equipment to test her theory, he would have to trust her. Her performance continued.

"You must believe me. Let me call for help, he needs to get to a hospital." Monique placed her left hand over her chest in a plea for him to listen. Her eyes locked on his. She willed her eyes to water, and sensed the emotions swelling as the flushness of her face took hold. She only wished a mirror were in reach to witness the effect. She batted her eye lids, but he didn't see them. Her cell phone rang as did Ted's. He looked at the lit screen on the table. Tenor pushed the end button on Ted's phone. Tenor picked up the phone throwing it down at the man who would not have felt it if it had hit him in the face. Monique's phone rang again.

"You're not listening!" He angrily said to her. Tenor's face was fire engine red. "He is the enemy, and you are too if you answer that."

Monique gingerly removed her cell from her belt on her right side. With the same two fingers that pulled the phone from its holder she extended her hand for him to take it from her. She made slow movements to show Tenor she had nothing to hide on her that could hurt him. Her left hand extended, shoulder height and straight out to the side, showing her total honesty and surrender.

"Here Brody. You answer it. It's Chad, I'm sure he wants to talk to you, not me."

Tenor was taken back by Monigue calling him by his birth name. There was an obvious surprise in his facial expression. For a moment, Monigue thought he was coming back to reality.

"It's been a while since I've heard that name. I like it better than Tenor."

He took the phone from Monigue, pressed the green button key, and lowered the Glock to his side.

"Hello."

Chad paused only slightly when his call was answered. He was expecting Monigue.

"Hello, who is this?"

"Hello Chad, it's me Tenor, but you can call me Brody."

Chad looked at Megan. The expression on both their faces were indescribable. Megan pulled into the passing lane overtaking several cars. Chads placed his left hand on the dash after winching his seatbelt tighter. He replied to Tenor without forethought to what he was to say.

"Tenor. What and why are you with Ted at the airport? More importantly, why did you leave us at Union Station?"

Chad encouraged Megan to pass another vehicle. They were close enough to the airport not to pass more cars, just to pull into the airport drive. Megan quickly pulled to the curb at the circle drive. It wouldn't have mattered if there were a restricted parking signs. She opened her car door, but Chad was still belted in. They both heard Tenor reply to the questions Chad ask him.

"I would say it's hard to hear you with all the people around you, but that's not the case. I'm at the airport, but you of course know this fact. Huh, Chad?

"We are on our way to the airport now. We need to talk. Don't go anywhere."

Megan looked at Chad with bewilderment. She closed her door, looked at Chad and shouted, "We are here! Let's go talk to him!"

"Something's wrong. He's using Monigue's phone, and he didn't mention anything about why he was using it."

Megan came close to cursing like a sailor. Megan listened to Chad talk to Tenor. He was listening and not talking. Tenor was on a rant. He lit into WITSEC and the government controlling his life and not taking him seriously as he was trying to help them with whatever they were attempting to accomplish. He was angry and Megan could hear every word spewing from his mouth. Much of it had long past the letter R rating for language. Megan's phone rang while Tenor continued with his shouting.

Chad attempted to bolt from the car to the airport lobby, but remained seated until he could release his seat belt. Megan had already circled the car but decided to wait for Chad. The both entered the airport lobby, nearly slamming into the slow automated sliding door entranceway.

CHAPTER 50

Monigue observed Tenor concentrating more on his phone call to Chad and not her. Tenor continued his rant of disappointment. She didn't want to anger him more than he was already.

She was still not in close proximity to grab the gun without the possibility of a discharge. She experienced absolute fear running through every vein in her body. All calmness long since fleeted. She was transfixed to the danger in front of her. Monigue was convince she would get shot and not survive at where she was standing. There was no escaping. She would let Tenor vent. Attempting to talk him off the ledge was frightening but that was the only option viable to her.

Chad reached the top of the stairs at a lightning pace. Megan didn't let any step separate the two of them as she reached the top. They positioned themselves on both sides of the conference door. The airport lobby seats were empty. Those once seated were now standing near the counter. Everyone were staring at Megan and Chad. Neither of them noticed people looking their direction as they climbed the staircase with handguns drawn. The shouting from an angry man inside the conference room would have predicated the emptying of the lobby.

Chad still had his cell on speaker although it wasn't needed. He didn't want to hang up the phone, afraid Tenor would harm Ted or Monigue once the connection went dead. He was also confident, Tenor didn't realize they had arrived at the airport. The shouting stopped and Chad quickly brought the phone up to speak.

In almost a whisper, Chad spoke so not to have Tenor suspect he was at the conference room door. "Tenor, you're obviously upset. Put Ted on the phone so I can tell him we are joining you at the airport."

"Not happening. You are part of the problem. I'm done."

"What are you talking about Tenor. Megan and I both helped you get a fresh start. You were brought in to help us stop whatever the Patriots were planning. You could have declined, but you came to Kansas City anyway and joined us."

"I've been lied to again. You are part of the problem. You and Megan both are. Life isn't worth living if I can't be free to live it."

"You're angry, you're not making since. Let's talk about this Tenor."

Megan looked down from her perch to the airport receptionist counter and employees. There were three people working the counter, and all were talking on a desk phone and looking up at her and Chad. Megan immediately pulled a lanyard from beneath her vest allowing the dangling shield to be seen by the employees. Those in the lobby now stood near the counter and on their cell phones looking as well. Chad mirrored Megans move and pulled his hidden shield in hopes of calming some of those staring up at them.

Inside the conference room, Tenor turned his back on Monigue and stared down at Ted. Monigue took the risk and reached to the small of her back, and firmly gripped her Glock. The loaded magazine in the pocket of the vest allowed her to clear the gun from any clothing obstruction. It was another training tip which served her and others well at range qualification. At this distance, Monique didn't need to aim, but she pointed at center mass.

"Tenor, stop!"

He turned to look at Monique. The determination on Tenor's face was one of resolute. His face lost all expression. It was a dangerous calm. He let out a breath as he turned again looking down at Ted.

Megan entered the code on the combination lock. It quietly chirped and she pulled the door open allowing Chad to enter, gun drawn.

Tenor heard the door unlock and open as did Monigue. He turned and looked toward the door and saw Chad enter pointing his gun at him. Monigue steadied her eyes and continued to aim her gun at Tenor.

"Drop the gun!" Chad commanded.

Tenor looked at Chad as if he hadn't heard him shout. Monigue repeated the same demand.

"Tenor, Ted needs help. Put the gun down!"

Megan entered the room with her gun drawn, but Chad and Monigue were between her and Tenor. She was surprised to see Tenor holding a gun as well. Neither she, nor Chad could see Ted who was prone on the floor.

Tenor looked down and without any telegraphed warning, pointed the gun down at Ted. Monique pulled the trigger twice in quick succession. Her second shot exploded simultaneously, as one from the gun Tenor held. Tenor fell on top of Ted after Chad fired once striking Tenor center mass.

Megan instinctively ran to the conference room door and shouted for the desk attendants to call an ambulance. Everyone in the lobby heard the gunfire. The police were on the line and were already enroute.

Within minutes sirens could be heard. Airport EMS were a short distance from Hanger 10.

It took little time for the scene to be chaotic and crowded with EMS and uniformed officers. An additional ambulance was requested by the airport EMS.

Megan directed arriving emergency personnel from the entrance to the airport lobby. She also notified Intercontinental CP and advised them of the critical incident unfolding at the airport. Other MoTAF members remained in their sectors in case other incidents took place.

Monique and Chad cleared the crowded conference room when EMS arrived. After several minutes passed and other EMS filled the room, a gurney carrying Ted emerged to start the stair descent. His Kevlar vest had been removed exposing the large impact site of the expended bullet from his own handgun. Electrodes were affixed to his chest and torso. The AED monitor rested between his legs as did an oxygen tank. Moisture filled the oxygen mask that was pulled tight over his face. Ted was unconscious. EMS held the gurney tight as they gingerly maneuvered down the stairs to a waiting ambulance.

Megan returned inside the airport and hastily confronted Chad and Monigue. They were both standing together outside the conference room door.

Megan spoke out of breath, "Today didn't go down as any of us thought it might. Did Tenor make it?"

Monigue looked at Megan and replied while Chads eyes were sunken looking downward. "No Megan, Tenor didn't make it. He was gone before the ambulance even arrived. There was nothing I or Chad could have done to help him."

"EMS wouldn't let me talk to Ted. They said he was unconscious."

"He had his vest on Megan," Chad looked up and continued, "He took a round to the right of the breast plate. He's in serious condition."

"Yes, but the vest stopped the bullet, so he should recover."

"He has internal injuries from the concussion of the bullet," Monigue answered.

"So, you're saying we'll just have to wait and see."

Monigue and Chad didn't say anything in response. All three leaned against the wall not speaking but reliving in their minds what had occurred only moments prior. Another day in Missouri's state archives yet to be concluded, another critical incident debriefing yet to be held.

Monigue stood and stared at Chad and Megan.

"What?" Asked Megan.

Chad looked at Monigue and waited for her to answer.

"Guys, there's something I need to talk to you about."

"Whatever it is, I'm sure it can wait."

"Actually, Megan, it can't. There's more to this day that hasn't been resolved. It has to do with Tenor."

"Tenor is gone. You guys were instrumental in saving Ted's life. There nothing to that storyline that needs to be clarified."

"I'm talking about the Kansas City International Airport. There is more to this day that was being planned by the Patriots. More of their plan which MoTAF was not briefed on."

Megan looked at Chad. He was shaking his head in disbelief. His eyes were misty from the shooting he and Monigue had experienced. The look he displayed was something she had never seen before. It was indescribable, it was more than anger.

Chad stood from his leaning position and stared Monigue directly into her eyes. "So, let's have it. What have you kept from MoTAF?"

"Chad, there are a lot of things out of my control. Decision making is one of them. It's left to those who are exclusively pegged for those tasks."

"In other words, you're not at liberty to discuss it."

As soon as the words came out of his mouth Megan stepped between them. She instinctively understood what Chad was referring to even though Monigue did not. It wasn't the time for him to explain it to her.

Monigue's cell was resting firmly in her belt loop holder. She grabbed at it before the ring stopped. She quickly stepped from Chad and Megan to answer the call from whomever was on the other end.

"Saved by the bell," Chad elevated his voice to make sure Monigue heard him. She descended the stairs not looking back. She heard his every word but needed to separate herself from them both.

Monigue let the phone ring till she reached the bottom of the stairs. She then hit the answer key.

"Hello, this is Monigue."

DC analyst were never at a point when they weren't in communication with each other. There were several avenues of connectivity. Things took on a new perspective for her. She couldn't allow what she experienced to change the scope of what their mission was and to what degree she would go to accomplish it.

Monigue understood after what she experienced, ones perspective on what's important can change. She understood her life was seconds from ending. That reflection would continue into the foreseeable future.

Monigue knew who was calling from the number displayed on her phone. It wasn't a specific person, it was a specific office. Her office.

The caller identified herself by her designated number and on the phone with the caller were two other office employees. They were wanting an update on all that was occurring. Monigue knew immediately, they had already been informed on several things, she didn't know to what extent they had learned what had happen so far. To her surprise, they heard what happened at the Kansas City Downtown Airport. The reason for their call was to know how she was doing. Monigue filled them in on the specifics and explained what could have been an alternative to the current outcome.

Dr. Theodore Morris succumbed to his injuries. Her receiving the call was to inform her about Dr. Morris. She was task the responsibility of informing those in Kansas City of Ted passing away at the hospital. He was in defib at the airport and the internal injuries he received from being shot further complicated his condition. All references to his participation would refer to him as a hero and not a patriot due to the nature of the ongoing assignment.

Monigue could not refuse or wanted to. There was more she had to inform members about. Particularly, all flight arriving and departing from KCI would proceed as normal. What MoTAF members were not aware of, Patriot members had theorized halting departure flights from KCI. The interruption would alter flights all over the country, thus causing international alterations as well.

No demands were being requested, other than electronic capabilities were vulnerable and not as secure as they professed them to be.

DC analysts uncovered malware scheduled to upload to airline networks. Airlines connecting to others would unknowingly allow the malware to attach to others across the country as updates were loaded into other airline systems. The upload successfully surpassed dangerous level of firewalls in furtherance of their intended disruption.

Monigue was to notify MoTAF members on all facets of the discovery and the untimely passing of Dr. Morris. Dr. Morris would have normally informed members in his unique way of transferring that information. She learned the arrest of a Patriot member and witness to the double homicide at the Jones - Confluence Joint State Park. The arrest allowed DC analyst to thwart efforts of potential catastrophic airline disruption. Monigue learned an interesting caveat. The Patriot member was to be offered WITSEC relocation and protection with his agreeing to cooperate with the government's investigation. Monigue was confident that agreement would be frowned upon by Missouri and their analyst counterparts. Her delivering the news of Teds passing and any agreement with WITSEC following the current day events would not be popular.

Chad and Megan spoke with the crowd of shocked employees and airport visitors. They requested everyone's assistance in answering police and detectives questions before they departed. The willingness to assist law enforcement was evident.

Monigue entered the airport lobby and met Chad and Megan. She hadn't prepared herself for delivering the update. There was no choice but to fill them in on what she was told before Chad could began asking unrelated questions.

She began with the good news update regarding the failed attempt by the Patriots disrupting the airline travel. The Patriots developed a well-planned and executed a near perfect attack. She wanted to inform Chad and Megan first, before joining other members at the Intercontinental Hotel for the full debrief. Each sector already informed Monigue they had no updates to report.

"Chad, Megan. I would prefer you sit down for bad news?"

"We have to go to the Intercontinental, why would we want to sit down?" Megan replied.

"Guys, I have information, you need to know about."

CHAPTER 51

MoTAF protocol playbook hadn't changed. The airport conference room crime scene investigation took over. Airport Police became secondary for investigation assistance, and public information inquiries. Media was shut down with no news breaking release of what occurred at Hanger 10. Print news was the only source of what happened in the sweltering afternoon summer heat. It was buried after the full-page furniture sale ad, and two thirds of the way past the loose-leaf newspaper ad inserts.

Every MoTAF member on assignment was present and accounted for. Monique, Chad, and Megan requested and received postponement of their critical incident evaluation until a suitable date could be scheduled. They all understood shooting incident protocol. The unspoken words between the three solidified their being members of an elite group. A critical incident group. Megan had her debrief several years prior because of the Jefferson City Capitol terrorism incident. Her debrief failed to uncover a demon that remained. The demon reappeared when she learned she lost her dear friend and confidant.

Chad had his own demons. His debrief from the same incident also proved beneficial. His circle of friendships, after leaving the foster care program, was therapeutic in a multitude of ways. Those friendships helped him with his self-imposed guilt. Not being able to prevent what happened to Ted awakened that monster.

Before entering the conference room for the debrief, Megan dialed a number from her cell's address book. She got the number from a highway billboard sign. On many occasions she dialed the number but never followed through connecting with someone.

After three rings her call was answered. A calm, soothing voice responded to every question she asked. Megan didn't leave her name or any information about who she was. More importantly, the man on the other end of the call didn't ask. His tone was exuberant on receiving her call. He gave her an address and confirmed the time for her to meet. Megan told him she would be there. He expressed sincere appreciation of her call and hoped to see her soon. He explained she didn't have to introduce herself or tell him anything about her. She was asked to show up and listen to what he had to say. She agreed.

Megan concluded her call and entered the Intercontinental CP. The small conference room was crowded, bursting at the seams with personnel. Several were standing and all seats were occupied. Floor fans were positioned under the large table, oscillating on high.

Monigue motioned to Megan and ask her to move to the front of the room alongside her and Chad. The room was quiet. There was a loss of life, and all understood the magnitude of their assignment. Although the Patriot mission had a hidden agenda under the cloak of recruiting, their designated effort failed. It wasn't until the debrief were other members made aware of the KCI international plot. It was revealed to the members the diabolical plot was foiled by diligent investigated techniques of analysts, local and federal law enforcement. Members listened about the murders occurring by Patriot Partners and how it related to their being assigned to assist and ultimately foiling the attack.

Monigue was sandwiched between Chad and Megan as she informed the packed room of the loss of one of their own. Delivering the news to Chad and Megan was difficult. Informing the remainder of those on assignment of Dr. Morris' death wasn't something Monigue wanted to do. Everyone either knew Dr. Morris or were aware of who he was and his relationship to the assignment. Everyone was shocked to hear the news. The successful mission was bittersweet. Members were reminded they would obtain digital copies of the assignment debrief. It was customary those on assignment were allowed the opportunity to respond to the debrief findings to improve operations and policy.

The camaraderie did not resemble a locker room following a team victory. There were no questions ask. The assignment concluded and members were dismissed. Some started dismantling equipment used to set up the command post. Others left carrying equipment after saying their goodbyes and extending hugs. The atmosphere was somber.

Megan made her way over to Chad, patiently waiting, not to interrupt his conversation with a comrade analyst. Chad wore his emotions on his sleeve as did several in the room. It was another attribute of Chad she was witnessing. Megan observed his conversation concluding and approached Chad extending a welcomed embrace. Megan's eyes were worse than bloodshot.

"How are you doing, Chad?"

"It looks like I'm doing just about the same as you."

"I can drive back home if you don't feel like it." Megan said.

"I may take you up on that. At least I might want you to drive part way."

"Do you think Ted's family has been notified?"

"I can assure you Meg, if we know, his family knows. I want to visit with a few more people then we can head back."

"Just let me know when you're ready," Megan replied.

Most of the drive back home was without conversation. Megan let her emotions flow without concern for what Chad was thinking. Chad refused to hold back as well. It was a solemn return. Music broke the mood and Chad change his XM radio to comedy. Megan smiled and laughed at some of the humor as did Chad. She hadn't displayed much of a smile until the music genre changed to comedy.

Chad broke the silence, "Hey, I distinctly remember you promising me some of your world-famous cobbler."

"It was my mother's recipe, and yes, it's famous in my opinion."

"Your opinion is all that matters. However —"

"There's no however. When it comes to my mom's cooking, there's no debate. I recall you boasting about your own culinary talents."

"I don't remember boasting, but I am comfortable around the kitchen."

"My, my. I do think your memory fails you. You'll have to prove it and show me what you got."

"Sounds like a challenge," he said.

"It is but I'm not letting you anywhere near my kitchen."

"That settles it. My kitchen it will be."

Megan smiled big. Her eyes were still bloodshot from the previous news.

"Megan, I've been waiting to tell you something. I called somebody you might know."

Her smile faded. "Relax Meg, I didn't call your childhood crush. I called your favorite winery in St. James."

"You should have your own comedy station on XM. I never had a childhood crush. Why did you call St. James winery?"

"I recall you telling me your favorite wine. I called the winery and got some delivered a while back. How about having some at your place over dinner?"

"As I said before, you're not getting anywhere near my kitchen. I'll take you up on any entree at your place though."

"Perfect. I'll be happy to accommodate if you bring the cobbler you've been bragging about."

"It's a deal, if you'll do me a favor," she responded.

"You drive a hard bargain. What's the favor?"

"I made an appointment to meet somebody, and I would like you to go with me."

Chad tried to come up with a funny or witty reply, but instead kept quiet.

Megan continued, "You've probably seen the billboard sign on 65 while driving north, just before you get to Kearney. I looked up the web site and it looks legit. It's an accredited focus group that meets monthly for social, personal, and clinical counseling. Sometimes I don't sleep very well. Will you go with me?"

"Absolutely. I don't sleep well myself. I'd be happy to go with you."

"It's short notice. They meet this coming Tuesday afternoon."

"No problem. I'll go with you."

CHAPTER 52

Tuesday came quickly. She pulled into the parking lot of the mini mall. The address was given to her by the man on the phone when she dialed the number from the billboard. Megan took a deep breath before exiting her car. She was early for her appointment. Chad was ready when she arrived at his place. Megan wasn't sure about agreeing to meet for the one-hour appointment. She didn't regret inviting Chad to go along with her. If the location had been a hotel, she would have kept driving through the parking lot. Calling a number on a billboard sign and the online information should have eased her mind. It didn't. The man on the phone sounded nice and said he looked forward to the meeting. She didn't tell the man she was bringing a guest. It was because of Chad, she was going through with it.

Chad could see the reservation on her face. The address on the door was of a dance studio. It didn't exactly send red flags up the pole but, he understood her reservations.

"We're only a few minutes early, Meg, let's go in and meet the guy. I'll just say I wouldn't let you come by yourself."

"You wouldn't let me come by myself, huh?"

"Hey, you can decide when we get in there what you're going to tell him. Remember, I'm just along for the ride."

'Not exactly. You said you don't sleep very well either. So, we're in this together buddy."

Megan smiled big as they both exited her car and walked to the dance studio. Chad opened the door with caution as if petting a snake, and not believing it was nonvenomous. Once inside, they observed several people helping themselves to drinks. There were trays of cookies and people were jockeying for open seating. There were more people than Meg or Chad expected. Chairs were positioned at tables and were aligned allowing people to view the podium at the front of the room. Curtains were draped over one wall of mirrors. It was an obvious location for ballet or dance class instruction.

A man walked to the lectern and asked people to make their refreshment selections and take their seats.

Megan recognized the voice. He was the man who she talked to on the phone when making her appointment. Megan passed on helping herself to the coffee, tea, and cookies. Chad didn't. He chose a few more cookies than he normally would have taken, in hopes that Meg would change her mind. She grabbed a chilled bottle of water resting in ice beside the other drinks.

All the seats to the rear of the room were already taken. It reminded her of a small church her mother would often talk about. Very few members would sit in the front row. It took courage to sit up front. If it weren't for Chad being with her, she would have given it serious thought to leaving. They took vacant seats in the second row and joined late arrivals who lingered getting refreshments. They weren't as early as presumed.

The welcoming voice greeted everyone and explained how those who were in attendance were related. The relationship was not by genetics but by circumstance. Everyone in the room lost something or someone close to them or were close to someone who has. Chad looked at Megan and immediately thought he had been duped. He recently learn Megan suffered from insomnia as he did. He did not expect to hear those words from the host that resonated so well with him.

The voice was comforting as he explained the gathering was the first step of many. The meeting they were attending would be the shortest of all their other gatherings. Each meeting was to help each other through their personal journey.

Megan listened and was drawn in by the man who was professional and experienced. Or so he seemed. He captivated the attention of everyone in the room. He explained that he had not introduced himself for reasons he would later explain.

He was in business casual attire. The buttons of his light blue shirt were not under pressure from a bulging waistline. The nicely pleated shirt was opened at the collar and tucked tightly around his waist. His brown belt, lightly clasped, and visible only between the unbuttoned navy sport coat. The man appeared to take care of himself. His cuffed kakis folded at his string tied brown shoes which fashioned his matching leather belt. He was in his mid or possibly late fifties, greying at his temples.

"Welcome. I will introduce myself in a little bit. But first, I want to recognize those of you who are returning to our group meeting. I recognize your faces and I thank you for coming as well as those joining us for the first time."

The host opened the room up for introductions. "For those who returned to join us, your participation will be vital to those in attendance for their first visit. For those attending for the first time, I encourage you to return and join us again. I also want you to know, if you choose not to return, you won't be alone in that decision."

The host looked directly at a gentleman who returned a nod to the host. The young man stood and told everyone his first name. When he sat, another guess stood and did the same, as did another, then another.

Megan whispered to Chad, "I'm not standing so don't even think about you introducing yourself either."

Chad smiled and continued looking to the front at the host who began to speak.

"We all have misgivings about opening up about our deepest fears. I want to tell you the story of my loss. The loss of a dear friend, but first I want to tell you who I am and a little about how I and others benefit from helping others like me to change their sorrow or misfortune into a positive."

Chad and Megan both became comfortable with being there. The host told of his battle scars and how others, like those who were in attendance, may also help others benefit from their own journey. His credentials were amazing, but he was able to explain learning his gift without gloating. He explained to the group, it was his own personal decision not to display certificates of learning for people to look at. His delivery was not without humor. It amazed Megan how everyone would smile or laugh, and soon thereafter, wipe tears from their cheeks.

Without anyone noticing, time quickly passed. Megan had already made the decision to return to the next scheduled meeting. Chad wanted to come as well, she would not need to entice him to join her.

The host gave everyone the next scheduled meeting date and encourage them all to return. He introduced himself and began to tell the story about his friend. It was an odd way of starting a meeting. It worked for him, or he wouldn't have repeated his strategy.

"My name is Seth. You can make up your own name of my friend and insert it into my story. It will give you my personal touch to why I'm able to stand before you today. I will not make up a name for my story, because I hold dear her real identity. Those of you who returned to be with us today have told me you won't tire of hearing my story. I hope the remaining will find it meaningful as well."

Seth began his story without using notes as he previously did when addressing the group. He didn't need any notes because it was his story. He looked at each person as the message resonated throughout the room. His story was different, but the loss reminded them of what some may have experienced or were dealing with. There were few dry eyes in the room, including the man at the podium.

The back story everyone was hearing caught Megan off guard. It was as if she had been told part of it before. The speaker said his friend was a coworker, and a good listener. This friend got him through some rough days when his only child, a daughter, passed away. She hadn't reached grade school age when she succumbed to the inoperable tumor. It broke his marriage apart. His ex-wife remarried and has a family with three children. The counseling helped, but he found himself spiraling downward with every progress he had made. The man repeated the loss of his child was the most painful experience. The separation and divorce took him deep into a valley. A valley where he saw no avenue of escaping.

The host told the group he and his friend became close. He told his friend his inner thoughts, his fears, and his friend shed the same to him. The group listened intently waiting not for his story to end, but to continue. All eyes continued to be transfixed on the man standing at the podium. He surprised them. He told them how his story didn't follow their current mindset. It wasn't a movie, although it seemed like a horror box office hit at the end.

Seth explained the coworker friendship was platonic. No inappropriate lines were ever crossed. She was beautiful inside and out. She was a passenger in a car when the driver lost control. His friend and passenger had seatbelts on but neither survived the crash.

"My friend would always say something to comfort me when I was troubled or was going through a difficult time. She was always a good listener. She taught me how to listen, and listen I did when she was having difficulty in her life. I learned things about my friend her family were unaware of. I learned her fears were not much different than my own."

Seth explained how they joked, laughed, and even shed tears. They were like a close brother and sister. There for each other if they ever needed. He explained his friend had a favorite phrase, he knew she would use on him. He would often turn the table and repeat her quote to her when the circumstance warranted. He paused. The pause became uncomfortably long. Then, the pause was interrupted by the first man who stood and introduced himself. This time he stood but didn't say anything. He just started applauding the host. Others joined and Seth smiled appreciatively and raised the palm of his right hand, then both hands to halt the standing ovation. He removed a handkerchief from his sport coat pocket and dabbed both eyes before walking over to a table near the back draped wall which hid the mirrors.

He picked up a wooden plaque that was face down. He walked back to the podium and hung the plaque at the front of the podium so it could be read by the group. He left it there. The plaque read:

"Peace Be Still."

Megan stared at the plaque and couldn't take her eyes off it. The man told the group his name again and repeated the date and time of their next gathering. The meeting concluded without fanfare although that is exactly what occurred. Several people, particularly those who were previous attendees, circled the host as if to comfort him, although it was more of congratulatory in nature.

Megan didn't stand to leave, she remained seated as did Chad. She was speechless. Megan kept looking at the three words carved into the wooden plaque. She pulled her phone from her purse and entered the next meeting date and time into her cell phone calendar. She willed herself to stand up. She wiped tears from her eyes without shame.

Looking at Chad, she ask, "Are you ready to go.?

"Yes, I'm ready. Are you OK?"

"I'm fine," she said looking at him with a teary-eyed smile. She grabbed Chad's hand and clasp her fingers tightly with his. When the door closed behind them she released his hand and embraced him affectionately.

"Thanks for coming with me. I can't wait to get to your place. You're going to enjoy the dessert I have planned."

THE END

Printed in the United States
by Baker & Taylor Publisher Services